# Secrets and Solace

**Love at Solace Lake, Volume 2**

Jana Richards

Published by Jana Richards Books, 2018.

# Praise for Jana Richards

**A LONG WAY FROM EDEN**

*"Jana Richards has penned a poignant romance that will have you believing in the power of love."* N.N. Light's Book Heaven

**SEEING THINGS**

*"Seeing Things is a book that will keep you at the edge of your seat."* Alice Klein, Sime-Gen Reviews

**THE GIRL MOST LIKELY**

*"Loved this book! Jana Richards writes with great wit and a sharp eye for detail, making her characters and story feel absolutely real."* Jill Blake, Goodreads Reviewer

**Get Your Free Gift!**

GET **HOME TO SOLACE LAKE**, your free prequel to the Love at Solace Lake series when you sign up for Jana Richards' newsletter!

# Prologue

ANGRY VOICES HUNG ON the humid summer air, as heavy as the scent of the pine trees in the forest surrounding her. Scarlet Lindquist tiptoed along the well-worn path, the soft earth muffling her steps. If Mom and Daddy caught her following them, they'd be mad. They'd told her to stay with Grandma at the lodge because they had things they needed to talk about. Adult things.

Her older sister Harper said Daddy's unexpected arrival at their grandparents' fishing lodge meant he was taking them home. He wouldn't have come all the way from Minneapolis if that wasn't his plan. Didn't he tell them how much he'd missed them since he went away?

Scarlet wasn't so sure. Harper hadn't heard the fighting between Mom and Grandma Dorothy. But she had. They thought she didn't understand, but she understood plenty; she was eight, not a baby like her sister Maggie. Mom said the marriage was over, and she was never going back. She was going to start a new life. Grandma said she'd be a fool to throw away her marriage. That she had a good life with Daddy, a secure life, and surely there could be forgiveness. Mom said Grandma didn't understand, that she'd never understood.

She hoped that didn't mean her parents were getting a divorce. Her friend Becca's parents got a divorce and she had to move between their houses every week, and they were constantly telling her how much they hated each other. Scarlet wished Daddy would come home, so things could be the way they were before.

She stopped and crouched behind a clump of trees. Her parents had arrived at The Point, a finger of land that stuck out into Solace Lake. Her mom kept her canoe here because it was easy to launch from the small sand beach on the very tip of the point, but today Scarlet saw that her mom's yellow canoe was tied to the dock. Grampa had built the dock at The Point for the use of his customers, the fishermen who came up to the lodge to catch the fish that lived in the lake. There was another dock closer to the lodge, but Grampa said fishers liked this one because the deep water at the end of the dock was the best spot on the lake to fish.

When she peeked between the branches, she saw that her parents had stopped walking and were facing each other on the beach. Scarlet held her breath, afraid they'd hear her and make her go away.

"I know what I said before, but I can't give you up. I don't want a divorce. We can try again. We can work this out." Daddy's voice sounded funny, as if he was crying. "You know I love you, don't you? I've always loved you. That hasn't changed."

"I know," Mom said. "But I can't go on like this, living a lie."

"It's not a lie! We have a family! The girls need us. Can't we try again? At least for them?"

"It's too late, Rob! You know it is!" She shook her head. "I'll never keep Harper and Scarlet away from you, no matter what happens between us. They need you."

"I can't bear it, Miranda! I can't lose you. I'm sorry I wasn't the husband you needed. I'm sorry I put my work first too often, but I can change. Can't you give me another chance?" He covered his face with his hands. "If you leave me and take the girls, I have no reason to live. I'd rather be dead."

She'd never seen her daddy cry before and it frightened her. She couldn't stop her own tears from streaking down her cheeks. She put both hands over her mouth so her sobs couldn't escape.

"Don't talk like that, Rob. It's not fair. You know as well as I do, we're no good together. I'm sorry, but it's the truth. You deserve someone who loves you to distraction, and that's not me."

They stopped talking and Scarlet heard only the birds singing in the trees. Then daddy sighed, his voice sounding tired and sad. "Do you love him?"

"Yes." Scarlet heard the hitch in her mother's voice. "I always have."

Who were they talking about? Did this mean they were never going home again? She didn't want to stay here forever with Grandma Dorothy and Grampa Bill. She hated the fishing lodge. She hated the bugs and the crawly things. She wanted to go back to their big house in Minneapolis and play with her friends. She wanted her daddy.

A sob escaped despite her hands covering her mouth. She curled into a ball and made herself as tiny as possible.

The branches parted and her mom peered down at her. "Scarlet, honey, what are you doing here? Didn't we tell you not to follow us?"

"Why can't we go home with Daddy?" Fear and anger made her shout.

"I'm sorry, honey. For now, we're going to stay here."

"I don't want to stay with Grandma and Grampa! I want to go home!"

Her mom pulled her up and gave her a hug, her arms so tight Scarlet could barely breathe. "We won't be here much longer. We're going to have a new home soon."

"Will Daddy be there?"

"No, honey, he won't. But you can visit him, and you can talk to him on the phone anytime you want to."

"Will Harper and Maggie come to our new home, too?"

"Yes, of course. We'll all be together."

*Except for Daddy.*

Mom kissed her cheek. "Go back to the lodge now. Daddy and I will be along in a little while."

Scarlet nodded. Over Mom's shoulder she saw her daddy. His hands were in the pockets of his jeans and his head was down. He looked sad, like he was going to cry again.

She scrambled out of her mom's arms and down the path to fling her arms around his waist. He sank to his knees and hugged her back. Then, he grasped her shoulders in his hands and looked into her face.

"I love you, Scarlet." He kissed her cheek. "No matter what happens, always remember that, okay?"

"Okay."

He gave her a brief, sad smile. "Good girl. Now listen to your mother and run back to lodge. We'll see you in a few minutes."

Tears ran down Scarlet's cheeks. "I don't want to leave you."

He kissed her again and then gave her one of his goofy grins. For a moment he was the Daddy she'd always known, the one who laughed a lot and told them funny stories. "Are Mom and I going to have to go out into the middle of the lake to have a private conversation? C'mon, go back to the lodge now, pumpkin."

She wanted to argue. She wanted to cry and scream and tell him not to leave her. But the sadness was back in his eyes, and she knew it wouldn't do any good.

Scarlet looked to her mom, hoping to appeal to her, but she'd stepped onto the dock and jumped into her yellow canoe. In the weeks since they'd been at the lodge, Scarlet had seen her on the lake lots, drifting around on the water.

Her father straightened to his full height, his movements stiff and angry. "Miranda, we haven't finished talking. Don't turn your back on me."

"I think we've said everything there is to say."

"That's your solution for everything, isn't it? Walking away and shutting me out. That's not going to work anymore."

With a sigh, Mom climbed back onto the deck. "Fine. Say whatever it is you need to say."

Scarlet turned and ran back the way she'd come, not wanting to hear them fight any more. She heard her mom call after her, but she ignored her and kept running. Partway back to the lodge, she saw Willy, Grampa's handyman, running in the opposite direction on another path toward her mom and daddy. They wouldn't like him listening to their conversation either.

Instead of going back into the lodge, she stumbled her way to the little fort in the trees that she and Harper had built by piling together sticks and branches. Even though it was next to the path between the lodge and Grampa Bill's shed, it was hard to see unless you knew where to look. She pushed aside the branches at the opening and went inside. She didn't want to go back to the lodge and face Grandma's questions about where she'd been.

Scarlet curled up on the dried leaves lining the floor of the fort and tugged on her ponytail, twisting her hair between her fingers. Where was this new home Mommy was talking about? Was it here in the country, close to Grandma and Grampa's fishing lodge, or someplace else? It was scary not knowing. Would she have friends there? When would she get to see her daddy again?

She fell asleep and was awakened with a start when she heard someone running along the path, sobbing. She stuck her head out of the fort in time to see Harper trip over a root on the path and skin her knees. Her sister was two years older and Scarlet had rarely seen her cry, even when she'd fallen out of the tree in their backyard and broken her arm. It scared her to see her crying now.

"They're in the water!" Tears streamed down Harper's face. "Willy said Mom and Daddy are in the water, and they didn't come back up. We have to tell Grandma!"

Scarlet ran behind Harper, her heart racing. Did Mommy and Daddy go out on the lake because she'd followed them? Because they didn't want her to listen?

If something bad happened to them, it was all her fault.

# Chapter One

*TWENTY-TWO YEARS LATER.*

Scarlet Lindquist struggled to hold back tears as she lifted her champagne flute in a salute to her sister and her fiancé. She hated public displays of emotion, especially when she was the one whose emotions were on display. But as maid of honor, she was expected to give a toast to the bride and groom at their rehearsal dinner and welcome Ethan Hainstock into her family.

"Please join me in toasting the happy couple. I wish you many years of love and wedded bliss. To Harper and Ethan."

The small gathering of family and friends of both the bride and groom rose together and lifted their glasses. "To Harper and Ethan."

She clinked her glass against her sister Maggie's and then turned to her left to touch Ethan's brother's flute, though she noticed the best man had passed on the champagne. A shiver trembled down her spine when her gaze locked with Cameron Hainstock's. His dark eyes openly assessed her. She was used to men's scrutiny; males had been staring at her since she was fourteen and developed breasts. But she sensed more in Cameron's gaze than simple sexual appreciation. It was as if he was trying to look inside her soul to determine what kind of person she was. She wondered what conclusions he'd made.

With the toast over, Scarlet tore her gaze away from Cameron's and gratefully resumed her seat. Her thoughts returned to the reason they were all gathered at Miller's, the resort down the road from their fishing lodge on Solace Lake in north central Minnesota. She and her sisters had inherited the lodge from their grandparents and were currently renovating it. Harper's relationship and subsequent engagement to Ethan Hainstock had happened so quickly. At first, Scarlet been suspicious of Ethan, but she'd come to like him, mainly because she could see how much he loved her sister. She was happy for Harper, she really was.

But to marry so soon? Scarlet hoped she was doing the right thing. Nobody deserved happiness more than Harper.

When they'd announced their engagement and said they wanted to get married right away, she'd been pleased, but cautious. They didn't have to rush into marriage. They'd only met a few months ago. It wouldn't hurt to wait. She had no doubt they loved each other, but was it enough? It certainly hadn't been enough for her parents. And she wasn't exactly a shining example of the power of love. She prayed Harper and Ethan would be the exception to the rule.

Ethan's sister Lydia got to her feet. "It's been a lovely evening, but it's time for us to go. Tomorrow's a big day, isn't it, Tessa?"

Cameron's five-year-old daughter nodded solemnly. "I get to be flower girl tomorrow."

Cameron leaned over to kiss his daughter's hair, the color the same deep chocolate brown as his own. An unwelcome emotion caused a lump to form in Scarlet's throat at the tenderness in his touch. "You're going to be the best flower girl ever."

"I know."

Everyone laughed at Tessa's earnest reply. Cameron lifted her out the booster seat and held her in his arms. "Come on, pumpkin. Time for this flower girl to hit the sack."

*Pumpkin*. Scarlet had a sudden flashback of being carried in her father's arms in the same way, her head resting against his shoulder in complete trust.

She swallowed and pushed the memory from her mind.

Cameron turned to face her. "Ethan said you needed help decorating the wedding tent tomorrow. What time did you want me to be there?"

She blinked in surprise. "I didn't know you'd volunteered to help."

Harper touched her arm. "I know you, Scarlet. You're planning some decorating extravaganza, aren't you?"

"Maybe." Her sister really did know her. She wanted Harper's wedding to be beautiful, and very special. Besides, she loved decorating.

Ethan put his arm around Harper's shoulders. "I thought maybe Cam and Drew could give you a hand."

Scarlet glanced over at Drew, Ethan's twenty-one-year-old nephew. He was acting as Ethan's groomsman and had been paired with Maggie in the wedding party. He flashed her a smile and a thumbs-up, and she smiled back. She enjoyed working alone, liked making the ideas in her head come to life. But there was a lot to do and, though she hated to admit it, she could use some help. She only wished Cameron's presence didn't make her feel so...unsettled.

She forced a smile. "I appreciate the help. I'll be at the tent around nine a.m. The tables and chairs we're renting are supposed to be delivered between ten and eleven, and I'd like to get most of the decorating finished before then."

Cameron nodded. "We'll be at the lodge at nine."

"Thanks. I'll see you then."

Ethan clapped his brother on the back. "Good. Thanks, Cam."

Scarlet smiled as she watched her sister and her soon-to-be husband cross the room. He was dark to her fair, tall to her petite, brown eyed to her blue. But in every way that was important, Harper and Ethan were a match. A perfect team. Ethan had made Harper's dream to bring the fishing lodge back to life his dream as well. Together, they were turning the old lodge into an eco-friendly resort the whole family could be proud of.

To have someone to share her dreams, someone to have her back and love her no matter what seemed like a fairy tale to Scarlet.

"They're a good-looking couple, aren't they?"

> Cameron's deep voice broke into her thoughts, chasing away her fanciful notions. *Nothing but wishful thinking.*

"Yes, they are."

He adjusted a limp, nearly asleep Tessa in his arms. Her head lay against his broad shoulder, while one hand rested on his chest, as if she wanted to feel the beat of her father's heart. For some reason, the thought made her heart ache.

"Is Harper pregnant?"

She jerked her head up at his whispered question. "What? No, of course not!" In her surprise, her voice was louder than she'd intended.

"I had to ask. They're getting married in a hell of a hurry."

At least, she didn't think Harper was pregnant. She and her sisters often withheld the truth about their lives from each other, especially when the truth was unpleasant, but she'd hoped they'd put those days behind them. Surely if Harper was pregnant, she would have shared the news with her and Maggie.

Harper had turned to give her a puzzled stare, alerted by sound of her raised voice. Scarlet flashed her a phony smile before speaking to Cameron again, this time in a lowered tone. "Do you think that's the only reason he'd marry her? Call me sentimental, but I believe they're marrying for love."

"They barely know each other. What would be the harm in waiting a few months? I don't want Ethan to get hurt."

She, too, had concerns, but she was too insulted on behalf of her sister to admit to them. He better not be suggesting Harper was only marrying Ethan for his money. Five years ago, Ethan won over a hundred and seventy-five million dollars in a lottery, though Harper hadn't been aware of that when they first met. Because of painful past experiences, he'd kept the secret far longer than he should have, afraid it would alter the way she saw him.

Scarlet straightened and looked Cameron in the eye. "I don't want Harper to get hurt *again*. He lied to her about the money and she's the one who walked away."

He leaned in close, his voice low and his eyes glittering. "But she came back, didn't she?"

Before she could respond, he turned and walked across the room. A moment later, he left the dining room of Miller's Resort with his family, Tessa still in his arms.

Anger swirled in her gut. Was Cameron Hainstock planning to make trouble for Harper?

Her hands fisted at her sides. *Not on my watch, he won't.*

# Chapter Two

CAM ARRIVED AT THE lodge at ten minutes before nine. At least Scarlet Lindquist couldn't accuse him of being late.

That was probably the only thing she wouldn't accuse him of.

He winced when he thought of their conversation the previous evening. He shouldn't have come right out and asked the question that had been worrying him ever since Ethan had announced his engagement. It had been rude and insulting. But he knew better than most the consequences of an unplanned pregnancy. He'd been relieved when Scarlet denied it.

He hoped she was right.

He parked his truck away from the construction chaos surrounding the lodge. Drew's car was nowhere to be seen. *Good.* He'd come a few minutes early on purpose, hoping to apologize to Scarlet for his rudeness. Though he was sorry for the way he'd acted toward her, it didn't change his wariness about his brother's upcoming wedding. Someone as rich as Ethan had to be very careful.

He made his way to the large white canvas tent that had been set up a short distance from the lodge on what had formerly been the parking lot. The sides of the tent had been rolled up to allow a breeze to blow through. Even at nine a.m. it was already hot.

Scarlet was inside the tent, fighting to untangle what looked like miles of mini-lights. For a moment, he studied her unobserved. She had the fair, creamy skin of a redhead, with a smattering of freckles sprinkled across her nose and cheeks. She wore a blue tank top and denim shorts that left acres of creamy thigh exposed.

He'd always been a sucker for a woman with great legs.

Cam struggled to focus on her face instead. She looked up when he cleared his throat, her expression wary.

"Hi. Thanks for coming. We've got a lot to get done."

"No problem." He shuffled uncomfortably from one foot to the other. "Listen, I want to apologize for what I said last night. I insulted you and your sister, and I'm sorry."

She silently continued to untangle the lights, her eyes on her task. When she finally lifted her gaze to his, her mouth was unsmiling and her chin lifted at a defiant angle. "Are you planning to cause trouble for my sister? Because if you are—"

"No." He held his hands up in surrender. "Hell, no. The last thing I want to do is interfere. I'm simply concerned. Ethan was engaged once before, and it was a disaster. The woman faked a pregnancy so he'd marry her and she could get her hands on his money."

Scarlet's eyebrows rose. "That's pretty intense. I didn't know." She set aside the lights. "I'm sorry he had a bad time, but Harper's not looking to use him. She loves him. She's a good person."

He nodded, accepting her words with a grain of salt. Of course Scarlet would defend her sister. Still, he hoped she was right.

"And you're wrong about why Harper went back to Ethan. You think it was because he handed over ownership of the lodge to her, free and clear."

"Wasn't that what happened?" When Harper broke up with him, his brother had papers drawn up, giving her everything. As far as Cam was concerned, it was the stupidest thing he'd ever done.

"Harper wouldn't sign those papers. She didn't want Ethan to think the money was more important to her than he was. She drew up her own papers. Ethan now owns fifty percent of the lodge."

That was a surprise. Ethan hadn't shared this information with him. He hadn't shared the information about giving Harper complete ownership either, but Lydia had filled him in. As Ethan's financial advisor, she'd been concerned.

This new information, if true, put Harper's relationship with his brother in a different light.

Drew walked into the tent, giving Scarlet a friendly smile. "Good morning. I see the decorating crew's all here. I hope I'm not late."

"No, at all. We're just getting started."

Cam noticed that the greeting Scarlet gave his nephew was much warmer than the one she'd given him. The smile she bestowed on Drew made his jaw clench. Trying to keep the edge out of his voice, he asked, "What would you like us to do?"

She lifted another string of white mini-lights. "My plan is to string these lights between the main supporting poles and some of the side supports and then cover the lights with tulle."

"With what?" Drew asked.

Scarlet grinned. "With tulle. It's a gauzy, see-through fabric. Trust me, it'll look really pretty and make this tent look better than the canvas hut it is right now."

She showed them where she wanted the lights strung. With the help of some staple guns and a couple of ladders borrowed from the construction crew, they got the job done.

"Looks pretty good, if I do say so myself," Drew said, looking up at the ceiling of the tent. He swatted at a mosquito on his arm.

Scarlet handed him a can of mosquito repellant. "Are you kidding? It looks great! But don't rest on your laurels yet. I have a few more things for you to do."

"Like what?" he asked, spraying his arms with repellent.

"I've got a couple of wooden arbors. I want to string lights through one and place it at the entrance to the tent."

"But the whole tent is open," Drew argued. "How are people supposed to know where the entrance is?"

Scarlet grinned. "Because we'll show them."

"Where does the other arbor go?" Cam asked.

"On the hill overlooking the lake where the ceremony is going to take place."

Cam and Drew strung the lights through the latticework of the arbor and set it in the spot Scarlet directed them to. She put the finishing touches on it by covering the lights with tulle. Cam could see her vision coming together, truly transforming the utilitarian tent into something beautiful.

After attaching the mini-lights to extension cords that were plugged into a generator next to the lodge, he and Drew tested the lights. When they were satisfied everything worked properly, they went back into the tent to find Scarlet. She was standing in front of the second arbor, a bundle of tulle in her hands.

"What's next, boss?" Drew asked.

"We're almost done," she said with a smile. "I just have to figure out what to do with this second arbor. Harper wants things to be kept simple at the ceremony. She thinks the lake and trees are enough decoration."

Drew lifted a piece of material and let it drop. "Why not decorate the arbor the same way you did the other one, with this tulle stuff?"

"I could, I suppose." She gave Drew a patient smile. "But I'd like something different, something to set it apart and make it a little more special."

"Do you have any more decorating material?" Cam asked.

She turned cool eyes to him. "Yes, I've got a box of ribbon. Over there."

She pointed to a cardboard box sitting on the ground on the other side of the tent, and Cam went to retrieve it. There were several rolls of ribbon, some silver and some in a dark emerald green, the same color as Tessa's flower girl dress. Harper had purchased the dress at a bridal shop in Brainerd, and a local seamstress had hemmed it and made a few alterations so it fit his daughter perfectly.

"How 'bout we wind some of these ribbons through the arbor. It'll match your dresses."

"How did you know our dresses were this color?"

"I assumed they were the same color as Tessa's. Am I wrong?"

"No, they're the same color." She said the words reluctantly, as if unwilling to concede even this small point to him. "I was going to use the ribbon to tie green and silver balloons from the three support poles. I don't have enough for the arbor as well."

"What if we only make a balloon and ribbon display on the center pole? That way we'd have enough."

Her brow wrinkled. "I suppose that could work. What do you have in mind?"

Cam lifted some of the silver ribbon from the box. It was about three inches wide and had metal wire embedded on the edges of the fabric that allowed it to be manipulated and folded anyway he chose. He wove silver ribbon through the latticework in one direction, then the green in the opposite, creating a checkerboard affect. He stepped back to check it out. *Not bad on short notice.*

Scarlet walked around the arbor, examining it with a critical eye. "It looks good. I like it." She sounded surprised.

"Well, you know, Uncle Cam is an artist," Drew said with a grin.

She turned to look at him, lifting an eyebrow as if she expected an explanation. Cam shrugged. "I do some drawing."

"Come on, Uncle Cam. Don't be so modest." Drew turned to Scarlet. "He's an amazing artist. Get him to show you some of his drawings sometime. And he makes furniture."

"A man of many talents." There was a slight mocking tone in her voice. Cam inwardly sighed. He couldn't blame her. He hadn't given her much reason to praise him. Or like him.

"So, will this do for the second arbor, or would you like to try something else?" he asked.

"No, this is perfect. Thank you. All we have to do now is set it up on the hill."

He and Drew carried the arbor a short distance to a small, flat-topped hill overlooking the lake. Cam smiled as he set it down. It was a beautiful spot for a wedding ceremony.

He hoped the marriage wasn't as short as the wedding ceremony was supposed to be.

"Where do you want this?"

Scarlet walked to a spot near the edge of the hill. "Right here. That way it's behind Ethan and Harper and will frame the view of the lake."

He could see it. Scarlet had a good eye.

They secured the arbor with pegs. "Do we need anything else up here?"

Scarlet shook her head. "Only the flowers, but I won't be picking those up until this afternoon. The ceremony won't be more than fifteen minutes, so everyone will have to stand. I'm afraid if we bring chairs, they'll sink into the ground."

"What's left to do?"

"The last thing is blowing up the balloons and tying them to the center support."

"I was thinking," Cam began. "You have lots of balloons. We can use what's left of the ribbon on the center support and then make smaller displays with just balloons on the other two support poles. It would look more balanced that way."

Scarlet cocked her head slightly as she examined him. "You really are an artist, aren't you?"

"Told you," Drew said with a grin.

Cam looked away, embarrassed by her words. He rarely talked about his artwork and almost never showed it to anyone outside of his family. His voice sounded gruff as he spoke to his nephew. "Come on, kid. You're so full of hot air you should be able to blow up a few balloons."

The delivery truck with the rented tables and chairs arrived as they finished hanging the last of the balloons. He and Drew helped unload and place the tables and chairs around the perimeter of the tent. Scarlet had also rented a portable wooden dance floor that they set up in the middle of tent, between the first two support poles.

"I think that's it, gentlemen," Scarlet said when they'd finished putting together the dance floor. "Thank you for all your help. I couldn't have done this on my own."

"You're welcome," Drew said. He slapped Cam on the back. "I'm ready for lunch. How about you, Scarlet? You want to join us? I hear Miller's has a really good lunch buffet."

"Thanks, Drew, but I can't. I still have a lot of things to do before the ceremony at five o'clock."

"How about you, Uncle Cam? You ready for lunch?"

Cam hesitated. He didn't want any bad feelings to linger between him and Scarlet, not on Ethan's wedding day. It suddenly felt very important that she forgive him for his stupid remarks last night. "You said you had to pick up flowers?"

"Yeah, in Brainerd." She checked her watch. "I should probably leave soon."

"Why don't I pick up the flowers while you have lunch with Drew? I'll bring them back here and we'll help you with them. That way you won't be so rushed for time."

Her blue eyes regarded him with a mixture of surprise and curiosity, which was better than the hostility he'd seen in them earlier. "That would be very...helpful. Thank you."

"That's me. Mr. Helpful."

When she laughed, something twisted inside his chest, as if a muscle he hadn't used in a very long time unexpectedly jerked back to life.

*Damn.*

There was no doubt she was a beautiful, desirable woman. And that was the reason he couldn't let himself feel anything for her, or even like her. He'd made the mistake of falling hard for another beautiful woman, and she'd ripped his heart in two. But she'd also given him Tessa, and he'd spent the last five years walking a tightrope between heartache and joy.

A very uncomfortable place to be.

CAM FROWNED AT HIS reflection in the mirror, at the crooked, bulky knot he'd made in his tie. How the hell did other guys wear one of these damn nooses around their necks every day? "Can't I wear a t-shirt?"

"To my wedding? I don't think so." Ethan spun him around, untangled the tie and flipped up the collar of Cam's shirt. "When was the last time you wore a tie?"

He knew the date exactly. "Seven years ago."

Ethan's eyes met his. "Dad's funeral."

Cam nodded curtly. The last thing he wanted to think about, the last thing he wanted Ethan to think about on his wedding day, was their father. But the old man cast a long shadow, even from the grave.

Ethan skillfully looped the silk tie into a perfect knot, then gave it a tug, nearly strangling him. Cam stuck his finger between his neck and the collar of his shirt. "Geez, give me a break here."

"Fine." Ethan loosened the tie enough to ease the strangling sensation. "Have I ever told you what a big baby you are?"

"Have I ever told you you're a pain in the ass?"

"Many times."

A knock sounded on Cam's bedroom door before Drew stepped inside. "Are you two ladies ready? Mom says it's time to go."

Cam slipped on his suit jacket. "Don't be a smartass, Drew. Just because you're dressed up all pretty doesn't mean I can't kick your ass."

"In your dreams, old man."

*Spoken with the confidence of a twenty-one-year old.* Cam had been there once, a long time ago, as brash and cocky as his nephew. But these days, he sometimes felt as ancient as Drew believed he was.

"Give us a minute, will you?"

"Okay, but make it quick. Mom's starting to get antsy."

"We'll be right there."

Drew nodded and shut the door as he left.

Ethan frowned. "Is there a problem?"

"I need to ask you, are you sure?"

"About marrying Harper? Absolutely. More sure than I've ever been about anything in my life."

He'd answered with no hesitation. His face was calm and his voice steady. He looked...happy.

"Is it true that you and Harper have divided up the ownership of the lodge fifty/fifty?"

"Where did you hear that?"

"A little birdie told me." A long-legged, redheaded flamingo. "Is it true?"

"Actually, I own fifty percent of the lodge and Harper and her sisters share the other fifty percent. It was Harper's idea. Why are you asking about this now?"

"It doesn't matter. Not if you're sure."

"I am. I love Harper. I've never met anyone like her. She doesn't care about the money. She loves me for me. Do you know how rare that it?"

"Yeah, I do."

He'd once believed Laura loved him that way, but he'd been wrong. Very wrong. He prayed Harper Lindquist cared as much for Ethan as he did for her, and that she wouldn't abuse his love. "I want you to be happy."

"I will be. I already am."

Cam breathed a sigh of relief and clapped his brother on the shoulder. "Then, let's go get you married."

As soon as they opened the door, Tessa launched herself at him, hugging him around the knees. "Daddy! We'll be late for the wedding! Auntie Lydia says!"

Cam hoisted her into his arms. She smelled like a sweet combination of baby shampoo and roses. Lydia and his teenage niece Carrie had curled Tessa's long, dark hair into shining ringlets that bounced when she moved. She clutched her wicker basket with both hands as if afraid to lose some of the precious rose petals inside. The poufy, emerald green flower girl dress was silky in his hands and made Tessa look like a tiny princess. *His little princess.*

Cam kissed her cheek, his heart overflowing with love for his child. "Don't worry, pumpkin. They can't start without the flower girl."

"Or the groom," Ethan said.

"Yeah, he's kind of important to this endeavor," his brother-in-law Graham added with a grin.

"Come on, boys." Lydia slapped Cam on the butt. "You can crack jokes later. Right now, we have a wedding to get to."

Lydia hustled them into the waiting limousine and they made the ten-minute trip to the lodge. Guests had started to arrive and were milling around the wedding tent they'd decorated that morning. Since the lodge was a construction zone, the tent had been the only solution. Cam wondered why Harper hadn't opted for a fancier wedding at a posh hotel in the city or a destination wedding somewhere in the

Caribbean. His brother would have given her anything she asked for.

Maybe Ethan was right about the money not being important to her. He hoped so.

"Harper said the bridesmaids would be waiting in the tent," Ethan said. "You can take Tessa there."

He walked Tessa to the tent while the rest of the family made their way to the hill overlooking the lake where the ceremony was to take place. It was a beautiful summer afternoon, perfect for an outdoor wedding. The temperature was cooler in the shade of the trees surrounding the tent, the air scented with pine. As soon as he entered the tent his gaze locked with Scarlet's. His breath caught in his throat. If he'd thought her attractive before, in shorts and a tank top, she was magnificent now in emerald silk. The color brought out the vivid red of her hair.

Holding Tessa's hand, he approached her. Harper's youngest sister Maggie was there, as well. Where Scarlet had blue eyes and red hair, Maggie had dark brown hair and eyes.

"Ethan said I was to bring Tessa here so she can walk to the ceremony with you."

Scarlet nodded. "Yes, of course—"

"Daddy, I want to go with you!" Tessa clung to his leg.

He put a hand on her head and tried to sooth. At five, she was very wary of people she didn't know. Her mother's constant stream of boyfriends probably didn't help, he thought bitterly. "It's okay, pumpkin."

Before he could say anything more, Scarlet stooped so she was at eye level with Tessa. "Of course, you can go with your daddy now if you want to. But maybe it would be fun to walk with my sister Maggie and me. My name is Scarlet. Remember, we met last night at the rehearsal dinner?"

"Yes, I remember." Tessa let go of his pant leg.

"My sister Harper is going to marry your Uncle Ethan."

Tessa responded with an enthusiastic nod. "And I get to be flower girl."

"I know. It's exciting, isn't it?"

Tessa nodded again.

"If you come with me and Maggie to the ceremony, you can toss your rose petals on the ground as we walk up the aisle."

"Really?"

"Yes, really. If you get nervous, you can hold my hand if you want to. We'll all walk together to the same place where your daddy and Uncle Ethan will be. Okay?"

"Okay."

Scarlet extended her hand. "Let's shake on it."

Without hesitation, Tessa put her hand in Scarlet's. And just like that, she erased his daughter's fears.

He wasn't sure if he should be grateful or worried.

Scarlet rose to her full height, still holding Tessa's hand. When she looked at him, the smiling face she'd presented to his daughter was gone. "Harper should be here any minute, then we'll be joining you. It won't be long."

Cam forgot to breathe. Scarlet's skin was flawless and pale, the freckles he'd noticed earlier making her even more attractive. He had the insane desire to run his finger over her cheek and discover for himself if it felt as soft as it looked.

"Harper is here," Maggie said, breaking the spell.

Cam blinked and looked over Scarlet's shoulder. Harper had entered the tent through the back with Reese Hanson and his wife, who leaned heavily on a cane. He didn't know that Reese, the general contractor on the lodge renovation, and Harper were so close.

"Abby was our mother's best friend," Scarlet said, reading his thoughts.

"Right. Ethan mentioned that."

Ethan had also told him that Harper's parents had died in a boating accident when she and her sisters were very young. Maybe that's why Scarlet connected with Tessa so easily. She would know what it was like to be a child and feel alone and scared.

He forced himself to look away. "I should go. Bye, Tessa. I'll see you in a couple of minutes."

"Bye, Daddy," she said happily, still holding Scarlet's hand.

With one last glance at the two of them, he left the tent and made his way to the spot where the ceremony was to take place. Maybe he'd misjudged both Harper and her sister.

# Chapter Three

"AND NOW TO GIVE THE toast to the groom, please welcome our Maid of Honor, Scarlet Lindquist."

Scarlet rose to her feet and made herself smile at the Master of Ceremonies, Ethan's brother-in-law Graham. She clutched her wineglass with sweaty palms. The second toast she'd had to give in as many days and her nerves were on edge. In her line of work, she often had to speak in public and make presentations to clients, but she was completely confident and in control in her work life.

Right now, she was anything but in control. There was so much at stake, namely her sister's happiness. If she said something Ethan, or his family, took offence to, it may affect Harper's marriage.

God, she hoped Harper was doing the right thing.

Graham smiled encouragingly and handed her the mic. Scarlet's hands shook as she began. "What can I say about Ethan? I haven't known him long, but in that short time he's demonstrated his generosity and kindness. And if you look over at the lodge construction site, you'll know he's a man who's not afraid to take risks.

"He's also willing to take the biggest risk of all – love. Ethan accomplished a feat no other man has ever managed before. He made my sister fall in love with him. I know that if Harper loves him, he must be very, very special."

Her throat clogged with tears. She hadn't expected to get so emotional. She paused for a moment and ducked her head. From the corner of her eye, she saw Cameron give her a reassuring wink. Surprised, she blinked at him, then raised her head and looked out at the fifty or so people gathered to celebrate the wedding.

"On behalf of my sister Maggie, I'd like to welcome Ethan into our family." She lifted her wineglass. "To the groom."

"To the groom."

With the exception of the bride and groom, everyone in the room stood and offered a toast. Scarlet noticed that once more Cameron's wineglass was empty. Maybe he was more of a beer guy.

Ethan got up from his chair and enveloped her in a hug. "Thank you," he whispered. "Your welcome means a lot to me."

"Just make her happy, okay?"

"I will. I swear."

Scarlet kissed his cheek. Despite the money, and despite the lies he'd told Harper when they'd first met, she believed him.

When she and Ethan sat down, Graham spoke into the mic. "And now for the toast to the bride, I give you the best man, Cameron Hainstock."

Cameron got to his feet and walked to the podium, taking his empty wineglass with him. Butterflies danced in Scarlet's stomach. She had no idea what he was going to say, but she hoped he didn't embarrass Harper by making some crude remark about money.

He stuck his hand in the pocket of his suit pants, looking every inch the confident, self-assured male. His grey suit jacket fit perfectly across his broad shoulders, the cut of the pants accentuating his lean hips and powerful thighs. Scarlet swallowed and looked away. The last thing she needed to obsess about was Cameron Hainstock's body.

"I don't have any prepared remarks," Cameron began. "But I wanted to say that I've never seen my brother happier. I wish both of you much success in the new venture you've embarked on with the lodge project. But mostly, I wish you much happiness in your life together. May you always love each other as much as you do right now." He picked up his glass and held it high. "Welcome to the Hainstock clan, Harper. To the bride."

"To the bride."

Scarlet swallowed some of her wine, relieved no damage had been done. Harper rose to give Cameron a kiss on his cheek. Over Harper's shoulder, he winked at her. When he sat down without looking her way again, she wondered if she'd imagined it.

Ethan and Harper stood together at the podium holding hands. "We'd like to thank everyone for coming and for making this such a special day for us," Ethan said.

"We'd especially like to thank our families for everything they've done," Harper said. She smiled at Scarlet and Maggie. "Thank you, my darling sister Maggie for all your work on the wonderful food you created, and to my work family over at Miller's Resort for letting us use their kitchen to prepare it. It was a fabulous meal and I love you all." She paused while people applauded. "And to my sister Scarlet, thank you for transforming this dreary tent into a beautiful fairy wonderland. If anyone could perform a miracle like that, it's you. I love you both so much." Her voice choked with emotion.

Ethan put his arm around her shoulders and accepted the microphone from her. "I want to thank my family as well. For Cam, Drew and Tessa for being in our wedding party, for Graham's skills as Master of Ceremonies, and to Carrie and Lydia for making us all look pretty and getting us to my wedding on time. Without your support, today and every day, I'm not sure how I'd get by. I love you all." He waited while everyone applauded. "That concludes the speeches for this evening. Now we can party!"

The dishes were quickly gathered and the food from the buffet tables packed in containers and taken away. The buffet tables were folded and removed from the wooden floor to allow for dancing. A four-piece band, set up in one corner of the tent, began to play. Graham, as Master of Ceremonies, announced the first dance.

"Ladies and gentlemen, Mr. and Mrs. Ethan Hainstock will now dance their first dance as husband and wife."

The assembled group clapped and cheered as the bride and groom stepped onto the floor. The singer crooned the old Elvis song "I can't help falling in love with you." Ethan and Harper didn't take their eyes off each other as they slowly waltzed their way around the small dance floor.

"They look so in love," Maggie whispered.

Scarlet linked fingers with her sister. "I know."

Her chest tightened. The way Ethan was looking at Harper, like she was his life, his everything, made her chest ache with longing.

She closed her eyes. *You had your chance, and you threw it away. Twice.*

Graham spoke into the mic again. "Would the rest of the wedding party please join the happy couple?"

Ethan's nephew Drew was at Maggie's side immediately, holding out his hand. Scarlet stifled a grin. He was a good-looking kid, but she was pretty confident he didn't have a snowball's chance in Hell with her beautiful younger sister.

Maggie politely accepted his hand and let Drew lead her out onto the floor. A moment later, Cameron was beside her.

"Would you like to dance?"

She looked up at him. His mouth was unsmiling and his dark eyes didn't give any hint as to what he was thinking. The idea of being in his arms caused gooseflesh to rise on her arms and her stomach to flutter in excitement.

She gave herself a mental scolding. *Stop it.* She didn't even like Cameron Hainstock. He could be abrupt and rude, and she still worried he'd cause Harper trouble in her marriage.

But he was also over six feet of hard-muscled male and she was only human. A few butterflies in the stomach didn't mean anything.

Scarlet gave a quick nod and got to her feet. She suppressed a shiver when his hand rested on the small of her back. A moment later, they were out on the dance floor and she was in his arms.

"I saw your face," he said.

"Excuse me?"

"You were afraid I was going to say something to embarrass your sister during my toast."

There was no use denying it. "The thought had crossed my mind."

"I would never embarrass Ethan on the most important day of his life. He tells me he loves Harper, and I have to accept it."

*Abrupt and rude.* "How very big of you."

To her amazement, he laughed. The smile transformed his face, making him look years younger, and almost...nice.

"You surprise me, Scarlet Lindquist."

"Really? How's that?"

"For one thing, you have a sense of humor."

"I'll have you know, I have a fabulous sense of humor. Everyone says so."

"Secondly," he said, ignoring her comment, "you were kind to my daughter. I appreciate that."

"She's a sweet little girl. Why wouldn't I be kind to her?"

He kept his voice low. "Because I questioned the reason they were getting married so quickly."

*Yep, abrupt and rude.* "And you thought I'd try to get back at you through Tessa?"

"The thought had crossed my mind," he said dryly, mimicking her words.

"Wow, you really have a low opinion of me, don't you? You think I'm so petty I would be mean to an innocent child so I could stick it to you?"

"Don't take it personally. I'm suspicious of the motives of most women. I make an exception for my sister and my niece, and of course my daughter."

Scarlet stared up into his face. He was serious. He must have been hurt pretty badly for him to distrust the entire female gender. "Well, as long as it's nothing personal."

He grinned and spun her around. Scarlet laughed. At least she knew where she stood with Cameron.

Tessa ran out onto the dance floor and Scarlet watched as she tugged on Ethan's suit jacket. He picked her up and twirled her and Harper in a circle. Harper laughed and kissed Tessa's cheek.

"She's going to make you put her on your exception list," Scarlet said. "You'll never meet anyone more loving and genuine than Harper."

Cameron looked at her, then back at Harper, all traces of humor gone from his face. "I sure as hell hope you're right."

CAM USUALLY WASN'T much for dancing, but tonight was special. He danced with Lydia and Carrie and Maggie. He waltzed with Harper and told her she made his brother very happy. The glow of pure joy on her face gave him hope for Ethan's future. Maybe Scarlet was right about her.

He danced with Scarlet several more times. He liked the way they fit together, the way she seemed to anticipate his every move. It was fun to have a partner so in sync with him.

But it was only a dance.

All three of the Lindquist sisters danced with Tessa and from what he could tell, his little girl had a ball. But it was nearly midnight, way past her bedtime. He looked around the tent for her.

Apparently, his little princess had turned into a pumpkin. From across the tent, he saw her curled in Scarlet's arms, sound asleep. Scarlet had kicked off her heels and stretched her legs onto another chair, but she had to be uncomfortable. As he walked toward them, before she realized he was watching, she kissed Tessa's hair.

The simple gesture was filled with tenderness and affection. A strong sensation of longing nearly brought him to his knees.

He shook it off, angry with himself. It meant nothing. He'd only reacted that way because he'd never seen Laura show as much warmth toward Tessa. He forced himself to calm down before he approached Scarlet.

With his emotions in check, he knelt beside her chair. "Hi."

"Hi," she whispered. Her smile was tired. "Turns out Tessa is a party pooper. She told me she was going to dance all night, but here we are."

"Yeah. Here we are."

Their gazes met and locked. They were so close he could see green flecks in her blue eyes, smell her light floral perfume. He looked away and stood up. "I should get her home. The limo is waiting to take us back to my place."

Scarlet nodded. "She's had a big day."

An older man stumbled towards them, stretching his hand toward Scarlet. "Miranda? Oh, God, you're alive! I thought you were dead. I was so afraid you were dead."

The man had long graying hair and reeked of stale booze. He staggered into Cam, intent on reaching Scarlet. Cam grabbed his arm, not wanting this drunk to touch Scarlet or Tessa.

"No Willy, I'm not Miranda," she said gently. "I'm Scarlet, her daughter. My mother is gone, remember?"

His face twisted in anguish. "Gone?"

"She drowned in the lake, remember? A long time ago."

For a moment, Willy stared at her. Then, his face crumbled and sobs wrenched his body. He would have collapsed onto the floor, but Cam held him up.

"Who's this guy?"

"Willy Eklund. He used to work for our grandfather at the lodge years ago. It looks like he's had too much to drink. He...he has a problem with alcohol."

A nice way of saying he was a drunk. The bartenders shouldn't have let him have so much to drink.

Cam grabbed Willy by the scruff of the neck, ready to throw him out. He wouldn't let him cause a scene and spoil the wedding.

Scarlet reached up and touched his arm, her eyes pleading. "Please. Don't hurt him."

As she spoke, two men he'd seen around Minnewasta, but didn't know, appeared at his side. "We'll make sure he gets home safely so he can sleep it off," the taller man said. They grabbed Willy under his arms and half carried, half dragged him out the back entrance of the tent. Fortunately, not many of the guests noticed what had happened.

"I'm glad they're driving him home. I'd hate for him to be out on the road in his condition."

Cam's jaw clenched. He'd been that guy, the one who drank too much and then got behind the wheel. The knowledge shamed him now.

He pushed away the shame. That was a different life, and he was a different man. He stood a little straighter and turned to Scarlet. She was resting her chin on Tessa's head, a despondent expression in her eyes. "Are you okay?"

"Everyone says I'm the one who looks the most like my mother."

He heard the pain in her voice. He sank to his haunches beside her chair once more. "I've been told I look exactly like my dad when he was my age."

> Unfortunately, his looks weren't the only thing he'd inherited from his father.

She looked at him as if she understood what he meant. "It's a burden, isn't it?"

He was saved from having to reply when Ethan and Harper stepped hand in hand onto the middle of the dance floor. Graham handed Ethan the cordless mic.

"The band tells us they're going to play one more song before packing up, so we'd love to see everyone out on the dance floor one last time. We're hosting a brunch at Miller's Golf Resort tomorrow morning at eleven, and we'd like to invite everyone to attend. Thank you for making this such wonderful day for us. Please drive home safely."

Cam turned to Scarlet, hoping his face didn't show his chaotic thoughts. "Here, let me take her from you. She must be heavy."

He scooped Tessa into his arms and held her securely against his shoulder with one arm. She woke, her eyes at half-mast. "Love you, Daddy. To the moon and back."

He kissed her forehead and repeated the mantra they used every night she spent with him. "To the moon and back, pumpkin."

She went back to sleep, once more as limp as a ragdoll. Despite the encounter with Willy, or perhaps because of it, he wasn't ready for the night to end. At least, he didn't want Willy's drunken performance to be the last thing either he or Scarlet remembered. Before he could change his mind, he held his free hand out to Scarlet.

"You heard the man. It's the last dance. Tessa would be disappointed if we didn't take her out for one more spin."

She smoothed Tessa's poufy skirt, a smile tugging at her lips. "So, it's Tessa who would be disappointed?"

"Of course. What can I say? I'm an indulgent father."

She chuckled and grasped his hand, and he led her out onto the floor.

He twirled them around in a slow circle, careful not to jar his daughter and wake her. Without her heels, Scarlet felt almost petite in his arms. But she fit perfectly there. Like she belonged. He tugged her a little closer.

*Idiot! What are you doing?* Scarlet Lindquist didn't even like him. The two of them had simply been caught up in the romance of the evening. And if he was honest with himself, lust was his predominant emotion. She was an incredibly beautiful, desirable woman. It was only natural he'd be attracted to her. He wasn't dead yet.

The song ended and the band said their goodnights. Scarlet put her hand on Tessa's back. "I guess it's time to get this little one home."

"Yeah, I guess so."

"Will you be coming to the brunch tomorrow morning?"

"Yes. The whole family will be there."

"That's good. I guess I'll see you then."

"Yes. Where are you staying tonight?" A second after the words left his mouth he realized how inappropriate they were. He didn't want her to think he was asking for an invitation.

The thought brought him up short. *Was* he asking for an invitation?

A tiny frown wrinkled her forehead. "Maggie and I are staying in one of the cottages overlooking the lake. Ethan and Harper are in the other one." She pulled away. "Thanks for the last dance. I'll see you tomorrow at brunch."

With that, she hurried back to the table to find her shoes. A few moments later, she joined Maggie and they walked out of the tent together. Without sparing a second glance at him.

# Chapter Four

SCARLET CRAWLED OUT of bed at seven the next morning. Padding barefoot into the kitchen, she put on some coffee, needing a strong jolt of caffeine to start her day. While she waited for the coffee to brew, she sat at the kitchen island, folded her hands on the counter, and rested her head on top of them.

Maggie's bedroom door opened. "Good morning, Sunshine."

Scarlet lifted her head and glared at her younger sister. "Do you have to be so damn chipper this early in the morning?"

Maggie grinned. "I guess I'm a morning person. Would you like something to eat?"

"I'm saving myself for brunch. I just want coffee."

Maggie grabbed a cup from the cupboard. She filled it with coffee and handed it to Scarlet along with the sugar bowl. Try as she might, Scarlet couldn't wean herself from sugar in her coffee. She added her usual two heaping teaspoons, then after a moment of hesitation, added another spoonful. She needed a little extra this morning.

Maggie climbed onto the stool beside her. "Didn't you sleep well?"

"No. It took me forever to fall asleep. Probably all the excitement yesterday."

Truth was, every time she closed her eyes she saw Cameron Hainstock's handsome face. His dark eyes seemed to look straight through her, as if he could see all her secrets. The strange thing was that when she looked at him, she believed she could see his secrets, too. He'd been hurt, no doubt by Tessa's mother, but she also sensed something darker. An involuntary shiver raced down her spine.

"The tent people will be here at nine to take it down, and Reese's guys should arrive about the same time to take the tables and chairs back to the community center," Maggie said. "We need to take down the decorations. Do you want to shower first, or should I?"

"You go ahead. I'll finish my coffee first."

"Okay." She hesitated, remaining on the stool. "You danced a lot with Ethan's brother last night."

"So? You danced a lot with Ethan's nephew. He has the hots for you, by the way."

Maggie grimaced. "Yes, he made that abundantly clear. I let him down easy."

"How so? He's a nice guy, and very good-looking. He lives in Minneapolis, doesn't he? It's not that far away."

"He's only twenty-one, Scarlet. Just a kid."

"You're twenty-four, not eighty-four. What's the big deal? Why not have some fun with a good-looking young man?"

"Drew is very nice, but I'm not interested in him that way. It wouldn't be fair to lead him on. I need someone more... mature." She frowned at Scarlet. "How did this conversation get to be about me? We were talking about you. You looked very interested in Cam Hainstock last night."

"I was being polite, for his little girl's sake."

Maggie lifted one dark eyebrow in disbelief. "Yeah, right. Cam's very attractive, and he seemed pretty into you."

"We don't like each other. We're too different."

Her sister studied her. "I know you've had some unhappy experiences, but don't let it keep you from trying again."

Scarlet set down her coffee cup with a thud, causing some of the liquid to slosh over the side. "Let's call a spade a spade, Maggie. I broke off two engagements. I hurt two perfectly nice guys, though I'm relieved to tell you they've both gone on to find new loves and are now blissfully happy. They dodged a bullet when I ran out on them."

"You're being awfully hard on yourself."

"Why shouldn't I be? When it comes to love, I'm about as screwed up as it gets." She folded her arms on the counter and rested her head on them once more.

"Maybe you just need to find the right man."

Cameron's face appeared in her mind's eye. When he'd asked her where she was spending the night, she'd seen the gleam of interest in his eyes. She raised her head and opened her eyes to dispel the image. "You should have your shower."

Maggie stared at her for a moment, then nodded and slid off her stool. She headed for the bathroom and a few moments later Scarlet heard the water running. She let out a sigh of relief.

No matter how attracted she might be to Cameron, she wouldn't act on it. With her track record, she'd only bring him more heartache. She couldn't do that to him. And she couldn't do that to his daughter.

IN A COUPLE OF HOURS, the decorations were removed, the tables and chairs carted away and the tent dismantled, giving Maggie and Scarlet enough time to change and drive the short distance to Miller's Resort for the wedding brunch. When they arrived, Maggie headed to the kitchen to check on the food, leaving Scarlet alone in the private dining room that had been set aside for the event. Fortunately, an urn of coffee had already been set up. She poured herself a cup and added the sugar, sighing with pleasure as she sipped the sweet, dark brew.

"Daddy, Scarlet's here!"

Tessa ran toward her and hugged her legs. Scarlet's coffee cup wobbled in her hand, nearly falling onto Tessa's head. She managed to set it on the table before causing any harm to the child.

"Good morning, Tessa. I'm glad to see you, but you have to be careful when someone has something hot in their hands. You could get burned."

The little girl's eyes turned cautious, and she shrank away from her. "Are you mad at me?"

Her question and her demeanor surprised Scarlet. She laid her hand on Tessa's shining dark hair. "No, of course not, sweetheart. I didn't want to hurt you. If I sounded mad, it was because I was scared."

"Tessa, you shouldn't bother Scarlet."

She looked up into Cameron's unsmiling face. He was dressed more casually in dark jeans, a cornflower blue cotton shirt and a black blazer. The look made him even more masculine and sexy than the suit had. Scarlet stiffened her spine. "She's not bothering me." She smiled at Tessa. "Are you hungry? We've got waffles with strawberries."

"Can I have whipped cream on my strawberries?"

"I'm sure that can be arranged."

Tessa smiled brightly, her earlier upset forgotten. "I'm going to tell Auntie Lydia!" She ran across the room where Lydia and Graham and their children were entering the dining room. Other guests had begun to arrive as well.

Cameron stepped closer. "I'm sorry. Tessa is a little sensitive about raised voices."

"Why is that?"

His mouth formed a straight, angry line. "From what I can tell, her mother raises her voice a lot."

"Are you saying she's verbally abusive?"

"I don't have any proof of that."

"But you suspect."

He looked into her eyes, and Scarlet saw the anger and turmoil before he carefully wiped his face of emotion. "Today is about celebrating Ethan and Harper's marriage. Let's leave it at that, okay?"

She nodded. This wasn't the time or the place to talk about Tessa's mother. "Okay."

Ethan and Harper entered the dining room hand in hand, looking relaxed and happy. Harper wore a simple cotton sundress the exact shade of blue as her eyes. Scarlet could probably count on the fingers of one hand the number of times she'd seen her sister in a dress. It was a different look for her, one that suited her well. The happiness glowing in her eyes also suited her well.

About thirty-five people arrived for brunch, mostly family, close friends, and people both Ethan and Harper worked with, in the present and the past. A couple of Ethan's aunts and uncles and several of his cousins from Wisconsin who had attended the wedding were also there. Seeing them laughing with Ethan and Harper caused an unexpected lump to form in Scarlet's throat. Her parents had both been only children, and all four of her grandparents were gone now. Harper and Maggie were the only family she had.

And now Harper had a new family. They would occupy her time and attention from now on.

She swallowed and looked away, busying herself by helping Maggie and the catering staff carry out the food from the kitchen and set up the brunch buffet. When everything was ready, Maggie stood at the front of the room and raised her hand.

"Good morning, everyone! Thank you for coming out for brunch on this beautiful Sunday morning. The staff here at Miller's Resort has prepared a lovely feast for us, including an omelet station where Chef Sherry will create an omelet for you to your exact specifications. So please, help yourself and enjoy!"

Guests quickly formed a line and began dishing up food. Though she'd been famished earlier, Scarlet's appetite deserted her. She got into line anyway and put a few things on her plate. She hated the melancholy mood that had unexpectedly struck her. This day was about Harper and her happiness. For her, Scarlet would push away the blues and slap a smile on her face.

She'd do anything for her sisters, even if it meant faking it.

Someone touched her arm as she was standing in line. Scarlet turned to see Abby Hanson and her husband Reese. She tried to hide her shock at Abby's frailness. They'd been at the wedding yesterday and she'd seemed fine, though tired. Scarlet knew she'd been recovering from surgery, albeit very slowly. But this morning, Abby looked terribly weak, as if simply getting here had taken every ounce of energy she possessed. She leaned heavily on a cane and on Reese's left arm.

"Good morning, Scarlet," Abby said. "I didn't get a chance yesterday to tell you how beautiful you looked. Your mother would have been so proud of all three of her girls."

Scarlet's eyes suddenly burned with tears, and she had to blink several times to keep from crying. She stooped to give Abby a one-armed hug, and swallowed back the raw emotions. "Thank you, Abby. I appreciate you saying that."

"Harper looks happy, doesn't she?"

Scarlet glanced at her sister. She was laughing up at Ethan, her love for him shining in her eyes. "Yes, she does. I think they'll be very good together."

"I think you're right." Abby patted her arm. "We're holding up the line. We'd better get moving before the hungry hoard gets restless."

Scarlet nodded before turning to the buffet and throwing a few more things onto her plate she wasn't sure she'd be able to eat. Harper waved at her as she left the buffet table.

"Come sit with us."

Large round tables that accommodated conversation had been set up around the private dining room. Scarlet sat next to Harper. A minute later, Tessa scrambled up into the chair next to her. Cameron set a plate with a waffle covered in strawberries and whipped cream, and a smaller plate containing carrot and celery sticks with a small pot of ranch dip in front of her before taking the seat beside her.

"I got lots of whipped cream on my strawberries, Scarlet!"

Scarlet couldn't help but smile at the little girl's excitement. "It looks yummy."

"Daddy says I have to eat some vegetables, too."

She caught Cameron's eye. "That's a good idea. You won't grow big and strong if you only eat whipped cream."

"Can you cut up my waffle for me, Scarlet?" she asked.

"Sure."

Scarlet used Tessa's knife and fork to slice the waffle into bite size pieces. When she looked up, Cameron was frowning, as if he didn't approve of her helping his daughter. *What was his problem?* Tessa had asked and she'd helped. No big deal.

Lydia and Graham and Reese and Abby sat in the remaining seats at the table. Maggie, Scarlet noted, had been convinced to sit with Drew and his sister and several young cousins at a neighboring table. She smiled. Drew was nothing if not persistent.

Harper turned to her. "Ethan and I added up the donations this morning, and it comes to over five thousand dollars."

"That's wonderful. Do you want me to deliver the donations to the shelter while you're away?"

"That would be great. Thanks."

Harper and Ethan had asked that guests to their wedding not bring gifts. Instead, they requested donations be made to the women's shelter in St. Cloud. It was Harper's way of paying tribute to their mother. Would Miranda be alive today if she'd had the help of a women's shelter? Scarlet pushed aside the thought. Today wasn't the day for such reflections.

"Everything was wonderful yesterday, Harper," Abby said. "Your bridesmaids were particularly lovely."

"I know. Not many brides have bridesmaids as beautiful as mine." Harper laid her hand on Scarlet's shoulder. "I can't tell you how excited I am to have you staying at the lodge for the next few months. It means the world to me."

Scarlet caught her hand and held it. She had no idea whether her sister's efforts to bring the old fishing lodge back to life would pan out, but she'd do everything in her power to help.

"You're going to be staying at the lodge?" Cameron asked. He didn't look happy.

"Yes, I'm taking a leave of absence from my job in Chicago until the first of November. I'm going to be working on a marketing plan for the lodge, something to help advertise its reopening and rebirth, and get it ready to launch into the world." She sipped her coffee. "Did you know

Maggie has decided to join these two crazy kids and work full-time at the lodge? She's developing a menu."

Cameron's brow wrinkled. "No, I didn't know that."

"We're getting the whole family involved in this project," Ethan said. "Cam's going to build the new luxury cottages."

Scarlet didn't know he was a contractor. "Will you be using the same plan to build the new cottages as the two existing ones?"

"I think we need to come up with something less generic. I'm working on some sketches. Then Harper and Ethan can decide which option they want to build."

"I'd like to see your sketches. Maybe I can get an artist to do a rendering of the new cottages from your sketches. That way, I can show potential guests the kind of luxury accommodation they could expect."

"No need for another artist, Scarlet," Harper said. "Cam's sketches are amazing. The new cottages are going to fit in beautifully with the vibe we want to create. Each one is going to be completely self-sustaining with its own solar power plant and composting toilet."

Cameron pushed food around his plate. "All that is going to cost thousands more than conventional building methods."

"Yes, but in the long run it will save money in heating and cooling costs," Harper argued.

"You're not getting the whole 'eco-tourism' thing, Cameron," Scarlet added. "The sustainability of Solace Lake Lodge is what will make it different from this resort and all the other resorts in the state. I plan to play it up big."

"What's wrong with a resort like Miller's? This place is beautiful."

Scarlet shrugged. "There's nothing wrong with this place, but if we want to stand out and carve out our own place in the market, we need to be different. Being eco-friendly will appeal to a lot of people. It may cost more to begin with, but I believe the investment will pay off, in a lot of ways."

"Lucky for you, Ethan's got a steady supply of money." Sarcasm dripped off his words.

She stared at him, anger flaring in her gut. Suddenly, the idea of spending the next five months at the lodge and having to see Cameron Hainstock every day was more than she could bear.

"What else do you have in mind for your marketing plan, Scarlet?" Lydia asked.

She wrenched her attention away from Cameron and directed it toward his sister, grateful for the diversion. "I'm going to set up a website and social media accounts for the lodge to get the word out about the renovations, and hopefully get people excited about coming here. I also want to attend some wedding shows and trade fairs. I'm hoping to market the lodge as a year-round destination for all kinds of events and conferences."

Lydia nodded in approval. "Excellent idea. It was a beautiful setting for Ethan and Harper's wedding. Why don't you give me a call next week, and we'll talk a little more about your plans and figure out a marketing budget for what you need to do?"

"I'd like that."

"Good. I look forward to speaking with you." Lydia turned to Ethan. "Speaking of weddings, are you two going to tell us where you're going on your honeymoon, or am I going to have to beat it out of you?"

Ethan grinned at her. "No need for violence, Sis. I didn't say anything because I was keeping it a surprise for Harper. I told her this morning. We're going to Paris for our honeymoon."

"That sounds very romantic, Harper," Abby said. Scarlet saw the wistful look she gave Reese and the way he squeezed her shoulder.

"It does, doesn't it?" Harper caught Ethan's hand. "Ethan knew I've always dreamt of going to Paris, and now he's making my dreams come true."

"You're lucky to have a husband rich enough to buy you whatever you want, whether it's an eco-friendly lodge or a trip to Paris."

The biting sarcasm in Cameron's voice shocked the table into silence. Thick tension instantly descended on the group. Harper's face went pale and her smile disappeared. Scarlet wanted to yell at him, or throw something at him, but with Tessa sitting next to her and listening to every word, she couldn't say or do anything. How dare he imply that Harper only married Ethan for his money? Anyone with eyes could see they were devoted to each other.

Ethan rose to his feet, his eyes blazing. "Damn it, Cam—"

"Cam," Abby interrupted. "Did you know that Harper's parents went to Paris on their honeymoon? Miranda always talked about taking Harper one day, but of course she never got the chance."

Cameron had the good grace to look uncomfortable. "No, I didn't know that."

"Harper and Ethan will be able to see the sights that Miranda talked about for so many years, and they'll be able to make their own memories there."

Ethan sat down, though anger burned in his eyes. Harper covered his fisted hand with hers. When she smiled, Ethan smiled back, his tense posture relaxing.

He turned back to his brother, the smile fading. "The money belongs to both Harper and me now, and the very best use for it is investing in the future of the lodge. Part of that future is sustainability, like solar energy. If you've got a problem with that, then maybe we need to reconsider our deal to have you build the cottages."

Scarlet held her breath while she, and everyone else at the table, waited for Cameron's answer. Tessa picked up on the mood. She abandoned her half-eaten waffle and kneeled on her chair to put her small arm around his shoulders.

"Daddy?"

Cameron laid his hand on her head, but looked at Ethan. "There's no problem."

Ethan gave a curt nod, but said nothing else. Cameron pushed back his chair, picking Tessa up as he got to his feet. "I have to get Tessa home to her mother."

No one said anything as he left the dining room. Tessa waved at Scarlet over Cameron's shoulder, and she waved back. Her heart ached at the little girl's unhappy, confused face. Tessa didn't understand what was going on, but she had sensed the strain between the adults and it obviously upset her. Scarlet suspected Tessa already had enough upheaval in her young life. Damn Cameron for exposing her to more tension.

And damn him for turning what should have been a joyous family occasion into a war zone.

# Chapter Five

THE BLADE IN CAM'S table saw abruptly stopped, the plywood sheet stuck in the middle. When he straightened and removed his ear protection, he saw Ethan standing near the door to his woodworking shop, the saw's electrical cord in his hand.

Cam sighed. He should have guessed he'd be getting a visit from his brother after his performance this morning. "Pulling the plug, E? Is that your way of telling me you want me to listen? Very subtle."

"I'm not going for subtlety." Ethan tossed the cord to the floor. "I'm going to use words even an idiot like you can understand. Leave my wife alone."

"Look, Ethan—"

"Do you know how much you hurt her? In front of the whole family, at our wedding brunch, you opened your big mouth and said she was only interested in my money. You were rude and insulting, and you don't even know what the hell you're talking about."

"Ethan—"

"The honeymoon in Paris was my idea. Harper wanted to stay home and work on the lodge, but I wanted to give her a break. Things have been hectic, and they're going to get even more hectic once the lodge reopens. I wanted to give her something special because I love her and because she deserves it. Harper never once asked for any kind of a honeymoon. Hell, if it had been up to her, we probably would have had an even smaller wedding. I had to fight her for the simple wedding we finally did have."

Ethan stopped to catch his breath, his chest heaving. Cam knew he'd been out of line this morning, but the words had tumbled out of his mouth before he had a chance to stop them. When he'd heard Ethan was paying for an expensive trip, in addition to the wedding he'd just paid for and on top of all the money he was investing in Harper's lodge, something snapped. All he could think of was Bree, Ethan's former girlfriend, the one who'd done her best to sink her teeth into his lottery winnings and ruin his life.

If he was honest with himself, he also thought of his ex-girlfriend, Tessa's mother. Laura never did anything unless there was something in it for her. If that was what Harper was doing, she was far cleverer and less obvious than the other two women.

But his timing sucked. He should have kept his opinions to himself, at least until after the weekend. He didn't mean to spoil Ethan's wedding brunch. "I shouldn't have spoken. It wasn't the time or place."

Ethan regarded him warily. "If I can't trust you to be respectful to Harper, I can't have you working at the lodge."

Cam looked down at his dusty work boots. He needed this job so he could stay in Minnewasta and be close to Tessa. If it meant placating Ethan, then that's what he'd do. "I'm sorry, E. I should have kept my mouth shut."

"Not good enough."

Cam lifted his gaze at Ethan's response. "I said I'm sorry. What more do you want from me?"

"I want you to give Harper a chance. I want you to get to know her and realize what a remarkable person she is. If you can't figure out for yourself that Harper isn't trying to use me, then we're done."

Cam went cold inside. "What are you saying?"

"I won't sit back and watch you humiliate her again. You're my brother and I love you, but I'm married to Harper now. She's everything to me. If you make me choose between her and you, it's going to be her."

The coldness quickly morphed into white hot anger. "Did she put you up to this?"

Ethan shook his head and laughed, but there was no humor in it. "You really don't get it, do you?" He looked away. "Harper and I are driving to Minneapolis tonight. We'll stay overnight at my condo and then tomorrow morning, we're catching a plane to Paris. We'll be gone about ten days. I want you to work with Scarlet to finalize the plans for the cottages and begin demolition. I'm hoping by the time I get back you and I can have a civilized conversation about money and family. I'll see you then."

He walked out of the shop and closed the door behind him. Cam stood rooted to his spot. Ethan wasn't just his brother. He was his best friend. Without his help, he'd likely be drunk in some gutter somewhere. Or dead.

Anger and fear churned inside him. He didn't have a lot of friends, and he only had one brother. He couldn't afford to lose him over some woman.

He wiped his hand across his mouth. Damn, what he wouldn't give for just one drink right now. But if he started, he couldn't trust himself to stop at one.

SCARLET HELD UP A LACY black satin bra and its matching thong. "Since when are you a sexy underwear kind of girl?"

Harper grabbed the undergarments from her hand. "Since always. Victoria isn't the only one with a secret."

Scarlet chuckled. "I'm guessing Ethan's enjoying your choice of undies."

"I haven't heard any complaints." Harper smiled as she tucked the bra and thong into her suitcase. A moment later, her smile disappeared as she checked her watch. "I don't like this. He's been gone for over an hour."

"Maybe that's a good thing," Maggie said. "Maybe it means Ethan and Cam are actually talking instead of beating each other senseless."

"Oh, God! Do you think Cam would actually hit Ethan?"

Scarlet shook her head. "No. Absolutely not."

She wasn't sure exactly why she believed so strongly, but she knew in her heart Cameron would never physically hurt his brother. Perhaps it was because of the way he was with Tessa. For all his outward gruffness, he was a kind and gentle father.

And a loyal brother, with a somewhat overdeveloped and misplaced protective instinct.

"Scarlet's right," Maggie said. "They're likely hashing things out, probably over a couple of beers. You know how guys are. They'll grunt at each other a few times and then all will be well. By now, they're watching a ball game on TV."

Harper sat on the edge of the bed, her head bowed. "I hope you're right. I know Cam doesn't like me. He thinks I'm only after Ethan's money, but he couldn't be more wrong. I love him, in spite of the money."

Scarlet shoved aside the suitcase to sit next to her. "You don't have to convince us. We know you love Ethan and more importantly, he knows it."

"Yeah, he does." She wiped away the tears that escaped down her cheek. "But I don't want to be the cause of trouble between him and his brother. They've always been very close."

"You haven't done anything wrong. Cameron's the one with the problem."

"Yeah, but—"

"No buts. Cameron is going to have to get over himself and realize that not everyone in the world is trying to exploit Ethan."

"I'm not sure I'll ever be able to convince him."

"You will. You're the least greedy person I know."

Maggie sat on the other of Harper and rested her head on her shoulder. "He'll soon realize what a sweetheart you are. You're the kindest, most generous sister a couple of girls could ever have. What would Scarlet and I have done without you all these years?"

Harper put her arm around Maggie. "You mean without me to referee your fights? I shudder to think."

From a young age, Harper had tried to take a maternal role in their lives, attempting to make up for their lack of a mother. Scarlet hadn't always appreciated her efforts. On more than one occasion, particularly in her teens, she'd told Harper she wasn't her mother so she should quit acting like it. But she always knew when she needed help, or when her heart was broken, Harper would be there for her.

Scarlet put her hand on her sister's shoulder. "Forget about Cameron Hainstock. Go with your husband to Paris and see the sights. And have lots and lots of wild monkey sex."

"Monkey sex?" Harper gave a surprised laugh. "Seriously?"

"Okay then, go at it like rabbits. Use whatever animal euphemism seems appropriate. Have fun with Ethan and don't think about anything except each other while you're gone. We'll hold down the fort here."

"You're right. Ethan deserves this holiday."

"Not to mention the wild monkey sex."

Harper laughed again and swatted Scarlet's arm. "Have you got sex on the brain or something?"

"Maybe. It's been a while." Since the breakup with her last ex-fiancé over two years ago to be exact. "I have to live vicariously through you."

"Don't worry about Scarlet," Maggie said. "I'll make sure she stays in line while you're gone. It's my turn to be the mature one."

"I can hardly wait to see that," Scarlet said with a wink at her younger sister.

Harper put her arms around both of them. "Thank you, guys. I needed the pep talk. And the laughs."

"What are sisters for?"

Silently, Scarlet swore Cameron Hainstock would not cause her sister one more minute of heartache.

WHEN ETHAN ARRIVED back at the cottage, Harper walked into his arms without saying a word. He held her close and rested his chin on the top of her head. He looked like a man who'd just lost his best friend. Or his brother.

Scarlet didn't want to intrude on a private moment. She grabbed Maggie's hand and whispered, "Let's wait outside."

Maggie nodded and they quietly left the cottage. While Maggie gathered some wildflowers growing in front of the cottage, Scarlet sat on the front steps and watched the lake through the pines. The sun sparkled on the water, like diamonds on the waves. When she was a little girl, she'd asked Grampa Bill if she could go in the water and catch a diamond. He'd laughed and said it was only an illusion. Make-believe.

She wondered if Cameron was as gutted by the fight he'd had with his brother as Ethan appeared to be. Then, she wondered why she was worried about him. He was the one with the problem. He'd insulted her sister, and Ethan had set him straight. Scarlet was happy he'd stood up for Harper, but a part of her didn't like the idea of Cameron being alone, on the outs with his family.

She shook her head, not understanding why she cared.

Harper emerged through the front door with Ethan close behind carrying two suitcases. Scarlet rose to her feet and she and Maggie followed them to his truck. He stowed the suitcases in the back seat and turned to Scarlet.

"Harper tells me you two volunteered to hold down the fort while we're gone."

Scarlet glanced at Maggie who raised her eyebrows. What exactly were they getting themselves into? "We'll do our best."

"Reese will be fine. He's got things under control at the lodge and the project is on schedule. If there's any major questions or concerns, I'll have my phone with me, so you can reach us anytime."

Scarlet nodded, but the lodge would have to burn to the ground before she'd interrupt their honeymoon.

"Cam and his crew are scheduled to begin the demolition on the remaining old cottages tomorrow. I told him he was to work with you on finalizing the designs for the new cottages."

"Me?" She blinked at him in surprise. "I don't know anything about construction."

"But you understand what kind of design will attract people to the cottages," Harper said. She threaded her arm through Ethan's, as if lending support.

Ethan swallowed. "I need you to keep an eye on Cam. Make sure he doesn't go off the rails."

"What do you mean?" Tension filled her chest. "What are you afraid he'll do?"

"He...he has trouble with alcohol."

"Trouble?"

"He's an alcoholic. He hasn't had a drop in over three years. He's turned his life around so he can be a good dad for Tessa." Ethan sounded worried, but the look in his eyes was fierce, proud even.

"Are you afraid that because you've argued with him he might start drinking again?"

He shrugged and looked away. "I don't know. I don't think so, but..."

"We don't have to go," Harper said. "We can stay right here and make sure everything's okay."

"No. We're going. There's no way I'm going to cancel this trip."

"But if you're worried, how are you going to enjoy yourself?"

He caught Harper's hand and kissed the back of it. "If Cam's going to drink, it's not going to matter whether I'm here or not. Maybe a cooling off period will be best for both of us."

"You're sure?" Harper asked.

"Yes. Absolutely sure."

Harper sighed and then smiled. "Okay then." She turned to Scarlet. "Are you going to be okay with this?"

Scarlet wanted to shout that she was so not okay. She didn't want to be anyone's babysitter, and she wanted to be Cameron Hainstock's minder even less. But she didn't want Harper and Ethan to worry. And strangely, she didn't want Cameron to be alone. She pasted on a smile, hoping Harper wouldn't see her worry. "Of course, I am. If I get in over my head, Maggie will help me. She's going to be the mature one, remember?"

"I remember." She pulled Scarlet into a hug. "I love you."

Scarlet kissed her cheek and whispered, "I love you, too. Remember, wild monkey sex."

"You bet." Harper released her with a smile.

Ethan embraced Scarlet. He whispered in her ear. "Look after him. Okay?" When he let her go, he said, "If things get really bad, call Lydia. I'll text you her number."

She nodded, unease settling in her stomach. She hoped she never had to make that call to Cameron's sister.

After hugging Maggie, they got into the truck and headed off down the road. Scarlet and Maggie watched until the truck was no longer visible.

"Well," Maggie said, heaving a sigh. "It looks like we have our work cut out for ourselves the next couple of weeks. What do you think we should do first?"

Scarlet put her arm around Maggie's shoulders. Her younger sister's petite frame always made her feel like an Amazon. "I think the first thing we should do is bake cookies. Chocolate chip."

"You want to make chocolate chip cookies?"

"Well, technically, you'll be making the cookies. My role is strictly supervisory."

"Okay, fine, I'll bake cookies. Can I ask why?"

"Cameron's crew is starting the demolition of the old cottages tomorrow. I think it would be a nice gesture to offer them a treat, a way of beginning on a high note. Maybe Cameron will see it as a peace offering."

"Sounds like a good idea."

"That and I have a real craving for chocolate chip."

Maggie laughed. "Of course, you do. Come on. I'll let you lick the spoons."

Scarlet squeezed her shoulder. "Have I ever told you you're my favorite younger sister?"

Maggie slipped her arm around her waist as they walked back to their own cottage. "I already knew."

# Chapter Six

CAM ARRIVED AT THE lodge at eight a.m., pulling a flatbed trailer with an excavator strapped to it behind his truck. He'd rented the machine for a few days so they could quickly knock down the old cottages and haul away the debris. Once he and his five-man crew cleared the sites, the fun stuff could begin – building the new cottages.

Ethan's parting words about working with Scarlet to finalize the designs rang in his ears. A ball of anxiety formed in his gut. What would she think of the floorplans he'd drawn up? Would she like the sketches, or would she think they were amateurish? He didn't have any formal instruction as an artist but he was a draftsman, having trained in building design. Combined with his knowledge of carpentry and construction, he believed he'd created a beautiful, functional product. But would Scarlet?

He wished he knew why the hell it mattered to him so much.

He drove the truck and trailer up the hill road overlooking the lake, past the two recently built cottages. When he arrived at the first cottage slated for demolition, his crew was already there. Some of his tension eased. They were a good bunch and needed this work almost as much as he did.

He waved at Charlie as he got out of his truck. "You ready to do this?"

"You bet!"

Charlie helped him remove the tie-down straps from the excavator and lower the ramp. Cam hopped on the machine and backed it off the trailer. He maneuvered it to the old cottage and, lifting the bucket, pushed it into the roof of the front porch. It fell in a heap onto the porch floor. A couple of more pushes and the roof and walls of the entire cottage were down, too.

The dumpster company arrived with the bin and he dumped wooden debris and pieces of concrete foundation into it. When he'd removed all the debris he could with the machine, he and his men cleaned up the small bits and pieces remaining. By the time they were done, it was difficult to tell there'd ever been a structure there. Cam insisted on neat and efficient work and refused to cut corners or accept sloppiness from himself or his crew.

The crew was about to move to the next cottage when Scarlet and her sister Maggie approached carrying a couple of thermoses and a picnic basket. With her red hair pulled back in a ponytail and her clean-scrubbed, make-up free face, she looked as harmless as the girl next door.

*Looks could be deceiving.*

"Hi!" she said with a grin. "We come bearing gifts."

Maggie set the picnic basket on the ground and pulled out several ceramic mugs that she passed around. Scarlet followed behind filling the cups with coffee from the thermos, and Maggie offered cream and sugar to anyone who wanted it. Then, Scarlet passed around a plastic container of cookies. Cam helped himself to one and bit into it. Chocolate and butter and sugar exploded on his tongue in an orgasmic mix of flavors.

Not a good idea to be thinking about orgasms with Scarlet nearby.

"Hmm. Good."

"Maggie made them," Scarlet said proudly. "She's the best. She's going to make the Solace Lake Lodge kitchen famous far and wide."

"Scarlet, stop." Maggie turned to him, a blush staining her cheeks. "I'm just filling in, developing some menus with local ingredients until Ethan and Harper find a real head chef willing to relocate to Minnewasta."

"Stop being so modest. You'll make a fabulous head chef."

"Enough, Scarlet."

Interesting that Maggie looked embarrassed rather than pleased at Scarlet's praise, not to mention a little stressed. He understood the stress. She was being asked to take on a crucial role in the makeover of the lodge. If she failed, the lodge might fail, too.

If he didn't deliver eight beautiful, rustic, yet modern cottages by next spring, the lodge may not be able to accommodate the number of guests it needed to. And if the cottages he built weren't to customers' tastes, no one would want to stay in them.

He'd been under pressure before, but an extra burden of tension weighed upon him with this contract. This was Ethan's baby and he wanted to do a good job for him, especially after the conversation they'd had yesterday.

Maybe he wanted to prove he wasn't a total screw-up.

Scarlet poured more coffee for everyone and after topping up her own cup, she sat beside him on the flatbed trailer. He heard her sigh as she stared down at her sandals. Cam couldn't help smiling when he saw her pretty pink toenails, a striking contrast next to his dusty, scuffed work boots.

"It feels weird to be tearing down Grampa Bill's cottages. He built them all by himself, you know, and he was so proud of his work."

"I wish we could have saved them, but they were too far gone." He crossed his feet at the ankle. "I didn't realize your grandfather built these cottages."

Her smile was tinged with melancholy. "He did. He was a handy guy. He did all the maintenance and carpentry work that needed to be done around here. He loved this place the way Harper does."

She looked out toward the lake. "I don't know why I'm feeling so sentimental about these old shacks. Grandma used to make me and Harper clean the things within an inch of their lives. It was our job to change the sheets and towels every day when we had fishermen staying. There'd be Hell to pay if we didn't do the job to her exacting standards."

Cam read between the lines and guessed her relationship with her grandmother had not been as loving as with her grandfather. He totally understood.

He followed her gaze out toward the lake. The best thing about these cottages was the view. He especially liked the sense of privacy each cottage had. There was plenty of space between the cottages, and lots of trees and bushes separating them. He wanted to take advantage of the setting to make guests feel like they were the only ones for miles.

Scarlet cleared her throat, then turned to him, all business once more. "So, did Ethan mention to you that he wanted us to work together to pick a design for the cottages?"

"Yeah, he mentioned it." He tried to sound blasé but his stomach twisted in a knot. He tossed out the remainder of his coffee.

"I wasn't real clear on how this was going to work. Do we have to hire someone to draw up blueprints from your sketches?

"No, I've taken care of it."

She lifted her eyebrows. "I didn't know you were an architect."

"I'm not. I'm a draftsman. Mostly I draft residential home plans, but I've also done some commercial buildings."

"Oh, I see. Can we look at your plans now?"

"Ah, sure. As soon we move the equipment to the next cottage. You want to come along?"

She hopped off the trailer. "Sure. Give me a second."

While she helped Maggie gather the empty cups and thermoses and pack them in the picnic basket, Cam guided Charlie as he drove the excavator back onto the flatbed for the short drive to the next cottage. Normally, he would simply drive the machine the short distance, but the pavement on the road between the cottages was already breaking up. He didn't want to hasten its demise by repeatedly running the steel tracks of the excavator over it.

Once Maggie lifted the basket and was on her way back toward the cottage, he jumped in the truck and rolled down the window. "Hop in."

He couldn't help noticing her long, exquisite legs as she hoisted herself into the cab. She was wearing shorts that ended at a perfectly respectable mid-thigh, but on Scarlet they looked anything but respectable. He wrenched his gaze away from her bare thigh and turned the ignition.

He drove slowly to the next cottage and parked in the flattest spot he could find. Charlie and Jim unloaded the excavator.

"I've got to go over some cottage plans with Scarlet. Can you operate the excavator?"

"No problem, boss."

He retrieved a long cardboard tube from behind the front seat and pulled out the rolled-up plans. Scarlet followed him to the flat bed where he smoothed the curled papers with his hand so she could see them. She touched the sketch of the exterior elevation of a two-story cottage.

"Did you draw this?"

"Yeah." He swallowed past his throat's sudden dryness.

"It's beautiful. Wow." She picked it up and looked at it more closely. "I can really see what it would look like in this setting. Do you have a floor plan for it?"

"Yeah, right here." He shuffled through the papers to find the corresponding floor plan. While she examined the plan, he examined her. He wasn't sure why her praise was so important to him, but it was. The tension in his gut eased.

"This feels very spacious," she said. "With two bedrooms and a bath upstairs and a master bedroom and bath on the main floor, we could easily accommodate a large family, or even two families. We could put a sofa bed in the great room for extra guests. The only thing I'm not sure about is the two-story style. I'm worried that it will look a little out of place with the two existing bungalow cottages."

"I thought of that," he said. "If we clad all the cottages with the same exterior siding and the same roofing material, we can create cohesiveness without having to be identical."

"Okay. What are these other plans?"

"Plans for different styles of cottages I want to build. My idea is to build several styles to fit the needs of different guests. We'll match the style of cottage to the size and shape of the lot, and it will look like it's meant to be there. Like I said, we'll use the same exterior siding to tie them all together." He cleared his throat and shuffled his feet, nervousness making him twitchy. "Of course, if you feel that, from a marketing perspective, it's a better idea for all the cottages to be the same, we'll use only one set my plans. Or, we can use the plans Harper bought online for the two cottages she built last year. That way, we'll have ten identical cottages."

He rolled up the first set of plans and put them back in the tube, then spread his favorite sketch in front of her. It was a smaller cottage with only one bedroom and one bath, but Cam loved the soaring vaulted ceilings that gave the cottage an open airy feeling while still maintaining the coziness of the place.

"Oh, this is cute," Scarlet murmured. "I love the way the fireplace chimney goes all the way up to the peak of the vaulted ceiling. It's beautiful."

"I thought we could clad the fireplace in stone much like the fireplace in the main dining room of the old lodge. It would give the place a real north woods vibe."

"That would be great. The problem is that this cottage is too small. It's really only big enough for one couple. Even with a sofa bed in the great room, it probably wouldn't be suitable for families, or even for a couple of buddies who want to come up here to fish or snowmobile. We have to appeal to as many people as we can."

"But don't you think there'd be a demand for something this size? A couple isn't going to want to pay extra for room they don't use. And it would be perfect for a person alone who wants a cottage rather than a hotel room in the lodge."

"I'd rather build a bigger cottage and give some people too much space than a smaller one we might have difficulty renting."

He had to admit her argument made sense, but he wasn't ready to concede yet. "Because it's smaller, it'll be cheaper to build."

She studied the sketches and the floor plans, her forehead wrinkled with concentration. "It is awfully cute. Let me think about it."

He'd take that. For now. "Maybe you'd like my third design better. It's got the same vaulted ceiling and stone-clad fireplace, but it's got two bedrooms."

Cam set the other sketch aside and pulled out the third. Scarlet nodded as she studied the floor plan, then turned to smile at him. The full impact of her high wattage smile gave him an unexpected punch in the gut.

"This is perfect. It's got all the elements I love about the second design with the extra space we need for guests."

"I'm glad you like it."

"I do." She pulled the plans for the smaller cottage closer and examined them again. "But I really love this design. It's so cute."

"I think it would be popular, and even though it's smaller, I don't believe there will be any problem renting it."

She drummed her fingers on the drawing. Then she straightened and met his gaze. Okay."

"Okay?"

"Identical is boring. Let's build all three of your designs. We want eight new cottages, so I propose building three of the two-story, three of the two-bedroom A frames, and two one-bedroom A frames. Along with the two cottages we already have, we should be able to accommodate any guest's needs. I believe Harper and Ethan would agree."

Cam was both pleased and relieved. "You've made a good decision."

"I think so, too. It'll give guests some choices." Her expression turned thoughtful again. "I think Grampa Bill would approve."

"Yeah?"

"Yeah. He was a very practical innkeeper, but he appreciated beauty too, especially the splendor of this lake. He'd think your cottages were special enough to fit in here."

Of all the things she'd said, this comment gave him the most pleasure. He had to swallow and look away before he could answer.

"I appreciate that."

"So, that wasn't so painful. We managed to make a decision without coming to blows. What happens now?"

"I'll finalize the designs and get them approved by the county building department. I need to figure out where the electrical outlets and lighting fixtures go, stuff like that."

"And don't forget the solar panels and some kind of battery storage area."

He'd like to forget about them. "I'm concerned that with all the trees here, we're going to have more shade than sun. How are solar panels supposed to work without sun?"

Her smile disappeared, replaced by a stubborn set of her jaw. "There'll be plenty of sun on the roofs of the cottages."

"I think tying the cottages to the regular power grid would be a hell of lot simpler and more reliable in the long run."

She crossed her arms over her chest. "I feel like we've had this conversation before. The whole theme of this place is sustainability and eco-friendliness. Are you saying you aren't capable of building these cottages to accommodate solar energy?"

Anger and pride rose in his chest. "Of course, I can build them. I can build anything. But I think going solar is a waste of money."

She lifted her chin. "You're wrong about that, but it really doesn't matter what you think. Ethan and Harper are your clients, and they want solar energy. So either get with the program or step aside so they can hire someone who can build what they want."

For one prideful moment, he seriously considered doing exactly that. But then common sense intervened. He needed this job and so did his crew. And he wanted to prove to Ethan he was reliable. A team player. He wanted him to know he could count on him. Lord knew that hadn't always been the case. "Fine. We'll use solar energy."

"Try not to sound so enthusiastic about it."

"What the hell do you want from me, Scarlet? I said I'll do it."

She threw up her hands. "Why do you have to be so pig-headed?" Cam saw her glance toward his crew, but fortunately, with the noise of the excavator, they hadn't heard their exchange. She lowered her voice. "Why do you hate my sister so much?"

"I don't hate her."

"Is it the money? Because I'm telling you, she loves Ethan in spite of the money."

"Money like that brings out the crazy in people."

"My sister is not crazy. She was in love with Ethan before she knew anything about his lottery win. Harper's a good person, the best. She's honest, and she doesn't lie."

"Ethan is honest, too."

Her eyes flashed. "Oh, yeah. Except for lying about his real name and true identity, real honest."

She stood in front of him with narrowed eyes and hands fisted at her sides as if she was ready to do battle with him on her sister's behalf. For reasons he didn't fully understand, it made him smile. "Okay, you've got me there. It wasn't one of Ethan's shining moments."

A reluctant answering grin tugged on her lips. "No, it wasn't. But the point is, Harper forgave him for lying. Eventually. She came to understand why he thought he couldn't tell her the truth. Maggie and I have forgiven him too, because we see how much he loves Harper. So, why can't you believe she loves him as much as he loves her?"

Cam heaved a sigh as he looked toward the lake once more. His feelings were complicated. He wasn't sure he understood them himself.

"I'm not going to give you any more grief about the solar energy, okay?"

"Okay. Ethan texted me the name of the solar energy company he's been in contact with. Do you want me to set up a meeting with them so we know what their requirements are before you start building?"

He nodded. "Yeah, sure. Let's get the ball rolling."

"I'll call them today." She looked down at his sketches once more. "These are really wonderful, Cameron. You should be proud of them."

"I am."

She glanced toward him again, her smile amused. "Good. Have you always been an artist?"

*"You think you're some kind of artist or something? Don't be stupid. Why are you wasting time drawing pictures of cartoon characters? Nobody wants your stupid little pictures, boy."*

With a force of will, Cam blocked out his father's voice and his derisive laugh. The old man had been gone more than seven years, and he still messed with his head. "I'm no artist."

She cocked her head to one side and studied him. He resisted the urge to squirm under her scrutiny. Barely.

"I'm sorry you feel that way." She pulled her sunglasses from the neck of her t-shirt and slipped them on. "I've gotta run. When do you think the demolition will be done?"

"We should finish in a few days. No more than a week."

"Sounds good. I'll let you know when we're to meet with the solar company."

He suppressed a groan. "Great."

She laughed and patted his arm. "Try to hold down your enthusiasm. Have a nice day."

The sexy sway of her hips as she walked down the road kept him rooted to the spot, unable to look away. He watched her until she rounded a corner and disappeared from view.

*Damn.* The last he needed was to be attracted to Scarlet Lindquist.

# Chapter Seven

SCARLET SPENT THE REST of the day at the public library in Minnewasta trying to deal with their unreliable Wi-Fi network. She managed to set up a Facebook page and upload pictures she'd taken of the renovation so far to chronicle its progress. But when she began work on choosing a theme for a website, she lost the connection. She spent a frustrating half-hour trying to reconnect before asking the librarian for help. The librarian was sympathetic but unable to offer any suggestions. She explained that the Wi-Fi network was temperamental and their IT guy wasn't scheduled to visit for another week. She then suggested that if Scarlet come back the next day, it might be working better.

Scarlet thanked her and packed up her laptop. If she was going to create a website and get social media platforms up and running, she'd need an Internet connection that was far more reliable than the one at the library. Maybe she could find a coffee shop with a more reliable connection, but it certainly wasn't the ideal solution. She'd have to drink a lot of coffee in exchange for tying up one of their tables.

There had to be a better solution. She could drive to Brainerd or maybe St. Cloud and check out their public libraries. If that didn't pan out, she might have to go all the way to Minneapolis. Perhaps she could stay at Ethan's condo.

But all of those options were inconvenient and, strangely, she didn't want to be away from the lodge. She wanted to be part of the action and see the progress on the lodge and the new cottages as it happened.

Even stranger, she found herself reluctant to leave Cameron.

She told herself it was because Ethan had charged her with the responsibility of keeping an eye on him, but that was an excuse. Something drew her to him. Maybe it was his tenderness as a father, or the passion she saw in his drawings.

Nothing good could come out of a liaison with Cameron Hainstock. They were no good for each other. He was an alcoholic, and she was totally unreliable when it came to relationships. She had two ex-fiancés who could vouch for that.

Getting involved with Cameron was a really bad idea, especially since they wouldn't be alone in any relationship. Both of them had to consider Tessa. And there was no way she'd do anything that might hurt Cameron's daughter.

THAT EVENING AFTER dinner, Scarlet told Maggie she was going for a walk. Maggie raised a hand in acknowledgement, barely looking up from her cookbook. She'd been absorbed for days in developing signature dishes for the new kitchen in the lodge. Her sister was feeling the pressure of coming up with something wonderful, even though she kept saying she didn't want the job as head chef. She maintained she'd be perfectly happy to play second fiddle as sous-chef to a more experienced head chef. Because she'd been so adamant, Ethan had been searching for a head chef. So far, no one had been willing to take a chance on a fledgling restaurant in an unproven resort in the middle of Minnesota.

Maggie didn't want to disappoint Harper and Ethan any more than Scarlet did.

She made her way down the road toward the old cottages to see what, if anything, was left. The cottage closest to the one she and Maggie shared had been completely leveled. A dumpster sitting next to the cleared site was heaped to overflowing with the remains of the old building.

At the next cottage site, the building had been flattened and most of the debris taken away, probably to the dumpster she'd just seen. Only the cement foundation and a few rotting timbers remained. Scarlet guessed the crew was waiting for another dumpster to be delivered so they could finish the job.

The excavator had been left at the third site, the cottage knocked to the ground. For some reason, this one hit her hardest of all. She hadn't expected the painful jolt at seeing the cottage reduced to rubble. There was nothing left to show that her grandfather, and her parents, had existed at all.

Scarlet walked on to next cottage, which remained completely intact. She climbed the stairs to the front porch, noting the sponginess of the floorboards beneath her feet. The door to the cottage didn't close properly, probably hadn't for years, and had allowed snow and rain, and rodents and insects to enter. Cameron was right. These cottages were too far gone to save.

But that didn't make their destruction any easier to bear.

She snapped several pictures of the interior with her phone and with the SRL camera she'd brought. Perhaps she'd use them on the website and on social media to show the before and after of the lodge. Or maybe she'd keep these pictures for herself, as a way to capture a tiny piece of her family's history. As a way to remember.

*"I love you, Scarlet. No matter what happens, always remember that, okay?"*

Her father's last words to her played in her head. Had he been thinking about killing her mother when he'd spoken those words? Scarlet pushed the thought away and concentrated on taking more pictures.

She heard the sound of a vehicle approaching and stepped out on the front porch. She was surprised to see Cameron's truck. He stopped in front of the cottage and hopped out.

"Hi," she said as she walked down the stairs. "What are you doing here at this time of day?"

"I need to take some measurements of the lots so we can finalize our plans. And I wanted to see what progress the boys made. I spent the rest of the afternoon at home working on the plans."

"It looks like they've been busy. The dumpster is completely full."

He nodded. "A new one is supposed to be delivered tomorrow morning."

"That's good."

She glanced back at the old cottage. Soon they would be gone, nothing but dust in a landfill somewhere. Sadness pressed on her heart at the thought. They'd be gone the way her parents and grandparents were gone.

"You okay, Scarlet?"

Cameron's question surprised her, jolting her from her morose thoughts. She swallowed and turned to him, forcing a smile. "Yeah, I'm fine." She lifted the camera. "I was taking some pictures. I guess I went a little too far down Memory Lane."

"I'm really sorry we couldn't save these cottages."

She stared into his dark eyes and saw that he really did understand. "I know. I don't have to be a structural engineer to see this place is ready to fall down on its own. I'm being overly sentimental."

"You're entitled. Like you said, your grandfather built these cottages." He looked toward the cottage as if studying the sagging roofline. "When I was a kid, my family ran an inn on a beautiful lake in northern Wisconsin. My mother's father built the place."

"I didn't realize we had a common childhood experience."

"At least the lodge is still in your family. My father sold the inn when Ethan and I were in high school. What was left of it, anyway."

Scarlet heard the bitterness in his voice. She wondered what it meant and waited for him to continue. Instead, he turned and walked back to his truck and retrieved a tape measure and a spiral bound notebook.

"I'd better get busy with those measurements. I want to finalize plans and get them approved as quickly as possible so we can begin construction."

She set her phone and her camera on the front steps. “Can I help? I can hold the end of the tape for you.”

He grinned at her. “Sure. I’d appreciate a hand.”

They worked for over an hour taking measurements of each cottage site. Cameron drew a plot plan for each site, explaining that there had to be sufficient room for the new cottages that were to be built on the existing sites. He pointed to a few trees that would have to be removed, but he'd make careful use of the space so the number of trees that needed to be sacrificed was minimal. Scarlet snapped several more pictures, sneaking in a few shots of Cameron when he wasn’t looking.

After they finished measuring the last plot, Cameron dropped her off in front her cottage. “Thanks for your help. That went a lot quicker than I expected.”

“You’re welcome. I was happy to do it. I guess I needed a distraction this evening.”

“Yeah.” His eyes were warm with understanding. “I’d better get home so I can finish up.”

“Right.” She opened the cab door and got out. Before she turned away, she looked through the open window at him. “Will you be around tomorrow?”

He nodded. “I’ll check in on the crew.”

Their gazes met, clashed. A wild notion to wrench open the door and pour herself back inside flashed in her mind. She wanted to touch him everywhere, plaster herself over him, and feel him touching her, kissing her.

She blinked and stepped away from the truck. What was she thinking?

“Goodnight Cameron.”

She turned and ran up the stairs to the cottage, not sure if he said an answering goodnight.

"MY NAME IS CAM AND I'm an alcoholic."

"Hello, Cam."

Cam looked out at the small group of people gathered together on a Tuesday evening in a church basement in Minnewasta, each of them there to fight their own personal demons. Alcoholics Anonymous was like an exclusive club, one that he and the other people in this room wished they didn't need to belong to. Over the last three years, he'd heard many stories in groups like this. All the stories were different, telling tales of individual descents into alcoholism. But in many ways, they were all the same. The same struggle, the same heartache, the same stories of broken families and relationships.

"I've missed some meetings lately," he began. "I've been busy with work, but I know that's no excuse. I told myself I was fine. That I've been sober long enough to be able to skip a few meetings.

"But the other day, as I was huddled over my drafting table, I found myself craving a cigarette. I almost went out and bought a pack. I told myself I'd only have one cigarette, to ease my nerves. What could it hurt? That's when I got scared and knew I had to get myself to a meeting. That kind of rationalizing, telling myself I could stop at one, is the same kind of thinking that made me an alcoholic. The truth is, in my mind a cigarette and glass of coke and crown belong together, like peanut butter and jam. I can't have one without the other. Just like I can't go into a bar and tell myself I'll only have something to eat.

"I've been given an amazing new opportunity, a chance to prove myself, and it scares the hell out of me. What if I screw up? What if the pressure is too much for me? A lot of people are counting on me. I've been given a second chance, to work and own my own business, and to be a father. I can't mess that up."

The disappointment he'd imagined on Scarlet's face if he started drinking again had kept him from reaching for that first cigarette, and that first drink. He couldn't say why her reaction, rather than his brother's or his daughter's, mattered to him so much. But it had motivated him to attend the meeting tonight.

"So here I am. Thanks for listening."

Several other people got up to share their stories. He'd seen most of them around town in the months since he'd moved to Minnewasta; the place was too small for complete anonymity. But he was surprised to see Reese Hanson.

When the meeting concluded and everyone helped themselves to coffee and cookies at the back of the room, Cam approached Reese. "Hi. I didn't know you were a friend of Bill W."

"Haven't been at a meeting for a while," Reese said. He sipped his coffee before continuing. "I've been in AA for over twelve years. Thought I had my drinking licked, but things have been...difficult lately. I'm finding myself needing the group more than ever."

"Maybe next time you could share what's going on in your life with the group. It might help."

"I'm not sure anything's going to help." Raw pain flashed across his face before he masked it. "It helps being around the group."

"Is there anything I can do?"

Reese's smile was tinged with sadness. "It's kind of you to offer, but no, there's nothing you can do."

Cam nodded. He'd seen Reese and his wife at Ethan's wedding, and Abby looked frail. He knew she'd had surgery and was recovering, but maybe she was seriously ill.

He didn't want to push. If Reese didn't want to talk about his problems, he couldn't make him. Best to change the subject. "How are the renovations on the lodge coming along?"

"Right on schedule. We've run into a few hiccups, but we've been able to work through them. I'm really proud of the Lindquist girls for taking on this project. A lot of people would have sold the place and never looked back."

"That was mostly Harper's doing, from what I hear."

"I know," Reese said, "but her sisters have stepped in to help. They didn't have to do that."

"No, I suppose not."

Cam thought of Scarlet taking an unpaid leave from her job for five months. That certainly spoke of her commitment to the project and to her family. He hadn't known her long, but he knew her well enough to understand she'd give everything she had to help make the lodge a success. She was the kind of woman who made him want to be a better man.

He blinked at the thought. Where the hell had that come from?

Scarlet Lindquist was an attractive woman, but that was as far as his appreciation went. Aside from their shared desire to see the successful completion of the renovations on the lodge, they had nothing in common. In a few months, Scarlet would pack up and head back to her real life in Chicago. He couldn't, wouldn't, get involved with someone who had no intention of sticking around.

Regardless of how attractive he found her, he couldn't take any chances. He was a package deal. If he got involved with her, she'd also get involved with his daughter. Tessa was already too attached to Scarlet for his liking.

His smartest option was to keep a safe distance from Scarlet Lindquist. It was the best decision for everyone.

# Chapter Eight

MAGGIE STUCK HER HEAD inside the door of the cottage. "They're here! Come on, Scarlet!"

Scarlet slid her feet into a pair of flip flops and followed Maggie out onto the front porch as Ethan's truck rounded the bend.

"I hope they had a good time and didn't worry too much," Maggie said, lifting her hand to wave.

"It sounded like they were having fun."

Scarlet had kept in touch with Ethan and Harper by email and text message for the last two weeks. She'd kept her messages as upbeat as possible, talking about all the progress that was being made on the renovations and the new cottages. Ethan had inquired numerous times about Cameron, and she'd been happy to tell him he was doing great and accomplishing a lot. Scarlet was inexplicably proud of Cameron. In spite of the fight he'd had with Ethan and the pressure he'd been under to get the cottages built, he'd stayed focused and hadn't turned to alcohol.

Maybe he was a lot stronger than Ethan gave him credit for.

The truck pulled up to the cottage and Harper jumped out before the vehicle came to a full stop. She ran up the front steps and threw her arms around Maggie and then Scarlet. "I missed you both so much!"

"We missed you, too. Did you have fun?"

The happiness on Harper's face told Scarlet everything she needed to know. "So much fun. We thoroughly absorbed Parisian culture. I even bought a beret!"

Maggie laughed. "No way!"

"It's true. And I got gifts for everyone. Shopping in Paris is amazing!"

Ethan joined them on the front porch and hugged both her and Maggie. Scarlet squeezed his hand. "I hope you didn't worry too much."

"Not too much."

"Liar." Harper affectionately wound her arm around his waist. "He tried not to let on, but he was concerned about Cam."

"Maybe I was a little concerned, but we still managed to have a nice honeymoon, didn't we?"

Harper's expression was full of love. "We had a wonderful honeymoon, the best."

The look they shared spoke of their deep connection, and the respect and love they had for each other. Scarlet had to look away as an unexpected pang of jealousy hit her hard, her stomach burning with it.

She hated feeling jealous of her own sister. It was stupid and petty and pathetic.

Fortunately, Harper was too happy and excited to notice her discomfort. "Ethan, could you get the purple suitcase from the truck? That's the one with all the gifts."

"Sure."

He gave her a kiss and headed to the truck. When he was out of earshot, Harper turned to Scarlet, her eyes serious and her voice soft. "Is Cam really okay? Your emails made it sound as if everything was fine, but we wondered if you were saying that so we wouldn't cut our trip short. He hasn't started drinking again?"

"No, he hasn't." Ethan and Harper's belief that Cameron would turn to alcohol again at the first sign of trouble annoyed her. "Cameron is doing great. You need to give him some credit."

Harper's eyes widened. She cocked her head to one side and gave Scarlet an assessing look that made her squirm. Finally, she nodded. "Maybe you're right."

Ethan hauled a large purple suitcase up the stairs to the front porch. "This thing weighs a ton. How much stuff did you cram in here?"

"Only a few gifts." She winked at Scarlet. "Why don't we take it inside? I'm excited to show Scarlet and Maggie what I bought for them."

Maggie opened the door and Harper wheeled the suitcase inside. "You didn't have to buy us anything."

"I wanted to. I can't tell you what a pleasure it is to be able to buy things for the people I love without having to worry about how I'm going to pay for them." She reached for Ethan's hand. "I have a very indulgent husband."

"I hope you bought something for yourself, aside from the beret." It would be so like Harper to think about others before herself.

"Don't worry," Ethan said. "I made sure she bought a couple of new outfits."

"That silk dress is beautiful, but when am I ever going to wear it? It's not the kind of thing you wear to overhaul an outboard motor."

Ethan planted a kiss on her forehead. "I'll take you somewhere nice so you have a chance to wear it."

Harper smiled fondly at him, but said nothing. She opened the suitcase and began pulling out shopping bags. She pulled out two bags emblazoned with a stylized H.

Scarlet's breath caught in her throat. "Harper, don't tell me you bought us something from Hermès."

She gave them each a bag. "Okay, I won't tell you."

Scarlet pulled a silk scarf from the shopping bag. The soft, beautiful material was bursting with color. She'd never owned anything more decadent and purely unnecessary. But she loved it.

Harper draped the scarf around Scarlet's neck. "When I saw the blues and purples of this scarf, I thought of you. With your fair skin, it's perfect. It'll bring out the blue in your eyes, too."

Her throat closed with emotion. Trust Harper to find the most perfect, most personal gift for someone else while she was on her honeymoon. "It's beautiful, Harper. I love it. Thank you."

"You're welcome." She turned to Maggie. "Open yours, Maggie Cat."

Scarlet hadn't heard Harper, or anyone else, use the nickname their mother had given Maggie when she was a baby in a very long time. Maggie looked momentarily stunned, but she roused herself and pulled a silk scarf from her shopping bag. This one was in a vibrant red pattern that went perfectly with Maggie's dark hair and eyes.

"I don't know what to say." Maggie's eyes filled with tears.

Harper smoothed her hair from her forehead. "If you like it, you don't have to say anything."

"I love it," Maggie said, her voice choked with emotion. "Thank you. It's the most beautiful gift I've ever received."

Harper pulled her into a hug and held her. Maggie clung to her, her small shoulders shaking.

Poor Maggie. Scarlet knew how much pressure she'd put herself under over the last few weeks and Harper's generous gift had finally broken through her tough exterior. At one time, Scarlet would have said such pressure would never have fazed Maggie. Her sister had been confident to the point of cockiness about her talents as a chef. But something had happened in the last couple of years that had undermined her confidence. She wished Maggie would talk about it. Maybe now that Harper was home she'd open up to her.

A knock sounded at the door and Scarlet jumped to her feet to answer it, the scarf still around her neck. Cameron stood on the other side, a cardboard tube under his arm. He appeared outwardly calm, but Scarlet detected the tension in his jaw that told her he wasn't sure of his welcome. "Hi. Come in."

He hesitated. "I saw Ethan's truck, and I thought maybe he'd like to see the completed designs we've come up with." He patted the cardboard tube.

She was surprised at his use of the word 'we'. "I'm sure Harper and Ethan would both like to see them. We all would. Why don't you come inside?"

He nodded and stepped over the threshold. As soon as he entered, Ethan got to his feet and came toward him. He held out his hand, then pulled his brother into an embrace, clapping him on back. "It's good to see you."

Some of the tension in Cameron's jaw eased. "It's good to see you, too. Did you have a good time?"

Ethan grinned. "The best. Harper was just opening up her bag of goodies. She got the girls some gifts, and I think there's something for you in there, too."

He looked genuinely surprised. "For me?"

"Yeah, you. Come on in."

Harper stood and faced him. No one but those who knew her best would realize how nervous she was, but Scarlet saw the way she clutched a shopping bag in front of her as if using it as a shield.

"Hi, Cam," she said.

"Hello." Cameron cleared his throat. "Did you just get home?"

"Yes, we pulled in a few minutes ago. We flew into Minneapolis yesterday and stayed at Ethan's condo overnight. I'd heard about jet lag, but I had no idea it would hit me so hard. I think I slept for about fifteen hours straight."

"I hope you're feeling better."

"Yes, much better, thank you." She held out the shopping bag to him. "Ethan and I did a little shopping in Paris. For gifts. I'm sorry it's in the bag like this. I didn't have a chance to gift wrap it."

Cameron reluctantly accepted the bag from her, his brows knitted together in confusion. No doubt he was wondering why she would give him a gift when the last time she'd seen him, he'd accused her of marrying Ethan for his money. Scarlet wondered the same thing.

Ethan moved beside Harper and put his arm around her shoulders. It didn't take an expert on body language to understand he was telling Cameron that he stood with his wife, both figuratively and literally.

"Harper picked out all the gifts. I'm hopeless at that kind of stuff."

Harper smiled at him. "I don't know about that. You picked out my ring yourself, and you did a great job. I love it."

Ethan kissed her forehead. Then, he turned to his brother. "Go ahead. Open it."

Cameron gave a brief nod and pulled a large, flat, rectangular cardboard box from the bag. The box gave no clue as to its contents. Harper gripped Ethan's hand, and Scarlet was pretty sure she was holding her breath.

He set the box on the coffee table and opened the lid, revealing another box made of wood. Cameron sat on the sofa, then reached inside and pulled it out of the cardboard box. This box was really a case, with hinges on one side and a carrying handle on the other. Beneath the handle there appeared to be two drawers, each with a tiny pull. Cameron stared at the box as if he was afraid of opening it.

Scarlet stood next to him, hoping she could ease the tension she saw on his face. "I'm dying to see what's inside. Why don't you open it?"

He turned to look at her and she gave him a smile for encouragement. His mouth curved in a brief smile before he turned back to the box and unfastened the latches. When he opened the hinged box, Scarlet saw dozens of sketching pencils, straight edge tools, and what looked like erasers. Cameron opened one of the drawers to reveal colored pencils and pastel crayons. He carefully studied the box but didn't say a word. Scarlet couldn't tell if he was pleased with Harper's gift or not.

The way Harper was stepping from one foot to the other with her hands clutched together, Scarlet knew she couldn't tell either. "You're such a talented artist, I thought you might like this." Her voice was hesitant.

"I do like this. I like this very much." Finally, he lifted his head and looked at Harper. "Thank you. It's a very thoughtful gift."

Scarlet's shoulders relaxed. She hadn't realized how much his response mattered.

Harper expelled a breath and her smile was one of relief. "You're welcome. We have a few things for Tessa, too." She dropped to her knees and began rummaging through the suitcase. "I'll gather them together and you can give them to her. I might have gone a little overboard. It's such fun buying things for a little girl."

"Maybe..." Cameron cleared his throat. "Maybe you'd like to give your gifts to her yourself. She's going to be with me on the weekend. I can bring her to your cottage on Saturday if you like."

Harper looked up at him, surprise and pleasure shining on her face. "That would be wonderful. I'd like very much to spend some time with Tessa."

He nodded, ran his fingers over the sketch pencils one last time, and closed the lid. Scarlet noted the reverent way he placed the wooden artist's box inside its protective cardboard covering. He may not have come right out and said so, but he was deeply touched by Harper's gift.

"I'm excited to see your final drawings for the cottages," Harper said to him. "That means we're a step closer to actually building them. Why don't you show us?"

He nodded and after putting his box carefully on a chair near the door, he retrieved the tube containing his sketches and opened it. The rolled-up papers slid onto the coffee table when he tipped it over. Ethan unrolled the paper and held the curling corners down with his hands. Harper knelt beside the table and ran her finger over the roofline of the A-frame cottage sketch.

"This is beautiful," she breathed. She turned to Ethan. "Can you imagine what this is going to look like when it's built? It's going to fit in perfectly."

"This one is set on plot number three," Cameron said. "Those are the trees that are actually on that plot right now. That spot of land is large enough for this cottage."

Scarlet was as proud of the sketches as if she had drawn them herself. She snapped a picture of the sketch with her phone. "For the website," she said when Cameron raised an eyebrow at her. "Assuming I get it up and running anytime soon."

Ethan shifted the papers to the architectural drawings depicting the interior. "This is nice."

Harper laughed. "Nice? This is freaking amazing! *I* want to live here!"

"We'll get Cam to build us a house," Ethan said with a wink in his brother's direction.

"I'd love a house like this. It's beautiful," Harper said. Scarlet heard the longing in her voice. "Maybe someday."

Ethan kissed her hair. "We'll make it happen."

She leaned against him. "Right now, I'm more concerned about getting these cottages up and running. When Reese is done with the event center, we'll have the owner's apartment to live in. It's going to be really pretty, and there'll be enough room for Maggie, too."

"I was thinking I'd find a place to rent in Minnewasta," Maggie said. "I don't want to cramp the newlyweds' style."

"You won't be cramping anything. There's plenty of space for the three of us."

Maggie gave a noncommittal shrug. "We'll see."

Scarlet understood her hesitancy. As much as she loved Harper, she wouldn't want to live with her and her new husband. They deserved some privacy, and so did Maggie.

Harper said nothing more, but the look she gave Maggie told Scarlet the subject wasn't closed, only shelved for the time being. Harper turned her attention back to the drawings. "You did an amazing job, Cam. Are you sure you're not an architect?"

He laughed. “Very sure. I went to trade school, not university. Even if my parents had had the money to send me to a school of architecture, I wouldn’t have made the entrance requirements. I wasn’t exactly a stellar student.”

“Then it’s all the more remarkable that you created something as beautiful and functional as this.”

Cameron mumbled his thanks. When the conversation turned to construction start dates and deadlines, Scarlet zoned out. She watched Cameron from the chair she’d pulled over from the dining room. She wondered if he believed Harper’s praise was genuine or if he thought she was trying to flatter him. Her sister didn’t operate that way. If she said his designs were beautiful, she meant it.

Maybe this could be the beginning of acceptance between Harper and Cameron. Scarlet vowed to do everything she could to help make it happen. Harper’s life would be so much easier if she got along with Ethan’s brother.

And Cameron's life would be happier if he could accept that Harper really loved his brother. Although why his happiness mattered so much to her, Scarlet had no idea.

# Chapter Nine

AFTER CAMERON AND ETHAN left to check on the progress of construction, Scarlet and her sisters got ready for the afternoon coffee break. Harper helped Maggie pack oatmeal raisin cookies into a plastic container while Scarlet poured water in the coffee maker.

"So, everything really went well while Ethan and I were away? Ethan's not here, so you can be perfectly honest."

Scarlet ground her teeth in irritation. Harper's inclination to think the worst of Cameron annoyed the hell out of her. "I already told you. Everything was fine. Really."

"Really?"

Scarlet rolled her eyes. "Yes, of course! Do you think I'm lying to you?"

"No, of course not, but—"

"But nothing." Scarlet found her purse and rummaged in it until she found a business card. She thrust it at her sister. "Here. Take this. You deal with it."

Harper reluctantly plucked the card from Scarlet's fingers. "An interior decorator? What's this for?"

"Before you two left on your honeymoon, Ethan gave me the name of the decorator who designed his condo in Minneapolis. I'm supposed to meet with her this week to talk about the design of the new cottages, but I'm delegating that job to you. I've got my hands full setting up the website at the moment."

Harper pursed her lips. "Scarlet, I'm no good at decorating. You told me that yourself every time you came to the lodge for a visit. Why do you want me to do this?"

"I told you. Because I'm busy."

"I don't doubt that you are. But I have a feeling you have an ulterior motive."

Scarlet stared at the stream of dark brew filling the coffee pot. "If you're involved in the decorating, you'll have to work closely with Cameron. It'll give you a chance to get to know him better. I think Ethan worried needlessly about him."

"That could be, but none of us were around when Cam was drinking. Ethan was." Harper snapped shut the lid of the plastic container. "From what he tells me, it was a bad time for the whole family."

"What happened, exactly?" Scarlet wished she didn't want to know.

"Ethan said that Cam had been drinking since he was a teenager and though he overindulged more often then he should have back then, his drinking didn't become a serious problem until about five or six years ago. Around the time Tessa was born."

Scarlet shook her head in silent denial. That didn't make sense. Cameron adored Tessa.

Harper continued. "He was in love with Tessa's mother Laura, and he asked her to marry him when he found out she was pregnant. But she turned him down. She told him she didn't love him."

"Maybe that was better than going ahead with a marriage she didn't want."

"Cam didn't see it that way. They lived together for a while in Minneapolis, and Cam really tried to make it work. But a few months after Tessa was born, Laura had an affair with another man. Ethan said she didn't even bother to keep it a secret. For Tessa's sake, Cam turned a blind eye. Then, when Tessa was about a year and a half old, Laura packed her up and moved to Minnewasta. Cam was devastated to lose his little girl, and the woman he believed he loved. His drinking got out of control at that point."

"This Laura sounds like a piece of work," Maggie said in disgust.

Scarlet had to agree. Her heart ached for Cameron. The way Tessa's mother had flaunted her affair in front of him, it was no wonder he had a hard time trusting. But there was one thing she didn't understand. "Why would Laura move to Minnewasta, of all places? She doesn't sound like a small-town kind of girl."

"That's the thing. She *is* a small-town girl. You know her, Scarlet. We went to school with her. Remember Laura Constable?"

Scarlet stared at Harper. Laura Constable? She hadn't heard that name in a long time. She'd hoped to never hear it again. "Unfortunately, I remember her well."

"She came back to Minnewasta with Tessa to live with her parents."

"And then Cameron moved here to be closer to Tessa?"

"Yes. Apparently, he and Laura have an informal agreement of sorts. As long as he pays child support, she lets him see Tessa."

Maggie pulled a tray of cookies out of the oven when the timer sounded. "I vaguely remember her name. I gather she was as much of a bitch back then as she is today."

"Pretty much. She tormented me all through school. Teased me about my red hair, my braces—"

"The fact that we were orphans," Harper added.

Laura had taken great delight in reminding her, and everyone else, that her father had murdered her mother. "Yes. But I got back at her. I stole her boyfriend in our senior year and made sure she saw us making out behind the bleachers."

Maggie laughed. "Scarlet, that's terrible!"

She shrugged. Definitely not something she was proud of, but she'd been so focused on getting back at Laura that she hadn't thought about all the people she was hurting with her actions. Grandma Dorothy had been angry and embarrassed when the story spread around town. She'd used Colin, Laura's boyfriend, without taking his feelings into account. Worse, she'd hurt Michael, her boyfriend at the time. He'd forgiven her, and they stayed together. Right after graduation, he presented her with a ring and they'd become engaged.

Until she dumped him. Her first broken engagement.

Icy *déjà vu* chilled her, despite the warm summer day. She couldn't shake the worry that Laura would once more bring havoc into her life.

A LARGE TRUCK RATTLED past Cam on its way up the winding road leading to the cottage construction sites. The truck was one of several delivering the cement block that would be used to build the foundations for the cottages. Until now, the cottages had been simply an idea in his head and on his drawings. It was gratifying to see the first steps being taken to bring his dreams to life.

His plan was to build the foundations and frame all eight cottages at once. That way, he could finish the exteriors of all the cottages and close them in before winter, and his crew could spend the winter working on the interiors. It made total financial and logistical sense to work that way. He had to hire a framing crew, plumbers, electricians, and other sub-trades since the job was far bigger than his five-man crew could handle on their own. Instead of bringing in the sub-trades eight separate times, they'd come in once to do their jobs. The framing crew, for instance, would arrive in about a week, once the foundations were ready. They'd likely have all eight cottages framed within a couple of weeks after that.

They'd save time, too, by building the cottages at the same rate. The building inspectors could make their checks on all eight cottages at the same time, which would mean they wouldn't have to waste time waiting for an inspection to be done before they could move on to the next step of the construction.

It was going to be a challenge to juggle all the pieces of the build, but it was one he welcomed. He was going to do his damnedest to make Ethan proud.

Cam scaled the steps to Scarlet and Maggie's cottage two at a time and knocked on the front door. A moment later, Scarlet opened it and shook her head. "You don't have to knock, Cameron. We told you to walk in at meal times."

"I know, but it doesn't seem right. My Mama raised me better."

She grinned and opened the door a little wider. "I'll bet she did. Come on in. Lunch is almost ready."

For the last several days, he and Ethan, Harper and Reese had been congregating at Maggie and Scarlet's cottage for lunch. Some days, if he wasn't expecting to see Tessa in the evening, he stayed for dinner as well. He found himself looking forward to his lunch break every day, not only because Maggie was a great cook.

Admittedly, the highlight of his day was spending time with Scarlet. She was smart and funny, and he liked hearing her ideas. She practically overflowed with plans to market the lodge.

And when she smiled at him, something moved inside his heart, like ice breaking up on a lake after a long winter.

He'd never act on his attraction for her. There were too many complications between them, starting with the fact that she was his brother's sister-in-law. But for the moment, he'd let himself enjoy her company.

Not to mention her gorgeous long legs and delectable ass. Today, she wore a pair of cut-off denim shorts that showed off both assets to best affect. Cam swallowed as he sat at the dining room table, grateful for the napkin he spread across his lap that hid the evidence of his interest.

"How's your day going, Cam?" Maggie asked.

"It's going well. We're making good progress on the foundation work. How are things going with you?"

"You can tell me how my day's going after you've eaten my lunch. I went to a farmer's market in St. Cloud yesterday and picked up some organic strawberries. I thought strawberry shortcake would make a perfect dessert this time of year."

He'd eaten enough of Maggie's desserts to know her strawberry shortcake would be a treat. "I'm looking forward to it."

"Good. Why don't you ask Scarlet how her day's going?" Maggie said with a grin.

He turned to Scarlet. "What's going on?"

She waved her hand. "It's nothing, really."

"Nothing? You should have heard the salty language in the cottage this morning. My ears are still ringing."

"Don't be so overdramatic, Maggie." She softened her words with a grin. "I may have uttered an expletive or two."

"Or six."

"I was frustrated with my Internet connection here. Or lack thereof. It's too difficult to do what I want to do on my phone, so I was trying to set up a Wi-Fi hotspot by tethering my phone to my laptop. But after spending the morning on the phone with my provider, it turns out my phone doesn't have the right setting because it's too old. I haven't updated my personal phone because I've got the latest and greatest through work. Unfortunately, I wasn't able to bring that phone with me."

"I didn't really understand a whole lot of that," Cam said. "But is the main problem the fact that you can't get on the Internet?"

"Yeah, pretty much." She told him how she'd used the Internet at the public library in Minnewasta, with limited success. Even when the connection was working, she could only spend about a half an hour at a time on it.

"I've got a good Internet connection at my house. You could use my laptop."

She blinked at him in surprise. "Thanks. That's not a bad idea."

"I have my moments. You could work there this afternoon, if you like. The place is empty."

"I think I'll take you up on that offer."

He pulled his keys from his pocket and removed the house key. "Here you go. My laptop is set up in the spare bedroom. It's all yours for the afternoon."

"What's your address?"

"I'm on the outskirts of town."

She passed him a pad of paper and he wrote down directions to his house along with the passwords for the computer before handing it back to her. She ripped the paper from the pad. "Thanks, Cameron. This is going to help a lot."

"You can use my laptop anytime you like. I'm here all day anyway."

"That would be great. I've got a lot of work to do."

"I'm glad I could help."

Harper walked into the cottage and sniffed the air. "That smells divine, Maggie. What are we having?"

"Chicken Cacciatore."

"Wonderful. I'm starved." She helped herself to a glass of water at the sink and then sat beside him at the table. "So, how's your day going, Cam?"

"Good."

Harper gave him a polite smile and waited a beat, as if hoping he'd say more. When he didn't, she looked away and took another sip of her water. He wasn't trying to be deliberately uncommunicative or rude; he simply didn't know what to say to her. Or what to make of her.

He couldn't figure her out. He'd been convinced the staggering amount of money Ethan was dropping on the renovations to the lodge was her entire motivation for marrying him. But seeing them together, and the loving way she looked at his brother, he had to admit she cared for Ethan. But he wasn't entirely convinced the money didn't influence her decision.

Then, there was the gift she'd bought for him. No one had ever thought to buy him artist supplies before, not even his brother or sister. It had touched him deeply. The gifts she'd brought back for the family had shown a generous spirit. But then, she'd purchased the gifts on Ethan's dime. Again, Ethan's money seemed to be the common denominator. Would she have been as generous if it had been her own money?

Ethan and Reese entered the cottage, and Cam saw Ethan's gaze zero in on Harper. But instead of watching his brother, he watched Harper's face. A smile of welcome curved her lips, as if Ethan was the one person in the world she most wanted to see. If it was an act, it was an Oscar worthy performance.

Scarlet insisted she was the real deal. He honestly hoped his worries about Harper were unfounded. Ethan adored her and was obviously happy; he didn't want anything to change that. Still, he'd reserve judgement on Harper until he got to know her better.

Ethan dropped a kiss on Harper's mouth, lingering there for a few moments. Harper laid her hand on his cheek. Cam looked away, feeling like a voyeur.

"Get a room, you two." Scarlet's tone was without heat as she put a casserole dish on the table. "Some of us are trying to eat here."

"Sorry, Scarlet. I can't seem to keep my hands off my beautiful wife."

"You don't look the least bit sorry, and I couldn't be happier." Scarlet sat at the head of the table while Ethan sat beside Harper. Maggie sat beside Cam and Reese slid into the chair at the other end of the table.

"This smells delicious, Maggie." Reese helped himself to a huge helping of the casserole. "You're an amazing chef."

"I'll second that." Cam's taste buds did a little happy dance as he bit into a tender piece of chicken in a fragrant tomato and onion sauce.

"Me, too," Ethan said. "If you keep feeding me like this, I'm going to lose my girlish figure."

A pink blush swept across Maggie's neck and cheeks. "Thanks guys. I appreciate the vote of confidence."

"Abby's been asking about you, Maggie." Reese poured himself a glass of water from the pitcher Scarlet had set on the table. "She'd really like to see you. All of you girls."

Maggie ducked her head, avoiding Reese's gaze. "Yes, of course. I'd like to see her, too."

"How is Abby?" Harper asked. "I didn't really get much of a chance to speak to her at our wedding."

Reese put down his fork. "She's...She's getting along, but she doesn't get out much these days. She'd really like some company. If you could spare a few moments to visit her, Harper, I know it would mean the world to her."

"Yes, of course. I'll call her this afternoon and see when the three of us can arrange a visit."

"That's a great idea." Scarlet passed the salad to Cam. "I've been wanting to visit her. But don't make any arrangements for this weekend, Harper. I'm going to that wedding show in Minneapolis, remember?"

"Wedding show?" Cam had never heard of such a thing.

"Yeah, it's a trade show for people in the wedding industry – florists, wedding gown designers, and hotels and other venues that hold weddings. I'm hoping to interest brides in booking their weddings at the lodge next year."

"Weddings are good steady business," Harper said. "Once the event center opens, we'll be able to host weddings for up to two hundred and fifty guests. The problem is, we won't have enough rooms for that many people."

"I've been thinking about that." Ethan said around a mouthful of food. "I think that in Phase two of the renovations, we build another wing of rooms."

"This is the first I've heard of a Phase Two." Harper's brow wrinkled in confusion. "We haven't even finished Phase One. Shouldn't we wait to see if this new version of the lodge is profitable before we start spending even more money?"

"Well sure, we'll finish these renovations first and then move on to the next stage. We're in the hotel business, Harper. I know you only wanted to fix up the lodge, but it was way too small. We have to have facilities that make people want to come here. We have to spend money to make money."

"What if this place doesn't catch on? What if nobody wants to come here and we lose a fortune. *Your* fortune. There's no way I want to put more of your money at risk."

Ethan covered her hand with his. "I keep telling you, it's your money now, too."

"If it's my money now, I vote that we hang on to some of it. Perhaps some cautious investments elsewhere. We don't know what's going to happen next year when we open. We could totally fall on our faces."

Cam continued to eat but watched Harper's face closely during the exchange. *Interesting.* She looked sincere, concerned even, but a good actress could also play heartfelt.

Ethan intertwined his fingers with hers. "You don't have to worry. Lydia is the queen of cautious investing. She's taking very good care of our money. But I want you to know I care about this place as much as you do. This is our home, our business, and we're going to make it a success. There's nothing in this world I'd rather spend that money on than this lodge."

"Promise me we'll wait and see how things go, okay?"

He kissed her hand. "If it makes you feel better, we'll take it a little slower."

"Just till we know we're going to be okay. All right?"

"All right."

Their conversation surprised Cam. He'd assumed Harper was the one pushing to spend more money on the lodge, but maybe he'd been wrong. He glanced over at Scarlet. She was staring at him intently, one eyebrow raised in triumph. He could practically hear her 'I told you so'.

With a cocky nod, she broke eye contact. "I need advice from you all," Scarlet said. "While I'm in Minneapolis, I've arranged an interview on morning television at WCJC. I've sent them pictures of the lodge, as well as the progress on the current renovations, and Cameron's sketches for the new cottages. Does anyone have any suggestions about what we want to project in this interview?"

"You'll want to play up how we're striving to create an eco-friendly destination," Ethan said.

Scarlet nodded. "Yes, that's high on my list."

Harper pointed her fork at Scarlet. "What about the fact that it's a short drive from the city, but a whole different world out here?"

"I think that's a good selling feature. I'm showing a lot of pictures from your wedding, especially the tent next to the lake. I want to emphasize how beautiful an outdoor summer wedding at the lodge can be."

"How about telling them about the Maggie's amazing food?" Reese said.

"Thanks, Reese." Maggie smiled at Scarlet." You'll do great, sweetie. You're wonderful at this stuff."

"Thanks, honey. I appreciate that, but I'm nervous as hell. I've never been on TV before."

"It's understandable to be nervous, but I know you'll do a good job. There's no better representative of the lodge."

"Thank you, Harper. That's the nicest thing you could say to me."

Cam had to agree with Harper. Scarlet would make a wonderful spokesperson for the lodge. She was smart, poised, and beautiful, a natural for TV.

She was far too special to hang around here. She belonged back in Chicago, where she could use her talents to the fullest capacity.

The thought of her leaving in a few months caused uncomfortable tightness in his chest.

# Chapter Ten

WITH THE HELP OF CAMERON'S map, Scarlet easily found his house. The place he'd rented was farther out of town then she'd expected, about a mile and a half. The house was set back from the main road and surrounded by trees, separating it from neighbors and giving the place a sense of complete privacy. The privacy of his house shouldn't surprise her. Cameron guarded everything about his personal life. At least from her.

A huge garage at the back of the property dominated the yard and was at least twice the size of the modest bungalow. She wondered why he'd want something so large until she remembered Drew telling her that he built furniture. Was the garage his workshop? Curious, she walked to the garage and tried to peek in through one of the windows, but they were too high. A padlock on the door screamed 'Stay out!' Maybe if she asked nicely, he'd let her into this inner sanctum. Then again, it could be one more thing he closely guarded.

The yard itself was neat, if somewhat Spartan. The grass was clipped and the yard was free of clutter. The bungalow looked recently painted, though somewhat boring with its simple white siding and black trim. The only concession to color was the pot of purple pansies near the front door. Scarlet wondered if Cameron had planted them for Tessa.

Using the key he'd given her, she opened the front door and walked straight into the bungalow's living room. Like the outside, the inside of the house was clean and tidy. She stopped to admire a beautiful wooden coffee table set in front of the sofa. The piece managed to be rustic and modern at the same time and would be perfect for the new cottages. She made a mental note to ask Cameron where he'd purchased the table. A thought struck her as she examined it more closely. Had he made this table? If he had, the man was beyond talented.

Unable to stop herself from snooping, Scarlet wandered through the main rooms of the house. Cameron obviously ran a tight ship. Everything in the kitchen and living room was spotless and seemed to have a place and a purpose, with no extraneous stuff to clutter the landscape. With the exception of the coffee table and a gorgeous wooden dining table with wrought iron legs in the kitchen, the best that could be said about the furniture was that it was clean and serviceable.

Scarlet's curiosity got the better of her and instead of finding Cameron's office and getting on with her work, she checked out the bedrooms. The room that obviously belonged to Tessa was painted a pale purple and contained a twin bed with a beautiful white headboard and a purple bedspread emblazoned with unicorns and rainbows. Matching curtains hung on the window and a child-sized wooden table with two chairs sat against one wall. Toys were neatly stacked on shelves and in a toy box. The thought of him tidying up pink ponies and Barbie dolls in this very feminine little girl's room made her smile.

She examined an adorable wooden train engine painted bright red. After putting the engine back on the shelf, she left Tessa's room, and walked down the hall past the scrupulously clean bathroom to Cameron's room. It felt like an invasion of his privacy to enter the room that most reflected his personality. Scarlet hovered in the doorway, uneasy, but too curious to leave. Like the rest of the house, it was neat and contained the bare minimum of furniture. A beautiful headboard dominated the room. Tall and elaborately constructed, the headboard appeared to be made out of some kind of reclaimed wood in varying shades of brown and grey. The room had a masculine vibe that reminded her of Cameron.

She stared at the king-sized bed that took up the majority of floor space. She imagined Cameron in that bed, the brown comforter messed up and barely covering his naked body. His dark hair would be rumpled, the scruff of a beard lining his jaw. His face would be relaxed in sleep, peaceful, and even more handsome than when he was awake. Then his eyes would open, and he'd stare into her eyes, his sensuous mouth smiling in pleasure as he reached for her...

*Stop right there.*

Scarlet quickly backed out of the doorway and hurried down the hall to the office, her heart racing. That's what she got for snooping. As she booted up Cameron's laptop with trembling fingers, she promised to keep her mind on business while she was in his house.

THE NEXT AFTERNOON, Scarlet let Harper into the cottage. Maybe her older sister could knock some sense into Maggie.

Harper set her purse on the island. "Are you guys ready? I told Abby we'd be at her house around two."

"I'm ready," Scarlet said, "but Maggie says she's not going."

"What?" Harper turned to Maggie. "Why not? Reese said Abby specifically asked for you."

Maggie broke a couple of eggs into a bowl and turned on the mixer. "Today's a bad day for me. I'm in the middle of something."

"Couldn't you do that later? We won't be staying for more than an hour."

"I've already started. You know I'm trying to nail down my menu. I'll go another time."

Scarlet shared a look with Harper, lifting her shoulder in a shrug. She was as baffled by Maggie's behavior as Harper appeared to be.

Harper threw up her hands. "You knew we were planning to go this afternoon. What's really going on, Maggie?"

"I'm under a lot of pressure." Maggie dumped a cup of flour into the mixer, raising her voice to be heard over the machine. "You want everything to be perfect, so I'm trying to create the perfect menu."

"Maggie, you're not being fair to Harper. If there's pressure, you're putting it on yourself. Harper hasn't said anything about perfection. She's giving you the freedom to create the menu you want. Do you know how lucky you are?" Sometimes her baby sister could be a real brat.

Maggie refused to look at them. "Maybe Harper hasn't told me directly she wants perfection, but it's there, in every meeting, in every conversation about the lodge. The dining room has to bring people in. If no one wants to come here, it's going to be my fault."

Harper stepped behind the island and put her hand on Maggie's shoulder. "Honey, I'm sorry you feel such pressure. That's not at all what I meant to do. Tell me how I can make things better."

Maggie turned off the mixer and scraped the sides of her bowl with a spatula. Scarlet noted her pinched mouth and the trembling of her hand. "I'm sorry, but I can't see Abby today."

Scarlet grabbed Maggie's free hand and squeezed. "Is there anything we can say to change your mind? Anything we can do?"

Maggie shook her head, still refusing to look at them. Harper sighed and turned to Scarlet. "I guess we'd better go."

"Don't forget to take the basket of goodies I made for Abby," Maggie said. She swallowed, and Scarlet realized she was holding back tears. "She always liked my brownies. Tell her...tell her I'm thinking of her."

Harper picked up the basket from the counter. "We'll tell her. Are you going to be okay by yourself?"

"Yes, of course." She turned the mixer on once more and began adding ingredients, carefully avoiding their eyes.

Scarlet glanced at Harper. She looked as confused and worried as Scarlet was. As a kid, Maggie had spent a lot of time with Abby, especially after Grandma Dorothy died when she was fourteen. Scarlet had been away from home by then, but whenever she'd talked to Maggie on the phone, she'd spoken of Abby. So why was she avoiding her now?

They didn't have time to get into it. Without another word, they left the cottage and drove to town.

A short time later, they arrived at Abby and Reese's house. After Scarlet rapped on the door, they waited several minutes for Abby to answer and when she did, Scarlet sucked in a breath. She looked even frailer than she had the last time she'd seen her, and thinner. Today she wore no head covering of any kind, and Scarlet was shocked at how short her hair was. Her skin had a sort of yellowish cast that looked sickly. For the first time, she wondered if something was seriously wrong with Abby.

The thought must have occurred to Harper as well. Scarlet saw the shock in her expression before she quickly covered it with a smile. "Hi, Abby." She stepped forward to give her a hug. "Here we are, as promised."

"It's wonderful to see you." Abby opened her arms to Scarlet and she hugged her. She felt small and fragile in her arms, like a wounded bird.

Abby looked out the open door. "Where is Maggie? Isn't she with you?"

Harper glanced at Scarlet before she answered. "She wasn't able to come today, but she said to tell you she's thinking of you."

Abby's mouth turned down at the corners, disappointment dulling her eyes. "I've been thinking about her, too."

Harper held up the basket. "She baked some brownies and other goodies for you."

"Maggie was a talented baker even as a young girl. I imagine her talents have grown since then." She roused herself and offered them a smile. "Scarlet, honey, would you close the door? Let's go have some tea and brownies."

Scarlet obediently closed the front door and followed them into the kitchen. Abby filled the kettle but when she tried to move it to the stove, it fell back into the sink with a clatter.

Harper was on her feet in an instant, her arms around Abby. "Let us take care of the tea."

She led her to a kitchen chair and made her sit down while Scarlet rescued the kettle from the sink and put it on the stove. Simply walking across the kitchen seemed to wear Abby out.

"I'm sorry about that. You're guests in my home. I'm supposed to look after you, not the other way around."

Harper sat next to her and clasped her hand. "We're old friends. We don't need to stand on ceremony."

Scarlet found teacups and small plates in the cupboard, along with a sugar bowl and an empty creamer. She filled the creamer with milk from the fridge and brought everything to the table. Once the water boiled, she made tea and brought it to the table as well.

Abby gave her a grateful smile. "Thank you, Scarlet. I'm having a little trouble getting around these days."

Scarlet sat across from her. "How are you feeling?"

"Oh, I'm fine. Just not as much energy as I'd like. Keeps me pretty housebound."

Harper put some of Maggie's brownies on a plate and set it within Abby's reach. "Is your lack of energy related to the surgery you had last winter? Have you asked your doctor about it?"

"He's doing what he can for me." She patted Harper's hand. "Please, don't worry about me. I'd rather talk about you girls and what's going on in your lives."

Scarlet glanced at her sister. Harper gave a slight nod, as if to tell her there was no point grilling Abby about her health if she didn't want to talk about it.

"Oh, I almost forgot." Harper dug in her purse for a small gift-wrapped box that she handed to Abby. "I got you a little something when I was in Paris."

Abby looked genuinely surprised. "Oh, honey, you didn't have to get me anything."

"I wanted to. Go ahead and open it."

Abby ripped open the gift wrapping with trembling fingers to reveal a small blue jeweler's box. When she lifted the lid, a *fleur-de-lis* pendant on a silver chain sparkled in the afternoon sunlight. Scarlet wondered if the stones on the pendant were real diamonds. Abby must have wondered, too.

"Oh, Harper, this is too much." She tried to push the box away, but Harper put her hands over hers, stopping her.

"I want you to have it. For the first time in my life I was able to buy really wonderful gifts for the people who mean the most to me. You wouldn't deny me this one little pleasure, would you?"

Abby pursed her lips. "That's dirty pool."

"Maybe, but I want you to have this necklace as a token of my love. You're our oldest friend."

"Oldest? I'm not sure I like that."

Both Harper and Scarlet laughed. This was the irreverent, funny Abby they'd known and loved. The one they'd turned to when things got tough at home.

"Okay, the friend we've had the longest. Is that better?"

"Better." Abby carefully removed the necklace from the box. "Would you help me put this on?"

"Of course."

She bent her head to allow Harper to fasten the clasp of the necklace. Abby touched the pendant. "Thank you, Harper."

"You're very welcome."

Harper told her about the places they'd visited in Paris, like Notre Dame Cathedral and the Louvre. Scarlet talked about her plans to attend the wedding show in Minneapolis on the weekend. When she mentioned she was going to be on television, Abby made her write down the time and date on her wall calendar.

"I watch that show quite often, when I get up early enough. I'll set my alarm so I make sure not to miss it."

"I hope I don't make a mess of it."

"Of course you won't. You're like your mother. You can handle anything."

"It means a lot to me to hear you say that, Abby."

She squeezed Scarlet's hand. "You're both strong, accomplished woman, and Miranda would be very proud of you. That reminds me. I was looking at some old photo albums and I found some pictures of your mother. I thought you might like to see them." She pointed to a cardboard box in the corner of the kitchen. "Could you bring them to the table?"

Scarlet pulled the three albums from the box and brought them to Abby. With a grin, Abby opened the first album to a page that had been marked with a bookmark. "These go all the way back to high school. Talk about ancient history."

Every picture showed a smiling, vivacious Miranda, the center of attention. Abby touched Miranda's image with her finger. "She was the kind of person everyone wanted to be around. It was like she had a light shining inside her. We all wanted to be close to her so we could be warmed by her light."

For the thousandth time, Scarlet wondered how different their lives would have been if their mother had lived, if they had been allowed to bask in her light. What kind of people would she and her sisters be? Would she still be as afraid to commit to love as she was now?

"I forgot to tell you, Scarlet. I found several boxes of Mom's stuff hidden away in Grandma Dorothy's closet when I was cleaning out the lodge." Harper refilled her cup and Abby's from the tea-cozy covered pot. "I haven't had a chance to open them all, just one box with a lot of photo albums like these."

"I'd like to see them," Scarlet said.

"Any time. They're stored away in the second bedroom of our cottage."

They paged through the albums for a while longer, laughing at some of the antics of Abby and Miranda and their teenage friends.

"How is Luke?" Scarlet asked. "I haven't seen him since...I don't really know how long it's been since I've seen him."

"That's because my son doesn't have any interest in coming back to Minnesota." Abby's wistful smile held a touch of longing. "I don't see him often, but we talk on the phone all the time. He says there's nothing for him here. He's much happier in California, managing a small, boutique hotel in the Napa Valley."

Resentment made Scarlet unable to speak for a moment. She'd give anything to be able to see her mother one more time, even if it meant the inconvenience of flying halfway across the country. It would be a small price to pay, one that Luke didn't seem to appreciate.

Abby sagged a little in her chair, her face lined with fatigue. Harper looked at Scarlet and tilted her head toward the door in a silent message that said it was time for them to leave. Scarlet got to her feet. "We've really got to get going, Abby," she said, stooping to kiss the top of her head. "I've got to start getting ready for my trip to Minneapolis this weekend."

Harper stood as well. "I've got a million things to do at the lodge. This project is taking on a life of its own."

"I hope you'll come again," Abby said.

Harper kissed her cheek. "We will. I promise."

"And you'll bring Maggie next time?"

Scarlet and Harper exchanged a look. Scarlet had no idea why her little sister refused to visit Abby and from the look on her face, neither did Harper. But they'd do their best to convince her.

"Of course." Scarlet hoped she wasn't lying.

"Goodbye, girls. It was wonderful seeing you again."

After a few more hugs and kisses, they left. When they got into Scarlet's car and pulled away from the curb, Harper looked at her. "Abby looks so frail. It scares me."

"Me, too. I wish she'd tell us what's wrong."

Harper looked down at her hands in her lap. "I'm not sure I want to know."

Scarlet understood. She didn't even want to think about there being something seriously wrong with Abby.

"We've got to convince Maggie to come with us next time," Harper said.

"Got any idea how we're going to do that?"

"Maybe guilt will do it. We could tell her how disappointed Abby was that she didn't come with us this time."

"I hope it works."

Scarlet wished she knew what was going on with Maggie. And she wished Abby could be the same healthy, fun-loving ball of energy she used to be.

But she knew better than most that wishes rarely came true.

# Chapter Eleven

"BREAK TIME!" CHARLIE called. "The cookies are here!"

Cam wiped the sweat from his brow with the back of his hand and followed Charlie's gaze. Harper trudged up the incline toward the work site, pulling a small child's wagon loaded with coffee, cookies, and water for his men. Every day at ten in the morning and three in the afternoon, one or more of the Lindquist sisters would bring coffee and baked goods for his crew's break. His men looked forward to whatever treat arrived from Maggie's kitchen. He knew the sisters did the same for Reese's crew working on the main lodge and event center.

Cam looked forward to seeing them too, especially when it was Scarlet's turn to make a delivery. She was away in Minneapolis at the wedding show, trying to drum up business. He wondered how she was doing. She'd been nervous about the TV interview—

*Stop.*

*Stop thinking about her, stop obsessing over her. Just...stop.*

Besides, he could check how the interview went later tonight when he watched the morning show on his PVR.

*Way to stop obsessing, Hainstock.*

He heaved a sigh, dropped his framing hammer, and got in line.

Ethan waved to his wife. He'd been working with the crew for the last week or so, pounding nails, hauling boards, and doing whatever he could to help move things along. Cam saw the look of welcome on Harper's face as Ethan approached her. She kissed him and put her arms around him, even though Ethan had to be as sweaty and dirty as he was. Then, she poured water from a large Thermos that Ethan downed greedily. There were a few perks to being the owner's husband.

After the break was over and Ethan went back to work, Harper approached him, a large canvas bag in her hand. "Have you got a minute? I met with a designer in Minneapolis the other day, and she gave me these samples for the interiors of the cottages. I need your opinion."

That surprised him. "You want my opinion on interior design?"

She shrugged. "I'm as confused as you are. I'm no good at this stuff, but Scarlet insisted that if I needed help, you could steer me in the right direction. She said you have a good eye."

"She did, did she?" What was Scarlet up to?

"Yeah." His voice must have carried a note of derision because Harper stepped away, a blush staining her cheeks. "I'm sorry, I shouldn't have bothered you. I'll figure it out."

"Wait." He gestured toward the open tailgate of his truck. "Step into my office and show me what you've got."

Her blue eyes lit with surprise, and maybe a little relief. "Okay, thanks."

They walked over to the truck. Harper pulled fabric swatches, a chunk of granite, some subway tiles, and a small cupboard door from the canvas bag and laid them out on the tailgate. Lastly, she produced a piece of hardwood flooring and a sketch.

"So, after I told the designer about the cottages we're building and the vibe we're going for, she came up with this stuff. I'm having trouble figuring out what all these samples will look like in the space. What do you think?"

"What did you tell the designer you wanted?"

Harper blew out a breath. "I told her they were rental cottages in the woods near a lake, and that we're reopening the lodge with an emphasis on sustainability and eco-friendliness. I showed her your drawings of the cottages and said the finishes needed to tough and long-wearing."

"You decorated the other two cottages, didn't you?"

Her cheeks turned pink. "Not exactly. The lady at the furniture store in Brainerd where I bought everything offered to decorate in exchange for doing her taxes for a couple of years."

That made him smile. She really didn't have a clue. "What do you see when you imagine what the new cottages will look like?"

Her face went blank and she shook her head. "I don't know. I told you, I'm no good at this stuff."

Cam picked up one of the fabric swatches and tossed it aside. "I'm not talking about the details of the color scheme. What feeling do you want the cottages to have?"

She leaned against the truck and crossed her arms, her gaze fixed on Ethan some distance away as he resumed pounding nails. "I want the cottages to feel warm and homey, and a little bit rustic. When people come here, I want them to relax and feel like they're really out in the woods on a little adventure."

He handed her one of the stark, white subway tiles. "So does this scream rustic, homey, adventure-in-the-woods to you?"

"No." She handed the tile back to him with a frown. "It says this is a designer's idea of what a north woods cottage should look like. I think these are the same tiles Ethan has in his condo in the city, which makes sense since the same designer decorated it."

He grinned at her. "I agree. I think this stuff is too sleek and modern for what we want here."

"Right." She stuffed the samples into her bag. "Back to the drawing board. Maybe I can get the lady from the furniture store to help me again."

"You'll figure it out."

"I hope so. Thanks. You helped me get a handle on what we want here."

Charlie approached him carrying a chain saw. "Boss, we're trying to take down those two trees that are in the way on the next lot, but the chain keeps coming off. Want me to run into town and buy a new one?"

Harper set her bag on the tailgate. "Can I see that?"

Charlie frowned, but handed it to her. "You know about chain saws?"

"A little." She ran her fingers over the chain, obviously unconcerned about getting her hands dirty. "I think I know what's wrong with it. I'll take it to my garage and get it back to you in a few minutes. Can I leave my samples in your truck for now, Cam?"

"Yeah, no problem." If Charlie hadn't been able to fix the chainsaw, he couldn't see what Harper could do. He watched as she hoisted the saw onto her shoulder and headed back down the hill.

A short time later, Harper returned with his saw. Cam climbed down the scaffolding to talk to her, curious to see what, if anything, she'd been able to do.

"It works fine now," she said, handing it to him. "All it needed was a good oiling. If it runs dry, it tends to seize up and throw off the chain."

Cam accepted it from her and pulled the rope. The motor jumped to life, purring smoothly in his hands. He killed the engine. "Where did you learn about chain saws?"

She swept out her arm to encompass the forest that surrounded them. "Right here. A good chain saw comes in handy. You might have noticed we have a few trees."

He couldn't help grinning. "Yeah, I've noticed the trees. Who taught you about chain saw maintenance?"

"My grandfather. He also taught me how to change the oil in outboard motors and snowmobiles." She inclined her head toward the chainsaw in his hands. "He always said that if I look after my tools, my tools will look after me."

He smiled at her gentle rebuke. "Point taken. I'll make sure to look after it better. You really know how to change the oil on an outboard motor?"

"Sure, among other things. Grampa Bill taught me basic maintenance stuff."

"Did he teach Scarlet, too?"

Her laugh rang through the trees. “Hell, no! She wasn’t into the finer points of chain saw maintenance. I’m the only grease monkey in our family.”

Cam regarded her closely. She didn’t look like any grease monkey mechanic he knew. With her long blonde hair and big blue eyes, she looked more like a Barbie doll. But maybe there was more to this Barbie doll than he’d been giving her credit for. He hefted the saw. "Thanks for this."

“Anytime. In fact, if you’re interested in switching jobs, I could be persuaded to give up my decorating duties.” She grinned as she grabbed her bag of samples from his tailgate. “You’d probably be way better at it than me anyway.”

His lips twitched. “Nice try, Harper, but I’ve got my hands full here. I’ll be happy to take a look at whatever you come up with, though.”

“Thanks. I’ll take you up on that offer.” The smile swiftly died on her lips as her eyes fixated on a point over his shoulder. She sucked in a breath “Damn it. What is he doing up there?”

He followed her gaze to the scaffolding where Ethan stood several feet above the ground helping to guide a rafter lifted by the crane into place. He’d insisted on joining the framing crew and doing his share, despite Cam’s protests that he’d never done that kind of work before, and he’d only slow them down. To Ethan’s credit, he'd learned fast and fit in well with the rest of the men. Most of them had no idea he was the owner of the place and not just one of the guys.

“Ethan’s doing well. I had my doubts at first—”

"But is he safe?" She turned to him, her eyes full of worry. "He could fall off the scaffolding or get hit in the head—"

"That's not going to happen."

"How do you know?" She watched Ethan once more, her grip on the bag turning her knuckles white.

"I know because safety is job one on any of my construction sites. The scaffolding is double-checked before we let anyone on it. Ethan is wearing a harness, like all the other guys on the scaffold. And everyone on site wears a hard hat. We never take any short cuts with safety."

She nodded, but said nothing. Cam had the feeling she didn't believe him.

"Harper, I'm not going to let anything happen to him. I promise."

She turned to him and after searching his face, she nodded again. "I guess I'll have to trust that you've taken every reasonable precaution. But even so, I've got to go. I can't watch him up there."

"Understandable."

"Please don't tell him we had this conversation. He already thinks I worry about him too much."

"Also understandable. He is kind of a knucklehead."

She laughed softly. "Yeah, but he's my knucklehead, and I want to it to stay that way. I'll see you later."

After gathering empty coffee mugs, Harper packed everything, including her bag of samples, into the wagon and walked back down the road toward her cottage. Cam watched her until she disappeared around a bend. He grinned.

"I'll be damned."

She really did love his brother. He could hear it in her voice and see it in every worried glance she gave him. Moreover, he was beginning to believe she'd feel the same way with or without the money.

Sometimes it was good to be wrong.

SCARLET SLID HER DAMP palms against her skirt and hoped her nervousness wasn't terribly obvious. She sat next to the host of the morning show and answered her questions about the lodge.

"Scarlet, I understand the Solace Lake Lodge has been in your family for many years."

"Yes, that's right. My great-grandfather purchased the property right after the Second World War. My grandfather built the timber-frame lodge we're currently renovating."

Pictures of the lodge and the lake flashed on a screen behind them. "Tell me about the renovations you're doing," the host said.

Scarlet launched into what she hoped was a coherent and interesting spiel about the new cottages and hotel rooms, the sustainable nature of the lodge, the event center, the new dining room using local ingredients, and the new recreational facilities they had planned. She didn't bother to mention that some of those facilities, such as the new eco-friendly tennis courts, hadn't actually been built yet.

The talk about the new amenities coming to the lodge nicely segued to the topic she really wanted to talk about – hosting weddings at the lodge. She gestured to the screen.

"These pictures are from my sister's wedding a couple of months ago. As you can see, the setting on the lake is absolutely breathtaking. It's a lovely place to get married."

"I can see that an outdoor summer wedding would be spectacular at your lodge. What about at other times of the year, say if someone wants a winter wedding, for example. Could you accommodate them?"

Scarlet's palms began to sweat again. She hit the button to bring up an interior shot of the dining room.

"As you can see," Scarlet winced at her repetition. She swallowed and forged ahead. "We have a beautiful indoor dining room that will accommodate between fifty to seventy dinner guests, so yes, once the renovations are complete, we'll be able to host small weddings year-round." She hit the button again to bring up the architect's drawing of the event center. "And once our event center is complete, we'll be able to accommodate weddings for up to two hundred and fifty people at any time of year."

"When do you expect the event center to be completed?"

"Construction has just begun. We estimate it will take approximately a year to complete and be fully operational. We're going to begin to take bookings very shortly for weddings in the event center scheduled for October of next year. And I want to remind couples that even if they don't hold their weddings at our lodge, we have beautiful, private accommodations for a honeymoon or a romantic weekend getaway, all year long."

"I understand you're attending the Minneapolis Wedding Show this weekend."

"Yes, I am. I look forward to meeting with engaged couples and letting them know what we have to offer."

"And when will the Solace Lake Lodge be open for business again?"

"By the spring of next year."

The interview ended with Scarlet giving out the lodge's website one more time and mentioning that it was an easy two and a half-hour drive from Minneapolis. After thanking the host for the opportunity to talk about the reopening, it was over. When they went to commercial, Scarlet blew out a breath and sank deeper into her chair.

The host laughed. "That wasn't so painful, was it?"

"No, not at all. I was ridiculously nervous, that's all."

"Well, I would never have guessed. Why don't you come back in the spring when all the renovations are done and we can talk again?"

She'd be gone long before spring came. The unexpected pang at the thought of leaving surprised her, but she kept her smile firmly in place. "Thank you. I'm sure we can arrange something."

She shook hands with the host and left the studio. Using the GPS in her car, she drove to the convention center where the wedding show was being held. After checking in with the organizers, she found her table and was pleased to see it was on a main aisle that should receive good traffic. She made several trips to her car to bring in her supplies, and then set up her booth with the banners, brochures and pictures she'd made. The only thing she could do now was hope she'd done enough to attract couples to the lodge.

*MINNEWASTA 10 MILES.*

Scarlet sighed in relief at the highway sign's proclamation. After going full-tilt for the entire weekend, she was exhausted. She'd spent three long days manning her booth at the wedding show. When the show wasn't open, she not only promoted the lodge at the TV station, she'd set up interviews at a few radio stations. In hindsight, she'd probably packed too much into one weekend, but she was under pressure to get the word out in the short time she had. She desperately wanted the lodge to be a success.

She wished she could say with certainty that her efforts over the weekend had paid off, but the truth was she had no idea. She'd handed out brochures and business cards to anyone who would take one, and had talked and smiled until her face ached. Though several people expressed interest, no one actually said the lodge was definitely the venue they wanted for their wedding.

Yawning, she opened her window a crack and turned up the radio. She probably should have stayed another night at Ethan's condo and driven back in the morning after a good night's sleep, but she was anxious to get home.

Funny, she hadn't thought of the lodge as home in a very long time.

Signaling, she made the turn onto the secondary highway that would take her to the lodge. A sense of relief came over her. And anticipation. It was past eight p.m. on a Sunday evening. She thought of Cameron, wondered whether he had worked over the weekend. Wondered whether he'd still be on site.

She pushed away thoughts of Cameron, or at least she tried. Was he the reason she was so anxious to get home? Nothing good could come from feelings like that.

Her cell phone rang and was picked up by the Bluetooth signal in her car. She hit a button on the steering wheel to answer. "Hello?"

"Hi, is this Scarlet Lindquist?"

"Yes, it is."

"Oh, good. I'm glad I caught you, Scarlet. My name is Melissa Carson and I spoke to you at the wedding show. I picked up your brochure and showed it to my fiancé. Then we looked online at all the pictures of the last wedding there. It was really beautiful. My fiancé totally loves your place."

She tamped down her rising excitement. "I'm glad to hear it."

"We're planning to get married in late May, and we're inviting about a hundred people. Do you have any openings at that time for an outdoor wedding like the one your sister had?"

Scarlet did a little happy dance in the driver's seat. She wanted to scream and shout her joy. *Yes! Somebody believed in them.* Instead, she used her best professional voice to calmly answer Melissa. "Yes, we have openings in late May. What date would you like?"

She pulled over to the side of the road and grabbed a pen from the bottom of her purse. The only piece of paper she could find was the wrapper from the burger she'd picked up to go a few miles outside of Minneapolis. But it did the trick.

She wrote down Melissa's name and number and the date she wanted to reserve for her wedding. Her client didn't have to know that hers was the only date reserved right now.

"I'm on the road right now, Melissa, but I'll get back to you in a couple of days about the details. And then I'll have my sister Maggie talk to you about the food you want served. Does that sound okay?"

"It's perfect." Melissa sounded excited, and it was infectious. Scarlet squirmed in her seat as she tried to keep her enthusiasm under control. If this booking panned out, it could be the beginning of something amazing for the lodge.

"I'll talk to you soon." She hit the off button on the phone before letting out a scream of pure joy. When she got herself together once more, she put the car into gear to drive the last few miles home. She couldn't wait to tell her sisters the news.

*I can't wait to tell Cameron, too.*

She was in too good a mood to examine why the idea of sharing her news with him made her giddy with pleasure.

# Chapter Twelve

CAM AND ETHAN WORKED all weekend on the cottage closest to Maggie and Scarlet's. After working the last two weekends in a row, Cam had given his crew the weekend off. They'd deserved a break, and he wanted to head off any complaints about working them too hard.

Besides, the weather forecast had been iffy, calling for sporadic showers all weekend long. The forecast had been right, but fortunately each rain shower had been blessedly short in duration. Despite having to run for shelter a couple of times, he and Ethan had made good progress. They managed to sheath the exterior walls of the cottage with plywood. On Monday, when the rest of the crew arrived, they could do the same with the other seven cottages. It was gratifying to see his sketches come to life.

He ate a late Sunday night dinner with Maggie and Harper and Ethan and helped with the dishes once they were finished. The cottage felt empty and quiet without Scarlet. He missed her.

*Not a good idea.*

Despite knowing it wasn't a good idea to miss her, he couldn't help asking about her. "How did Scarlet do at the wedding show? Do we need to build another cottage?"

"Apparently, we're not in any danger of having to do that," Maggie said with a grin. "I talked to her last night and she said it was busy, but no one laid down their hard-earned cash to make a booking."

"When is she getting home?" He tried not to sound too interested in the answer.

Maggie washed a glass and set it in the drainboard. "Last I heard, she planned to stay overnight at Ethan's condo tonight and come home in the morning."

Surprised by his disappointment, he shook his head as he dried a plate. Missing her, and waiting for her, was plain stupid.

If he missed her now, what the hell was he going to do when she went back to Chicago?

When he'd dried the last dish, he hung up his towel and said goodnight. He drove down the narrow lane leading back to the main lodge. In the twilight, a small car approached and as it got closer, he realized it was Scarlet. After honking her horn, she stopped on the side of the road, then opened her door and ran toward him. Cam slammed on the brakes and threw his truck into park, his heart lodging somewhere in his throat. He flung open his door and reached her in two strides. He grasped her shoulders and hung on tight.

"Are you okay? What's wrong? I thought you were staying in the city tonight."

"I'm fine. I wanted to get home." She grabbed his arms, her face lighting up in excitement. "I got a booking. I got a booking! The bride just called me. Isn't that wonderful?"

Her smile robbed him of breath and for a moment he couldn't speak, only feel. Her face lit with a glow of happiness that made her so beautiful his chest ached with longing.

He cleared his throat. "That's great."

She laughed. "Great? Are you kidding me? It's freaking awesome!"

She threw her arms around his neck and hugged him. He held her tight, his body responding with lightning speed to the feel of her in his arms.

She leaned back a little to look into his face, her blue eyes shining in the half-light. "We're going to make it, Cameron. We're really going to make it."

The hope and joy and utter elation he saw dancing in her eyes made him do the only thing he was capable of in that moment. He kissed her.

For a second, she went completely still. But then she sighed against him and kissed him back, as if she'd been waiting for this. As if this kiss was as special to her as it was to him.

With a little sound of pleasure that went straight to his groin, she wound her arms around his neck and pressed herself against him. She opened her mouth to him and touched her tongue to his.

Cam lost it. He lost control, lost all sense of time, lost his mind. His pulse pounded through his brain, every beat telling him he needed to get closer to her, needed *her*. Scarlet held back nothing, meeting the thrusts of his tongue with wild parries of her own. Her hands roamed his body and when they snaked beneath his t-shirt to caress his overheated skin, he began to move her toward the shelter of the trees, needing to strip off her incredibly sexy power suit and sink himself into her. He needed to touch her, smell her, feel her soft, smooth skin, hear her cry out with her orgasm.

His cell phone rang. Cam ignored it, and it stopped. He cupped one perfect, luscious breast through the soft silk of her blouse, the weight of it filling his hand as if it had been made for him. Her scent, something floral with notes of spice, intoxicated him in a way that coke and Crown had never achieved.

His phone rang again. Through his passion-fogged brain, he recognized the ringtone. *Laura.* The ringtone he'd be sure to answer since she only ever called about Tessa.

Reluctantly, he ended the kiss and rested his forehead against Scarlet's as the phone rang for the third time. She whimpered, her breath as ragged as his. He kissed her forehead. "I have to take this."

Scarlet stared into his eyes, her hands pressed against his chest. Taking a deep breath to slow his heartbeat, he pulled his cell phone from his pocket and hit the talk button. "What's up?"

"What took you so long to answer?" As usual, Laura sounded pissed with him.

"What do you want, Laura?"

"When are you coming to pick up Tessa? I'm leaving first thing in the morning, and I need you to pick her up before her bedtime."

His brain still wasn't firing on all pistons. He put some distance between himself and Scarlet and turned his back on her, unable to think with her hands on him. "Wait. Where are you going? Why is this the first I've heard about this?"

She gave an impatient huff. "I told you I was taking a vacation."

Cam was pretty sure she hadn't mentioned going anywhere. He would have remembered something so important that affected his daughter. But it wasn't worth starting an argument about. "And you're going where?"

"California. A little vacation."

"How long are you going to be gone?"

"A couple of weeks."

"Don't you have to work?"

"I quit the job at the grocery store. It was nothing but a dead end. And before you give me a lecture, save it. I've heard enough from my folks."

"Fine." Cam grit his teeth. Laura's parents were salt of the earth and as baffled by their daughter's behavior as he often was. But she was their only child, and they'd indulged and spoiled her since the day she was born. They provided free rent and babysitting services and gave her money whenever she asked. Which was often.

"Are your mom and dad going to be able to sit with Tessa while I'm at work?"

"My folks left today for Rochester. My grandma had a heart attack or something, and my mom wants to stay with her for a while." He heard the impatience in her voice. "So, are you picking her up or not?"

"I'll pick her up." He didn't have to think twice about it. Tessa was his first priority.

"Make it fast," she snapped.

The line went dead. *Nice talking to you, too, Laura.* For the thousandth time, he wondered what he'd ever seen in her. Though, if he was being honest with himself, he hadn't been thinking with his brain when he'd first met her.

But their union had resulted in Tessa and for her sake, he'd deal with Laura.

He turned back to Scarlet. Unsmiling, she gazed at him with watchful eyes, her arms hugging herself. He wished they could pick up where they left off, but he had to go to Tessa.

Judging by her body language, kissing her again was off the table anyway.

"I have to go."

"I heard."

He couldn't leave her like this. He stepped toward her. "Scarlet—"

She held up her hand in a stopping motion. "Don't. I was excited about getting a booking and we got carried away, that's all. You should go."

It stung to hear her call the passion they'd shared "getting carried away". It was more than that. Way more.

He didn't have time to analyze her feelings, or his. With a last nod at her, he sprinted back to his truck and hit the gas. When he glanced in his rear-view mirror, she was still standing on the road, watching him leave.

SCARLET SAT AT THE kitchen island and nursed her coffee. It was past nine and she'd only managed to drag herself out of bed a few minutes ago. Maggie had already baked a few dozen different kinds of cookies and the sweet scents of chocolate and butter and sugar filled their cottage.

She sipped her coffee. She'd need a gallon of the stuff to make it through the day. Last night she'd tossed and turned, reliving Cameron's kiss over and over. She'd never experienced a kiss so wild, so elemental, so completely sexual. And yet, it was so much more than sex. All his needs, his passions, every heartache and triumph, communicated themselves to her through his kiss. How could such a physical act be so emotional?

She straightened her back, at the same time stiffening her resolve. It didn't matter. Nothing could come of the kiss. Nothing had really happened aside from sharing some saliva with a handsome man.

She inwardly winced at her crude assessment. And, she had to admit their kiss had meant much more than that. Maybe that's why it scared her so much.

She'd made so many mistakes in the past, and she didn't want Cameron Hainstock to be another, especially when he came as a package deal. If they started something and she, as usual, ruined it...If he started drinking again...Scarlet couldn't bear the thought of hurting him or Tessa.

No matter how amazing their kiss last night had been, that was as far as it went. For the next few months, she had to keep her distance. For both their sakes.

Maggie refilled her coffee cup. "You look like you had a bad night."

She reached for the sugar. "Couldn't sleep. I guess I was too wired after the weekend."

"Why don't you take it easy today? Have a nap this afternoon. You deserve it."

Despite her fatigue, she didn't think she'd be able to fall asleep. "I wish I could, but I've got a lot of work to do."

"Is everything, okay? I know you're tired, but you seem really off this morning. Did something happen this weekend to upset you?"

Maggie's dark eyes were full of compassion. Scarlet wished she could unburden herself to her sister, but what she'd shared with Cameron was too private. Besides, if she started talking now, the dominos would begin falling. If she tried to explain why his kiss had frightened her so much, the path would lead straight to her two failed engagements. She didn't want to go there.

Scarlet forced a smile. "I'm fine. Just tired."

Maggie held her gaze. "You know you can tell me anything, right? I'm always here for you."

She blinked to keep her tears at bay, embarrassed at feeling suddenly weepy. "I know."

As if her thoughts had conjured him from thin air, Cameron knocked on the door before opening it. Tessa bounced into the cottage in front of him. Despite warning herself to keep a safe distance from both of them, Scarlet's fatigue lessened and her heart expanded at the sight of the little girl. "Hey, Tessa. What are you doing here this morning?"

She climbed up onto the stool next to Scarlet's and grinned at her. "I'm staying with my Daddy for a whole two weeks!"

"That sounds like fun." She glanced at Cameron, but couldn't get a read on him. His face was carefully wiped of emotion, though he couldn't quite hide the tension in his jaw.

"Mommy's going on a holiday," Tessa said happily.

This time when Scarlet's gaze collided with Cameron's, he blinked and looked away. She turned back to Tessa with a smile. "It'll be fun having you here with us. You can help Maggie and me make cookies. Well, mostly Maggie."

"I'm trying to find a babysitter for her in town for the next two weeks," Cameron said.

"She'll be okay here with us." Scarlet ran her hand over Tessa's baby soft curls. "Between the five of us, she'll be well looked after."

"She's my responsibility. I'll look after her."

She looked up sharply, stunned by the anger she heard in his voice. "Of course, you will. I just thought you could use a little help."

"You're not Tessa's mother, so quit acting like you are."

Scarlet drew in a sharp breath at his cutting words. If he'd meant to inflict pain, he was doing a damn fine job. Cameron turned away and went to stand in front of the fireplace. He leaned one hand against the mantle, his head bowed.

Maggie lifted Tessa from the stool. "Sweetie, why don't you come with me for a walk? We can see what Uncle Ethan and Auntie Harper are doing. And then later, you can help me bring cookies and coffee to the crew."

With a worried glance at her father, Tessa put her arms around Maggie's neck. Maggie carried her outside and closed the door softly behind them.

Cameron ran a hand through his hair. "I shouldn't have said that." He began pacing in front of the fireplace. "Especially in front of Tessa. Damn."

She wasn't ready to let him off the hook quite so easily. "No, you shouldn't have said that. I care for Tessa, we all do. But I don't have some kind of mommy complex, if that's what you're worried about."

"I know. It's just that—" He stopped and shook his head.

"What?"

"Something's going on with Laura."

"What do you mean?"

He shrugged and looked away. "It's a feeling I got. Nothing's ever what it seems with her."

"It never was. One minute she could be your friend and the next she'd stab you in the back. Sounds like things haven't changed."

He turned sharply to face her. "You know Laura?"

Scarlet shrugged. "We grew up here in Minnewasta, remember? Laura and I went to school together."

He nodded, his expression bleak. "I never know where I stand with her."

Confusion made her head ache. Was he upset because Laura was going away? Was he worried she had someone new in her life? Was he still in love with her? The thoughts curdled the coffee in her empty stomach.

"About last night," he said, his face grim. "I took that kiss too far. It won't happen again."

His words were like a slap to the face. She hated how much they stung, how much they mattered. Obviously, she'd been affected far more by their kiss than he had. "Forget about it. We both got carried away." She swallowed and walked to the coffee pot to pour herself a cup she didn't want, her hand shaking slightly.

"I meant what I said about Tessa." She added sugar to her coffee and kept her gaze averted from his. "We can look after her here. She seemed excited to be spending time with you. Of course, if you'd rather find a babysitter in town, that's your prerogative."

Cameron slid onto one of the stools and folded his arms on the counter. "I would like to keep her close by. You're sure you can help?"

"Of course. Not by myself, but I know my sisters will be happy to spend time with Tessa. So will I."

He nodded. "All right. If Maggie and Harper are okay with the idea, I'll bring her to work with me."

"Okay."

Cameron ran his hand through his hair again, the gesture full of weariness. Maybe she wasn't the only one who'd lost sleep. "I'd better get to the job site. I didn't have the heart to wake Tessa this morning. She was so tired..."

Scarlet clearly read the worry in his voice. He was concerned about Tessa, though she seemed happy enough this morning and not bothered by her mother leaving. Tessa had reacted more to Cameron's simmering anger. She wasn't about to tell him that, though.

And she didn't know the whole story. He was her father and knew her best. She had to trust that he would do what was best for his daughter.

"I'll see you later." Cameron slid off the stool and headed for the door. He stopped with his hand on the knob, his head bowed. "Sometimes, when I'm upset, things come out of my mouth that I don't mean. Cruel things. You've been nothing but kind to Tessa, and you didn't deserve any abuse from me. I'm sorry, Scarlet."

He opened the door and walked out without looking back. Scarlet wrapped her hands around her cup, trying to absorb its warmth into her cold skin. Keeping her distance, physically and emotionally, was going to be far harder than she'd ever imagined.

# Chapter Thirteen

"SCARLET, LOOK AT ALL the little fish!"

Tessa stretched out on her stomach and peered over the side of the dock, her ponytail hanging mere inches above the water. Scarlet grasped the child's small waist to keep her from toppling in. "Yes, there's lots of minnows in the lake. They're babies now, but someday they'll be big."

"Just like me!" Tessa pulled herself up to a sitting position. Her sunny face never failed to lighten Scarlet's heart.

"You mean, you're going to grow up to be a fish?"

"No, silly. Little girls can't be fish. I'm going to grow up to be a lady."

"Oh, so that's how it works," she teased.

"You're so silly, Scarlet," Tessa said with a grin. She grasped her hand. "Can we walk on the beach again?"

"Sure. Come on."

For the last several days, Tessa had been coming to the lodge with Cameron every morning. While he worked, Scarlet and her sisters looked after her. Scarlet usually spent the mornings with her. In the afternoons, when she went to Cameron's house to use his laptop and Internet connection, Maggie and Harper took turns staying with Tessa.

It didn't feel like babysitting to Scarlet. Mornings with Tessa had quickly become the best part of her day.

Together, she and Tessa explored the forest surrounding the lodge, and Scarlet showed her places she'd known well as a child. Like the rocks on a hill overlooking the lake where she'd watched many sunsets and wondered if her parents were somewhere behind the brilliant colors.

Tessa's favorite thing to do was walking on the beach. She searched for pretty rocks and threw the ones she deemed as less pretty into the water. On hot mornings, they put on their suits and splashed around in the lake. With Tessa, she was a kid again, a happy kid free of worry. A kid who didn't realize how cruel life could be.

That's what she wanted for Tessa – to never experience the cruelty of life. It was impossible to shelter her completely, but as much as it was in her power, she would try.

They walked hand in hand along the edge of the lake, down the sandy beach until it disappeared into a mass of reeds. Then, they tramped down a well-worn deer path through the forest that circled back toward the cottages and the lodge.

"Do you want to go back to the cottage and see if Maggie has any cookies left?"

"Okay."

Tessa skipped on ahead of her, humming a little tune to herself. When they got to the cottage, Maggie was gone, but she'd left a plate with some cookies and a note that said there was fresh milk in the fridge. Scarlet lifted Tessa onto one of the stools and then brought two glasses from the cupboard.

She filled both with milk. Clinking her glass against Tessa's, she said, "Enjoy your cookie, sweetie."

"You enjoy yours, too." Tessa lightly clinked her glass against hers. "I love you, Scarlet."

Her unexpected words stole Scarlet's breath. For a moment, she could only stare at the child. Tessa calmly ate her cookie and hummed to herself, totally unaware of the emotional bombshell she'd dropped.

Scarlet didn't know what to do with love. Love was scary because it was too easily taken away. Even her sisters' love couldn't be taken for granted. She'd spent most of her life looking for love, then running away from it when it was within her reach. Her two ex-fiancés could attest to that.

But Tessa was different. She was a child, and she gave away her love without expecting anything back. Except maybe to be loved in return.

Scarlet wanted so much to be worthy of her love. She didn't want to be afraid anymore. But in a few months, she would go back to her old life in Chicago. If she let this bond between them grow, Tessa would be disappointed and hurt when she left. Then, Cameron would be angry with her. She needed to sever this emotional tie before it was too late.

The thought of no longer having these golden mornings with Tessa caused an ache in her chest. There was no way she could give them up.

She put her hand lightly on Tessa's head and gently smoothed the silky tresses. Her throat burned with longing when she spoke. "I love you too, Tessa."

SCARLET ADDED SOME pictures to the lodge's website and then tweeted them out to her fifty followers. The number was ridiculously small, but growing slowly. She was working on getting included on the website for the Minnesota Tourist Bureau, as well as a bed and breakfast association. Hopefully, locals and people from away looking for a holiday in the north woods would see the lodge on their sites and decide it was exactly where they'd like to vacation. And spend lots of money.

She was so engrossed with setting up a Pinterest page for the lodge that she was surprised when she heard the front door opening. Tessa burst into the office and threw herself into Scarlet's arms.

"What are you doing here?" she asked. She kissed Tessa's hair, loving the scent of baby shampoo.

"I could ask you the same question."

Scarlet looked up. Cameron leaned against the doorframe, his thumb looped into the pocket of his jeans, a sexy grin on his face. *Damn, did he always have to look so good?* "What do you mean?"

"It's past seven, Scarlet. You missed dinner. Maggie tried to call but there was no answer. I had to promise her I'd find you before she called the authorities."

"Oh, dear."

She set Tessa on her feet and grabbed her purse, rummaging inside for her phone. "It's dead. The battery doesn't hold a charge for long anymore, and I forgot to plug it in. I completely lost track of time."

"I'll give Maggie a quick call so she knows you're okay."

"Thanks."

Cameron pulled his phone from his pocket and called Maggie. "Hey, it's Cam. Scarlet's here at my house. Yes, she's fine. Her phone's dead and she lost track of time." He paused a moment, then placed his hand over the phone. "She wants to know when you'll be home."

"Tell her I'm leaving right away."

While he relayed her message, she stuffed her useless phone back into her purse and powered down Cameron's laptop. She picked up her tote bag and her purse and got to her feet. "Thanks again for the use of your computer."

"No problem. Like I said, you're welcome to work here anytime."

He gave her another sexy grin, the one guaranteed to turn her knees to water. Looking at his mouth reminded her of the kiss they'd shared. They'd both lost control that night. Much longer and they surely would have taken it further. If Laura hadn't called...

Scarlet didn't know whether to be angry with her, or grateful.

Both Cameron and Tessa walked with her through the kitchen, past the wooden table she loved so much. Scarlet stopped and ran her hand over the wood.

"I've been meaning to ask about this table. It's gorgeous and I think it would be perfect in some of the new cottages. Drew mentioned you make furniture. Did you make this?"

He shrugged. "Yeah, I made it."

His indifferent manner belied the tension on his face. *Interesting.* "It's beautiful, Cameron. What kind of wood is this?"

"Reclaimed pine. I make all my furniture from reclaimed wood."

"Do you sell your stuff in a store somewhere?"

He shifted from one foot to the other. "No, it's a very small business. Mostly I sell by word of mouth, but I do have a website. I've gotten a couple of orders through it."

Scarlet put her bags on the table. "Show me."

His brow furrowed. "Scarlet—"

"Please? I'd really like to see what you have on offer."

With a sigh, he pulled his phone out of his pocket and hit a few buttons. He handed it to her. "Here."

Scarlet scrolled through the pictures of furniture. It was pretty clear an amateur had created the website. The pictures were small and didn't do his furniture justice, not if the table was anything to go by. A coffee table caught her eye. She handed the phone back to him. "This looks like the table in your living room."

"It's the exact one. It didn't sell and I needed something for the living room, so I kept it."

"Daddy made me some toys," Tessa said. "Wanna see?"

"Yes, I do."

Tessa grabbed her hand and led her to her bedroom. She pointed to the train engine Scarlet had admired the first time she'd been at the house. She saw now the engine came with several cars that could be attached together.

"There. Daddy made me a train." She ran to her toy box and began rummaging, pulling out some wooden blocks. "And these, and my table and chairs. My Daddy can make anything!"

"Yes, I believe he can, sweetheart." She glanced quickly over her shoulder at him before walking over to Tessa's bed and running her hand over the headboard. "Did you make this, too?"

"Yeah, I made it."

He sounded almost angry, as if defying her to contradict him. He should be proud of the things he'd created.

"Cameron, do you have any idea how much someone in Chicago would pay for a headboard like this? You've way undervalued the furniture on your website. And your website could use an overhaul. I didn't even see a contact page when I was scrolling through. I could take better pictures for you, optimize your site so it's easier for people to find you." Ideas burst into her head. "Etsy is a website where people sell hand-made crafts. If we got you on Etsy, the things you make would blow people away. The toys alone—"

"No! I don't want to be on Etsy, whatever the hell it is. I don't need a new website."

"But I could help you—"

"No! I'm fine. I don't need your help."

"Yes, you do." What was wrong with him? She could make things better for him. Maybe she could even make money for him. "Your website needs work. I could get you on social media, make you a Facebook page—"

"No!" He ran his hands through his hair. "I don't need your help, and I don't need you!"

Scarlet sucked in a breath, his outburst rendering her speechless. For a moment she stood completely still, pinned to her spot by his angry stare like a butterfly trapped on a collector's board. His words reverberated painfully in her head. *I don't need you.*

Self-preserving anger took over, saving her from crying in front of him. "Fine. You want to do it on your own, be my guest." She brushed past him on her way out the door.

"Scarlet, don't—"

"Daddy? Please don't be mad at Scarlet!"

At Tessa's plaintive cry, she stopped and turned back. She'd been so angry she almost forgot that Cameron's daughter had heard their angry exchange. She knelt in front of her, wiping away a tear trickling down her cheek. "Honey, I'm sorry. Sometimes I can be very bossy. I shouldn't have tried to tell your daddy what to do."

"I don't want Daddy to be mad at you!" She launched herself into Scarlet's arms.

Cameron laid his hand on Tessa's head. "I'm not mad at Scarlet. Really. I shouldn't have yelled at her. I'm sorry."

She watched his grim expression over Tessa's shoulder. She wished she knew what was going on in his head. Was he really not angry with her, or was it something he said for Tessa's benefit? Maybe she had been bossy, but that was only because she was so excited about his work.

"Everything's okay, sweetheart." She pulled away from Tessa and smiled at her, trying to show her she meant what she said. "I'd better go home now. Maggie is worried about me."

She stood and met Cameron's gaze. Worry, and something she couldn't define, clouded his eyes. "I'll probably see you tomorrow."

"Yeah. Goodnight."

"Goodnight." She made herself smile. "Goodnight, Tessa."

Tessa hugged Cameron's leg. "'Night, Scarlet."

Scarlet hurried from the bedroom and grabbed her bags on her way out the door. Once outside, she ran to her car, wanting nothing more than to get away. Despite his apology, his *I don't need you* played over and over in her head like a scratch on a vinyl record.

Why the hell did she care? She didn't need him either.

But as she drove back to the lodge, she worried she was only lying to herself.

THE POUNDING OF HAMMERS and the noise of men and machines on the job site gave Cam a headache. He wanted to snarl at everyone to shut up the hell up and leave him in peace. But of course, he couldn't. The job had deadlines to meet, and they all had bills to pay. So, he stayed as far away as he could from the rest of the crew, only speaking when he had to.

He'd barely slept last night. The hurt he'd seen on Scarlet's face wouldn't let him rest. He'd done that to her. Him and his stupid pride, and his big, fat mouth. She'd only wanted to help and he'd turned on her. What a colossal fuck-up he was.

His self-induced brow beating stopped when a beat-up green Ford half-ton drove erratically down the lane toward the job site, narrowly missing vehicles parked along the side of the road. The truck veered off the road, coming to a sudden stop as the bumper kissed a massive pine tree. Cam ran to the truck but before he could get to it, the driver stumbled out of the truck and fell to his knees. When Cam helped him to his feet, the man leaned heavily against him.

"Miranda!" he shouted. "Where's Miranda? I need to find her!"

This was the same drunk who'd shown up at Ethan and Harper's wedding. He'd been looking for Miranda then, too. Scarlet's dead mother.

Ethan ran up to them. "Willy! What the hell's the matter with you? You know Harper doesn't want you to drive when you're drunk. You could have killed somebody."

"Harper will help me," Willy said, his voice thick and slurred. "She'll find Miranda."

Ethan exchanged a glance with Cam. "I'm sorry, Willy. Harper can't help you."

"Is he all right?" Cam turned to see Harper sprinting toward them. "I saw his truck go by. I was afraid he was going to hit someone."

"Everyone's okay," Ethan put his arm around her. "I'm sorry, sweetheart. He's looking for Miranda again."

Harper closed her eyes, her face full of pain. For a moment, she leaned against Ethan's shoulder as he held her. But then she roused herself, pulling away from him and straightening her back.

"I have to get him home, let him sleep it off. He can't drive anymore. He's going to kill himself or somebody else." Her voice hitched. "If I didn't stop him from driving and he killed someone, I'd never be able to forgive myself."

Ethan squeezed her hand. "We'll keep the truck here for now. I can contact the police, have them pull his license. You don't have to do it."

Cam pulled Willy up by the waistband of his pants when the man started to crumple to the ground.

"I don't want them to throw him in jail!"

"That might be the safest place for him." Ethan kissed Harper's cheek. "We don't have to do anything right now. We'll figure something out together. Okay?"

She nodded. "Okay."

Scarlet ran towards them. "Is everyone all right?"

Willy surprised Cam by pulling free of his grip and grabbing Scarlet's arm. "Miranda! Thank God you're okay. I thought you were gone. Thank God!"

He threw his arms around her, nearly knocking her over. Cam reached out to steady her, then stepped behind her to hold her shoulders securely with both hands. He wanted to peel Willy off Scarlet and toss him to the ground but for some reason, she and her sisters had a soft spot for the man.

Once again, he was reminded of how close he'd come to being in Willy's shoes.

"Willy, I'm Scarlet, remember?" She was close to tears, her expression stricken.

Willy stepped back, looking confused. "Scarlet?"

Harper put Willy's arm around her shoulders, and he rested his weight against her small frame. "We're going to take you home now."

Scarlet slipped her arm around Willy's waist to help support him from the other side.

Cam put his hand on her arm and she looked up at him in surprise. "Ethan and I can come with you. Make sure everything's okay."

It killed him that her eyes were shiny with tears. She shook her head. "Thanks, but we'll be fine."

He hesitated a moment before nodding and letting her go. The two women half walked, half dragged Willy back toward the cottages.

"Why wouldn't she let us help them?"

"I don't know about Scarlet, but Harper feels some sort of crazy responsibility for Willy. She's been looking after him for years, even before her grandfather died. She picks him up when he's too drunk to drive, pays his bills when he can't, sends him food." Ethan's mouth turned down in disgust. "Hell, she even got me to bathe him once. But no matter what I say, or what Willy does, she won't abandon him. She knows what it feels like to be left on her own, and she won't do that to Willy. All I can do is to help her do what she feels she has to."

Cam admired Harper's loyalty. Not many people would put up with the crap Willy was dishing out. But he wondered if she was enabling him with her kindness, making it easier for him to be a drunk. With her looking after him, he had no reason to change.

He should know. It was only when Ethan and Lydia threatened to wash their hands of him that he hit rock bottom and began climbing his way out of the pit of alcoholism. At that point he finally accepted Ethan's offer to pay for rehab. For the first time he worked hard on his sobriety because he knew if he didn't, he'd lose everyone who mattered to him. And that had scared him more than facing up to his alcoholism.

Scarlet's stricken face haunted him. Maybe Harper was loyal to a fault, but did that mean she expected Scarlet to be loyal to Willy, too? He was afraid that when Willy hit absolute bottom, he would take the Lindquist sisters with him.

# Chapter Fourteen

LATER THAT AFTERNOON, Cam drove into his yard and parked beside Scarlet's car, grateful she was still there. He needed to talk to her, apologize, and it had been impossible with so many people always around them. So he'd taken off, telling the crew he had something he had to take care of.

It was sort of true. He had to explain to Scarlet why he'd been so adamant the other day about her not helping him. Not to mention why he'd been so angry.

Maybe if he explained it to her he'd begin to understand it himself.

He got out of the car and sprinted to the side door leading to the kitchen. Like the other day, it was locked. Using his key, he let himself in. A moment later, Scarlet cautiously peeked around a corner and then, seeing it was him, slowly walked toward him.

"You scared me. Why didn't you tell me you were coming?"

"Sorry. I didn't mean to scare you." Cam closed the door, stalling for time. "Why do you lock the doors?"

She shrugged. "I'm a city girl. I always lock my doors. Did you forget something?"

"Yeah." He looked away, studying Tessa's artwork on the refrigerator before turning back to her and holding her gaze. "I forgot to apologize to you."

Her lips parted in surprise. "Apologize? To me?"

"Yeah." He motioned for her to sit at the table. "Can I make you some tea?"

"I guess so. Sure." She sounded anything but sure.

Cam busied himself filling the kettle with water and setting it on the stove. He brought a couple of mugs to the table and when the water boiled, he filled a teapot and threw in a couple of teabags.

"Do you take milk or sugar?" he asked as he poured tea into a cup for her.

"Sugar, please."

She sat back in her seat and waited, her blue eyes watching him with caution. Cam spooned sugar into his tea and stirred. He wasn't even sure where to begin.

He cleared his throat. "The other night...I know I need your help. I really don't know anything about websites and marketing. A friend set up my website for me, but I can't even figure out how to change stuff on it. It's way out of date."

"Then why were you so adamant about doing everything yourself?"

The words "*I don't need you*" hung in the air between them, though neither of them spoke them aloud. He'd hurt her yesterday, but today he wanted to be honest. "Embarrassment, I guess."

"Embarrassment?" That seemed to surprise her. "Because you don't know how to update your website?"

"No. I don't give a damn about that. Well, I do, but it's more of an annoyance than something that really bothers me." He hesitated a moment, then made up his mind to trust her. "Would you like to see my workshop?"

She sat up straighter. "Yeah. I would."

He led her outside and across the yard to the shop, stopping in front of the padlocked door to unlock it. Scarlet pointed to the bars on the windows and grinned at him. "You're giving me hassle about locking the house and you've got this place sealed tighter than Fort Knox."

"I've got thousands of dollars' worth of tools and materials in here. The most valuable thing in my house is the TV." He turned the key in the lock and removed the chains. Once inside, he turned on the overhead lights and disarmed the alarm system.

"And your daughter."

It was his turn to be surprised. "Right. And my daughter." Maybe it was time to install an alarm system in the house as well.

Scarlet stepped inside and Cam watched as she studied her surroundings. She turned in a circle a couple of times, then zeroed in on a fireplace mantel leaning against one wall. She made a bee line for it.

"This is really beautiful, Cameron." She ran her hand over the rough wood. "You made this?"

"Yeah." Her appreciation for his work eased the knot of nerves in his gut.

"I've never seen wood like this. Where did you get it from?"

"We salvage old buildings. The wood that mantel is built with came from an old barn in western Minnesota that Ethan and I and a couple of guys from my crew took down two summers ago."

"I love the colors, so many different shades of grays and browns."

"You only get that kind of color from years and years of exposure to the elements." He pointed to some finished headboards nearby. "The wood on some of these headboards came from an old grain elevator."

Scarlet went over and examined them. "This looks like the same wood as the headboard in your room."

Cam couldn't help but grin. "It is. So, you were in my bedroom?"

Her face flushed red before she turned away to examine the headboards again. "I might have done a little snooping, from the doorway."

He could picture her in his room, in his bed, naked and writhing beneath him. His body responded enthusiastically, his cock pressing against the zipper of his jeans. He turned away and shook his head to dispel the powerful, erotic image. *Change the subject, Cam.*

"The last couple of summers we've taken down a building or two and I spend the winters planing the wood and building furniture. So far, it's mostly a hobby. I haven't made much money at it."

"That's only because no one knows what you can do. No one has seen how talented you are. A great website and a good marketing plan could change all that."

"But what if it doesn't? What if the world doesn't beat a path to my door the way you think it will? What if I'm not as good as I hope I am?"

"What do you mean?"

He ran his thumb over the rough wood of the headboard, avoiding Scarlet's gaze. "I like construction work well enough, especially the creative parts of design. It pays the bills. But this..." He threw out his hand to encompass the workshop. "This is what I really want to do. When I work with a piece of old wood, I can hear it talking to me. It tells me what do to make it beautiful and useful again."

He stopped talking and turned his back, embarrassed at revealing so much to her. "That probably sounds crazy to you."

"No, it sounds like your creative process to me. And it sounds like you're afraid. What are you afraid of, Cameron?"

He still couldn't look at her. His art was too close to his heart, too vulnerable. "I'm afraid of falling flat on my face and making a fool of myself. Of dreaming bigger than my talent can reach. Of being a fraud."

"You're no fraud." He felt her move closer, though she didn't touch him. "I've seen the drawings you made for the cottages. Those were works of art. And all this...it's amazing. You have every right to believe in your talent. For what it's worth, I believe in your talent, too."

He turned to look at her. Her eyes were clear and calm, with not a hint of derision or doubt. "I appreciate that. But you're one person."

"Are you dissing my taste, Mr. Hainstock?"

He grinned, completely charmed by her. “I wouldn’t dream of it. But I know the things I’ve created aren’t to everyone’s taste.” They certainly weren’t his father’s taste.

“I suppose, but if someone doesn’t like something you made, so what? Art is subjective and you’re not going to please everyone. Personally, I think someone who doesn’t appreciate your stuff has no taste at all, but that’s only my opinion.”

He hid his grin. “Of course.”

She started examining the headboards stacked up against the wall again. “I think these would fit in perfectly in the new cottages. They’re rustic and charming, with a kind of urban chic that I think a lot of our guests would appreciate. Would you be able to make enough headboards and mantels for all the cottages?”

“Possibly. I think I have enough wood.”

“Do you have enough time?”

He shrugged. “I don’t need to sleep.”

She laughed. “That’s the spirit. I’ll take some pictures and tell Harper what we’ve decided. I think she’ll be relieved she doesn’t have to figure it out herself.”

“She doesn’t trust her own taste.”

“I could say the same about you, too.” When she smiled, he remembered the softness of her lips and the sweet taste of her kiss. Longing swamped him.

She spent the next few minutes taking pictures of the fireplace mantles and headboards in his shop. He helped her move a few pieces so she could get a better shot. At last, she stuck her phone in her back pocket.

"That should be enough to give Harper an idea of the vibe we're going for. I should get back to work. I've got some things I need to finish up."

"Me, too. Gotta make sure the boys don't goof off."

"Any time you think you'd like to redo your website, let me know and I'll help you out."

"Okay, thanks." He didn't know if he'd take her up on the offer, but her faith in him made him feel like he could do anything. "Scarlet, I appreciate everything you said. It means a lot to me."

A slight blush swept across her cheek, tempting him to touch the soft skin. He wanted to play connect the dots with the freckles sprinkled across her nose, kissing each one in turn.

They stared at each other, neither of them making a move for the door. Then, Scarlet lifted her chin. "Thank you for showing me your workshop, Cameron."

He answered honestly. "It was my pleasure."

He followed her to the door. After locking up, he jumped in his truck and waved at her as he sped out of his yard. He barely saw the road as he drove. All he could see was Scarlet greeting him at the door when he came home from work, Scarlet in his bed and in his arms. Overwhelming longing nearly had him turning around and going back to her.

He quashed that idea with brutal force. Scarlet had her own life in Chicago, and she was going back to it in a few months. She didn't belong in small town Minnewasta anymore, and she didn't belong with him.

Cam turned onto the main road and pressed down on the accelerator. He had to get the hell away from her before he changed his mind.

AFTER A STOP AT THE hardware store in town, Cam made it back to the worksite just as Harper and Maggie brought coffee and goodies for the guys. Tessa skipped alongside the little wagon they pulled, pigtails bouncing. Seeing his daughter so happy made him smile.

After they'd passed out coffee and juice and cookies, Cam approached Harper with the bag from the hardware store.

"Here. This is for you," he said, handing the bag to her.

Her eyes widened in surprise. "For me?"

He grinned. "Yeah, but don't get too excited. It's nothing special. Just restocking your supplies."

She reached inside the bag and grinned as she pulled out a plastic gallon container of chainsaw oil. "Thanks. I was running low."

"The perfect gift for the girl who has everything."

She laughed. "Hey, chainsaw maintenance is important."

"Don't I know it. I wanted to say thanks."

"No problem. I was happy to help."

Cam ducked his head, not quite able to look her in the eyes. Apologies didn't come easy for him, and this was his second of the day. "I also wanted to say I'm sorry. I thought you married Ethan for his money, but that's not the truth, is it?"

"No." Harper's voice was barely a whisper. "I love Ethan. I'd love him just as much if he didn't have a dime."

"I see that now."

Her gaze drifted to the half-finished cottage. "I'm not gonna lie. His money makes all this possible. Without it, I would have had to sell the lodge."

"I know."

"But if the money disappeared tomorrow, it wouldn't matter. I'd still love Ethan and he'd still love me. We'd figure something out. Together."

Cam nodded and looked away. "He deserves that kind of loyalty."

She touched his arm briefly. "So do you."

Scarlet's image flashed into his mind's eye. Would she be loyal, or would she play around on him like Laura had? He rejected the idea. He couldn't imagine her being unfaithful.

He shook his head. There was no point speculating.

Instead, he changed the subject. "Don't let your loyalty to Willy blind you, Harper. He's using you."

"Maybe that's true, but I can't simply cut him loose. I can't abandon him like everyone else in town has."

"If he knows you've got his back, he has no reason to change."

She pursed her lips together. "How do you know that for sure?"

"Because I've been there. I *was* Willy a few years ago. Until I was confronted with the hurt I was causing my family, until they told me that unless I straightened out they couldn't stand by and watch me destroy myself anymore, I wasn't ready to work on my sobriety. I had to stand on the brink of losing everything, and everyone, before I finally changed."

"Is that the only way? Threatening him? Abandoning him?" She shook her head, her face full of misery.

"It was for me."

"You think I'm enabling him, don't you?"

He wouldn't sugarcoat it. "Yes."

She studied her shoes. "That's what Ethan says. I don't know what to do."

"Why don't you go to an Al-Anon meeting and talk with people in the same position as you? I'll come with you if you want me to."

She lifted her gaze to his. "Really?"

"Sure. And I know Ethan would come too."

"Yeah, I'm sure he would." She sighed deeply. "Willy is the only thing we've argued about. I hate it."

"He's afraid for you. He doesn't want you to have to go through with Willy what he went through with me."

"I'll think about Al-Anon, okay?"

"Okay. Whenever you're ready, I'll be there."

"Thank you. For everything."

"My pleasure."

# Chapter Fifteen

THE MORNING WAS HOT and still, the water on the lake silent and smooth, with not a ripple to disturb the calm surface. Even the birds had decided it was too hot to sing. An eerie silence settled on the forest.

Early morning at the lodge had quickly become Scarlet's favorite part of the day. It was a time to quietly reflect, to watch the lake and feel the forest come alive. For the last couple of weeks, she'd set her alarm an hour early to drink a cup of coffee on the front porch and watch the sun rise over the lake, turning the sky from fiery red to endless blue. She hadn't realized how much she'd missed this.

Scarlet finished drinking her morning coffee and went back into the cottage to shower. In deference to the heat that would only get more intense as the day wore on, she dressed in one of her coolest outfits, a sky-blue cotton sundress with spaghetti straps. By the time she emerged from her room, Maggie was already in the kitchen making breakfast. She was surprised to find her alone.

"Hasn't Cameron dropped off Tessa yet?"

Maggie shook her head. "No. I haven't seen them. They must be running late today."

A moment later, Ethan knocked on the door of the cottage before letting himself in. "Have you seen Cam?"

Scarlet exchanged a worried look with Maggie. "No, not yet." She checked her watch; five minutes after eight. In the past couple of weeks, he and Tessa usually arrived at the cottage by seven-thirty.

"Have you tried calling him?" Maggie asked.

Ethan nodded. "Yeah, several times. No answer. We had a meeting scheduled at seven this morning with the mason who's building the fireplaces, but Cam didn't show."

Unease settled in the pit of her stomach. Something had to be very wrong for him not to show up without any explanation. Tessa could be ill, but if she was, he would have called Ethan.

"That doesn't sound like him."

"No, it doesn't. Unless..." Ethan shook his head and looked away.

"Unless what?"

He lifted his gaze to hers. "Unless he's started drinking again."

Scarlet shook her head before he'd finished speaking. "No, no way. He wouldn't do that. Especially not while Tessa is staying with him."

"Then why isn't he answering his phone?"

"Maybe his phone's dead, or he lost it. There could be a hundred different reasons."

"Maybe that would explain why he hasn't answered my calls, but it doesn't explain why he hasn't shown up for work." He headed for the door. "I'm going to look for them."

"Ethan, wait." Scarlet stopped him at the door. "Let me go. I need to use Cameron's laptop today anyway. I'll go to his house and see if he's there. I'll give you a call."

She didn't like to think about the possibility but if he had been drinking, she didn't want Ethan and Cameron to get into an argument, not in front of Tessa.

Ethan's jaw clenched. "I don't want to put you in the middle of this."

"You're not. This is my choice. I want to make sure Tessa is okay." She didn't want to examine too closely her desire to see to Cameron's welfare as well.

Ethan stared into her eyes, then gave her a curt nod. "Fine. But make damn sure you call me whether he's there or not."

"I will."

"I'd better get back to the work site, but I'll have my phone on me."

"Okay."

He hesitated, as if he wanted to say something else but in the end, he simply nodded and left the cottage. Scarlet let out her breath in a rush of relief.

Maggie touched her arm. "Do you want me to come with you?"

She covered Maggie's hand and gave it a quick squeeze. "Thanks, but I'll be fine."

"Call me, too. Okay?"

She enveloped Maggie in hug and kissed her cheek. "I will. I promise."

Grabbing her purse and her tote bag, she left the cottage and hurried to her car. She drove straight to Cameron's place. She arrived to find his truck parked in front of the house. Scarlet ran to the side door. The outside door was wide open with only the screen door closed. It was odd that Cameron would leave the door open on such a hot day when the air conditioner was running at full capacity. She knocked.

Then knocked again. "Cameron? Are you there?"

Still no answer. Scarlet opened the screen door and stepped inside. The house was still and quiet. Everything was as neat and tidy as usual. When she came to Tessa's room, everything looked the same. Until she noticed the open closet door. All of Tessa's clothes were gone and some of her favorite stuffies were also missing. Scarlet's heart beat frantically. Something was wrong.

She retraced her steps to the side door and ran down the stairs. With his truck still there, Cameron had to be close by. Perhaps he was making something in his workshop and lost track of time. She clung to that hope, even though the alarm bells ringing in her head were telling her something was terribly, terribly wrong.

The door to the shop was locked. She banged on it with her fist. "Cameron! Are you in there?"

No answer. Scarlet tamped down the rising panic in her chest and tried to think. Was there a back door to the workshop? She'd only been inside that one time, but she thought she remembered an overhead door at the back of the building.

She followed a path around the side of the building to the back and then she heard it, a thumping sound, as if something was being hit hard with force. When she rounded the corner and saw Cameron stripped to the waist, splitting a log in half with an axe, she nearly dropped to her knees in relief. Instead, she took a few cautious steps closer.

"Cameron? Ethan was worried when you didn't show up for work this morning."

His axe stilled for a moment, but he didn't look at her. "Go back to the lodge and tell Ethan I'm still alive. I'll be at work tomorrow."

He hefted the axe and split the next log in two, sending one half flying across the yard. Scarlet hesitated. Cameron was in a strange mood. She should take his advice and leave. But the tense set of his shoulders and the way he wouldn't look at her made her feel she had to stay. Whatever he was dealing with, he was dealing with it alone, and something told her he shouldn't be.

Whatever he'd told her in the past, and despite all his denials, right now he needed her.

She stepped closer. "Why didn't you go to work this morning? Is something wrong?"

He split another log in half. The ax landed on the stump with a punishing blow. He stood the half log on its end and prepared to hit it again. "Go back to the lodge, Scarlet."

"Cameron, where's Tessa? Why are all her clothes gone?"

A mixture of anger and despair crossed his face. He swung his axe over and over, turning the log on the stump to kindling. Scarlet held her breath and watched.

Finally, exhausted, his skin shiny with sweat, he stopped. He bent over and leaned on the axe for support, his head bowed and his chest heaving. His voice was barely a whisper. "She's gone."

Scarlet carefully removed the axe from his hands and tossed it to the ground. "Gone? You mean back to her mother?"

He straightened slowly and turned to look at her. The searing pain in his eyes made her gasp.

"She's gone for good. Laura's moving to California and she's taking Tessa with her. I'm never going to see my daughter again."

THE SHOCK ON SCARLET'S face, the disbelief and grief, made him wish he'd kept his mouth shut. The last thing he wanted was to inflict her with the same hell he was going through. He turned away from her, pushing her hand from his arm. "Go home, Scarlet."

"I'm not going anywhere." She grabbed his arm again, preventing him from picking up the axe, the tool he'd used to keep himself from reaching for a bottle. "I won't leave you alone."

Ignoring the sweat and dirt, she wrapped her arms around his waist and held him tightly, resting her head against his chest. His body stirred to life at her touch, disgusting him. His world was crumbling around him and all he could think was that he wanted to bury himself inside her until she screamed his name.

"Go," he said roughly. If she was smart, she'd run away and never look back. He was a bad-tempered, recovering alcoholic with nothing to offer her. He wasn't worth the risk.

She looked up at him, her blue eyes clear and steady. "No. I won't leave you."

He pushed her up against the wall of the workshop, not sure if he was trying scare her away or make her stay. "I don't want to hurt you."

She shook her head. "You won't."

Cam closed his eyes and groaned. He wrapped his arms around her in a vice-like grip, unable to resist her any longer.

God, he needed her.

He lowered his head and kissed her. There was no subtlety in the kiss, no gentleness or finesse. Only passion and raw need. But she stayed with him, returning his passion, giving solace. He greedily lapped it up, taking everything she had to give.

But he wanted, needed more. He lifted her and she wrapped her long, slender legs around his waist. He buried his face against her soft, sweet-smelling neck, inhaling her clean, floral scent. At the same time, he snaked his hand up her thigh and began to pull down her panties.

"Tell me to stop," he rasped. "Tell me now while I still can."

She kissed his jaw. "No, don't stop. Please don't stop."

"Scarlet—"

She stopped his protest with a kiss, one that was nearly as needy as his own. Tongues swirled and danced and mated, hands touched, caressed. In a couple of swift moves, her panties were gone and so were his sweatpants, and he was deep inside her. He drove into her over and over, harder and harder, pushing her against the surface of the workshop wall. She felt so good, so warm and wet and welcoming.

A moment later, her muscles clenched around his cock, and he heard her breathless cry as she came. "Cameron!"

As her long legs tightened around him, he followed her over the edge, spilling himself into her as wave after wave of exquisite pleasure washed over him. He clung to her, their bodies still joined.

He couldn't let her go. He needed her. His world was spinning out of control, and Scarlet was his only anchor in a turbulent sea.

Scarlet made a small sound of discomfort that jerked him back to his senses. He'd crushed her against the wall, hurt her. Immediately, he pulled out of her and set her on her feet. As he grabbed his sweatpants and pulled them on he called himself a hundred different names – bastard, coward, irresponsible fool. He'd used her to assuage his fear and pain and for that, he could never forgive himself.

"I'm—"

She put her finger over his mouth, stopping him. "No. Don't you dare say you're sorry. I'm not the least bit sorry."

"Damn it, Scarlet, I didn't even use a condom." God, what if they'd just made a baby? It would be his nightmare with Laura all over again. How could he be so stupid?

"I'm on the pill." She pulled her panties on under her dress, avoiding his eyes. "So you don't have to worry."

Relief hit him hard, followed quickly by an unexpected emotion. *Regret*. He shook his head.

She reached into her purse and pulled out her phone. "I'm going to call Ethan and tell him you're okay, and then you're going to tell me what's going on with Tessa."

He couldn't talk about Tessa. At least not yet. "I need a shower."

He brushed past her. Once he rounded the corner of the workshop, he ran the rest of the way to the house. If running away made him a coward, then so be it.

Cam stripped off in his small bathroom and stepped into the shower, turning the water to the hottest setting he could stand. He braced himself with one hand against the wall, letting the hard spray beat against the back of his neck. He didn't understand why Scarlet would want to stay with him. The memory of her soft skin and her sweet scent came back in a rush. She was an incredibly beautiful woman. But it was the hunger in her kiss that he remembered most. It was almost as if she'd needed him as much as he needed her.

The shower curtain rustled. Scarlet slipped into the shower and wrapped her arms around his waist, resting her head against his back. "Don't shut me out, Cameron. Stay with me. Talk to me."

He knew what she meant. He'd been trying to push her away since they met. So had she. But somehow, they always found their way back to each other. Maybe he didn't want to run anymore.

But sharing his thoughts, his burdens, even with family, didn't come easy for him. He and Laura had never had the sort of relationship where they told each other their deepest secrets, or fondest wishes. Cam didn't know if he had anything to give to Scarlet.

He turned in her arms to hold her and just like that he wanted, needed her again. He kissed her, pulling her hips against his erection, his body communicating the feelings he couldn't put in words.

He turned off the water and stepped out of the shower. After wrapping a towel around her, he lifted her from the tub. Scarlet rested her head against his shoulder and silently watched his face as he carried her to his bedroom. When he set her on her feet, he grabbed the towel and carefully dried her hair and body. But he couldn't stop himself from touching her silky skin. He kissed the pale freckles sprinkled across her shoulders, and inhaled her sweetness, trailed his hand down her stomach to the cleft between her legs. When he inserted a finger, he found her slick and ready. She moaned his name, the sound fueling his desire.

She leaned against him, her hands roaming across his chest. "Cameron. Please."

Cam pulled back the sheets, then lifted her into his arms once more and placed her in the middle of his bed before lying down beside her. He wanted to look at her – her pale, creamy skin, her perfect breasts with their rosy nipples, the triangle of red hair between her legs.

"You're so beautiful." His voice sounded thick with longing, even to his own ears.

"So are you." She laid her hand on his cheek, her blue eyes imploring him. "Make love to me, Cameron. Please."

He kissed her, softly, gently, loving the taste of her. This time when he made love to her, he wanted to take it slow. He wanted to take his time and make it good for her.

She deserved that much.

He trailed kisses across the delicate bone structure of her cheek and her jaw, over the golden freckles sprinkled lightly on her shoulder and collarbone. When he reached her breast, he licked the nipple with his tongue. She moaned and arched her back.

"Please, please, please."

He knew what she wanted and could deny her nothing. Taking the taut nipple into his mouth, he sucked and licked and gently pulled while she moaned and writhed, her hands gripping the sheets. Cam gave equal attention to the other breast before moving his explorations further down her body. Her skin was soft and smooth and her fragrance surrounded him with sweetness, as if he were enfolded in a bouquet of roses. He smiled to himself at the ridiculous, romantic comparison, but somehow it seemed right. Here, in his bed with Scarlet, every touch, every scent felt right. Perfect, even.

He positioned himself between her legs, his hands kneading her buttocks. The first touch of his tongue to her mound made her suck in breath, her legs trembling.

"Yes, yes. Please, Cameron. Please."

He wouldn't make her beg any longer. Spreading the folds of her delicate flesh with his fingers, he exposed the tiny nub of nerves and took it into his mouth. She screamed her release, her body shaking with her orgasm. He stayed with her, suckling and licking until she came again and again.

He couldn't wait any longer. Reaching across her to his nightstand, he found a box of condoms and quickly tore open a packet. She pushed herself up on her elbows as he slid the condom over his cock.

"Didn't you believe me when I said I was on the pill?"

"I believe you."

"Then why are you using a condom?"

He pushed her back against the pillows. "I also believe in insurance."

He kissed her tenderly and was gratified when she responded in kind. He pulled back to look into her face, wanting her to understand. "As much as I love Tessa, I was careless when she was conceived. She didn't ask to be born into the upheaval we've created. I won't do that again to another child, or to you."

She stared up at him again with an inscrutable look, one that wouldn't allow him into her thoughts. Finally, she caressed his cheek, the barest hint of smile on her lips. "I understand."

He kissed her again, and she wrapped her legs around his waist and held him tightly. He sighed with pleasure as he entered her, willing his body to hang on a little longer to prolong the ecstasy.

"You are so fucking sweet."

He heard her whisper against his neck. "So are you."

Then he started moving, setting a rhythm that she followed in perfect synchronization. His release built as he pushed harder, faster into her. But he held on to the last shred of his control, desperately wanting to bring her to release once more. He slipped his hand between them, inserting a finger inside her and finding the knot of nerves once more. He curled his finger, pressing gently against it. Beneath him, Scarlet's eyes flashed open and she gasped.

"Oh, God. What are you doing to me, Cameron?"

With that, she came once more. He gratefully followed her, spilling himself into her. He held Scarlet tightly as spasms rocked his body over and over. She was the only thing that made sense right now, the only thing that kept him from flying into a million pieces.

And for a few moments, he'd lost himself in her.

But now, as his body settled and his heart rate returned to normal, it was time to face reality.

Tessa was gone.

SCARLET NESTLED CLOSE against Cameron's side, her head resting on his chest. She could hear the steady beating of his heart, strong and reassuring. Their legs were entwined in the twisted sheets, joining them together. That was fine with her. She could stay like this with Cameron for days.

*I could stay forever.*

She pushed the thought from her mind. Forever was something she didn't do.

But she couldn't deny that what they'd just shared struck a chord deep in her soul. She'd never experienced such a deep connection with a man before. Making love to Cameron was more than a simple physical act. When they'd made love, they'd soared to another plane where they were emotionally and spiritually in sync.

Scarlet blew out a shaky breath. It was dangerous to fantasize about higher planes and relationships that lasted forever. Her track record with relationships on any kind of plane was abysmal. Better to enjoy this for what it was – great sex with a handsome man, no strings attached.

Besides, she had more important things to consider. Cameron needed her, and she needed to find out what was going on with Tessa.

She looked up into his face and laid her hand on his cheek. "Can you tell me what happened?"

His weary sigh told her how difficult it was for him to talk about his daughter. "Laura has a new boyfriend.

Apparently, he got a job in California and Laura's going with him and taking Tessa."

"Can she do that? I mean, as her father, don't you have some say about where she lives? I thought that was what custody agreements were for."

"We don't have a custody agreement."

"What do you mean?"

"We were never actually married. I wanted to marry her when I found out she was pregnant, but Laura refused." He gave a bitter laugh. "I guess she was waiting for a better offer."

"But even if you weren't legally married, you still have rights as Tessa's father. I'm not a lawyer, but I'm sure you have a say in where your daughter lives. We should contact a lawyer and—"

"Leave it alone, Scarlet."

She pushed herself to a sitting position and pulled the sheet around her breasts. "I don't understand. You love Tessa, I know you do. You're an amazing father. Why wouldn't you fight for her?"

He pushed himself up and sat on the edge of the bed, turning his back on her. "I said leave it alone. You don't understand."

"Then explain it to me. What don't I understand? Talk to me, Cameron!"

He turned his head, his eyes blazing. "You want to understand? Understand this. I'm an alcoholic. Every day is a struggle. Every day I think about having a drink, and every day I have to fight against the beast. What judge in his right mind is going to grant any kind of custody to an alcoholic?"

"So, you're not even going to try?"

He stood and faced her, completely oblivious to his nakedness. "Did you hear what I said? I'm an alcoholic!"

"Of course I heard you! I'd have to be deaf not to."

"Then why are you still here? Why aren't you running as far and fast as you can?"

*Good question.*

"Because I know you love your daughter and you'd do anything for her. I know you've been sober for three years and even though that beast is with you always, you're strong enough to slay that dragon every single day. You keep fighting because you want to be there for Tessa, and your family. And I'm proud of you."

Her last words were spoken on a whisper. Tears pricked at her eyes, but she sniffed them back. For a long minute, Cameron stared at her, as if he couldn't understand what she was saying.

Finally, he shook his head. "You knew about me, that I'm an alcoholic? All this time?"

"Yes. Ethan told us before he and Harper left on their honeymoon. He was worried about you."

He looked up at the ceiling. "He thought I was going to fall off the wagon because of our argument."

"But you didn't, did you?"

"No."

"Maybe you should give yourself a little credit. And maybe you should have some faith that a judge will see what I see when I look at you – a strong man who has his daughter's best interests at heart."

A mixture of surprise, confusion, and relief skipped across his face. At last, he sighed and sat on the bed once more, this time facing her. "I don't know why you have so much faith in me, but thank you."

"It's easy to have faith in you because I know what a good dad you are."

He turned away, closing his eyes and bowing his head. "I'm not sure that will matter anymore."

"What do you mean?"

"Laura says Tessa isn't my child."

For a moment, Scarlet couldn't speak. The fact that Laura would stoop so low astounded her. It angered her, too. How could she do this to Cameron?

"She's lying." She couldn't stop the quaver in her voice. "Tessa looks exactly like you. She has your dark hair and eyes."

He shrugged, the nonchalant gesture not able to mask his pain. "It could simply be a coincidence."

"I don't believe it's a coincidence. I think Laura's lying because she knows taking Tessa away from you is wrong. We have to fight for her. A DNA test will settle the argument once and for all."

He started shaking his head before Scarlet finished speaking, his jaw set in stubborn firmness. "No."

"If it's a question of money, I'm sure Ethan will help you."

"No. I'm not taking Ethan's money. This is my problem, not his."

"Tessa is Ethan's niece. Don't you think he'd want to help both of you?"

"Ethan's already done too much for me. I can't ask him to help with this, too."

She touched his arm, surprised at the tension locking his muscles. “Cameron, please. Don’t let your pride stand in the way of your daughter’s future. Do you think Laura is a good mother? Will Tessa be safe with her as her only parent?”

He hesitated, and Scarlet clearly read his feelings. “You’re worried about Tessa being alone in California with Laura and her boyfriend, aren’t you?”

“Yes.” He swallowed and turned his face away. “I don’t think she’d ever physically harm Tessa, but I’m worried about neglect. Laura isn’t exactly maternal.”

“Then you have to fight for her. If the tables were turned, if you’d been the one holding the winning lottery ticket instead of Ethan, and if he was fighting for custody of his child, wouldn’t you want to help him?”

His answer came swiftly. “Of course.”

“Then why can’t you believe he’d want to help you?”

He sighed and shook his head. “It’s not the money, not really. I know Ethan would want to help. If it was only a question of money, I’d get down on my knees and beg for Tessa’s sake. I’d beg the judge to give me sole custody. Hell, I’d even beg Laura to stay in Minnesota.”

“I don’t understand.”

“What if a DNA test proves that Tessa isn’t my daughter? What then? Would I lose all access to her forever? Since Laura and I were never married, she wouldn’t be my daughter in the eyes of the law. At least, if I don’t know, there’s still a chance she could be my daughter.”

The pain in his voice nearly brought her to tears. But tears weren’t what he needed right now. Scarlet snuggled close and laid her hand on his chest. "Tessa is your daughter no matter what any test says. She'll always be your daughter."

"I know." His voice choked with emotion. "But the legal system might not see it that way."

"All the more reason to get a good lawyer and find out for sure where you stand. Maybe the worry is worse than the reality."

He kissed her forehead. "Yeah. I can't pretend this will all go away. I know I have to do something."

Scarlet intertwined her fingers with his. "You're not alone in this, you know. You've got your family and for what it's worth, you've got me, too."

He gently tipped her chin to look into her eyes. His lips curved in a sad smile. "Thank you. That means a lot."

As he kissed her, Scarlet gave herself over to the emotion welling inside her. Right now, all she wanted to do was ease his pain. She'd worry about what happened next tomorrow.

# Chapter Sixteen

AT SEVEN THE NEXT MORNING, Cam pulled his truck up to Scarlet and Maggie's cottage. Scarlet pulled in next to him. For a moment, they simply looked at each other through the open windows of their vehicles. God, she was amazing. His body came to life just thinking about the things they'd done to each other. He realized with a start that until Scarlet came into his life, he'd never made love with a woman before. He'd had sex with plenty of women, but it had never felt so right, so spiritual that it transcended the physical.

*Spiritual*? He gave his head a shake and opened the door of the truck. He didn't do hearts and flowers. But he couldn't deny the way his heart lifted when he looked into her amazing blue eyes.

Scarlet joined him on the front porch and smiled in encouragement. "Are you ready?"

*Hell no.* "I'm ready."

She opened the door and stepped inside, and he followed right behind her. Conversation at the dining table stopped abruptly and four pairs of eyes stared at them with varying degrees of concern and displeasure. Cam resisted the urge to squirm.

Ethan folded his arms across his chest, his mouth pursed in annoyance. "So good of you to show up for work. Finally."

"Don't give him a hard time," Scarlet said. "You don't know what's going on."

"I can speak for myself, Scarlet. I don't need you to defend me."

His tone came out harsher than he'd intended. Her eyes widened in surprise, then carefully shuttered. Damn, he hadn't meant to be so tough on her, but he didn't want her to fight his battles for him. She was already far too mixed up in his life for her own good.

Harper rose to her feet and stood beside Scarlet, placing her arm around her waist. "What do you mean? What's going on?"

Scarlet simply raised her eyebrows at him and walked into the kitchen. Cam saw the rigid set of her shoulders and sensed her withdrawal as she poured herself a cup of coffee. Their magical night, and the bond they'd shared, was officially over.

The jolt of regret came as a surprise, but he pushed it away and focused on his brother. "Laura's taken Tessa to California."

For the next ten minutes, he explained the situation to Ethan, Harper, Maggie and Reese. Scarlet sat by herself on the sofa, sipping her coffee, and saying nothing. He glanced at her and saw her staring out the front window to the lake beyond. She was doing her best to distance herself from him, while he was keenly aware of every move she made.

"Laura's not going to get away with this. We'll fight her." Ethan's voice shook with anger. "We'll hire the best lawyer we can find."

"A good lawyer is going to cost a lot. I probably won't be able to pay you back."

"I don't give a damn about the money." Ethan grasped his arm. "This is about Tessa. I won't let Laura take away my niece."

Cam lowered his gaze. "The thing is, she may not be your niece. Laura says she's not mine."

For a moment, stunned silence filled the room. Then, Ethan swallowed and looked into Cam's eyes. "I think she's lying because she wants to scare you. But even if she's not, it doesn't matter. Tessa's our girl."

Cam nodded and looked away, barely able to keep his tears of gratitude at bay. "Yeah, she is. Thanks."

Ethan slapped his shoulder. "We'll figure it out. I'll call Lydia and have her ask around about lawyers. But in the meantime, we've got work to do. As soon as you eat breakfast, meet me at the job site."

"I'll be there."

With one last squeeze to his shoulder, Ethan kissed Harper and then left the cottage. A moment later, Reese drained his coffee cup and got to his feet.

"I should get to work, too." He grasped Cam's hand and shook it. "Don't let her take your daughter away. Fight with everything you've got. Tessa's too important."

"Thanks, Reese."

He nodded. "If there's anything I can do, just ask."

With that Reese left, closing the door quietly behind him. Cam's gaze connected with Scarlet's, and she gave him a tremulous smile. He breathed a sigh of relief. She might be distancing herself from him, but at least she wasn't angry.

For that he was profoundly grateful.

MAGGIE WHIPPED UP A couple of omelets and placed one in front of her. Scarlet picked at it, unable to eat. Cameron had no such problem. He devoured his omelet, thanked Maggie for making it for him, and then left as if he couldn't get away fast enough. As soon as he shut the door, both of her sisters turned on her.

"You slept with him, didn't you?" Harper accused.

"That's really none of your business."

"Like hell it isn't. Cam is my husband's brother. Anything that upsets Ethan upsets me."

"Why should Ethan be upset? I would never hurt Cameron."

"No, not intentionally." Maggie sat beside her at the dining room table. "But you have a pretty rocky track record when it comes to men. Two broken engagements makes you something of a flight risk."

"Who said anything about getting engaged? We slept together, that's all!"

"Ethan worries about Cam's drinking. After Laura took Tessa away from him the first time, he went off the deep end. His drinking got out of control. Now with what's happening again with Tessa, Cam doesn't need the extra stress of worrying about when you're going to take off."

Scarlet stared at Harper. Of all the people in the world, she thought her sisters would understand. Or at least give her the benefit of the doubt. Profoundly hurt at their lack of faith in her, at their assumption she would lead Cameron on and then toss him away, she pushed her chair back and rose slowly to her feet.

"Cameron's not going to fall to pieces. He's a lot stronger than Ethan gives him credit for. Now if you'll excuse me, I've got work to do."

"Scarlet, come on. Let's talk about this."

"I think I've heard enough."

She didn't wait to hear what else Harper wanted to lecture her about. She marched out the door and jumped into her car, kicking up dirt and stones as she tore away from the cottage. Hot tears of hurt and anger blurred her vision.

Miles flew by until she'd calmed down and her tears stopped. She pulled off the main road and found a parking lot next to a small lake. The sunshine sparkling on the water made her think of her grandfather and her long ago belief in diamonds beneath the waves.

She'd never told her sisters about the conversation she'd heard between her parents on the day they died. Maybe if she had, they'd understand why she'd run away from her engagements.

But then, she didn't fully understand it herself. Not really. So how could she expect them to?

With a sigh, she started her car and drove to Cameron's house to do some work. Since she hadn't done anything the previous day, she was behind. She walked around the house, to Cameron's bedroom where they'd made love, the covers slightly askew from hastily fixing the bed that morning. The towels in the bathroom were still damp from their shower together. She could almost feel Cameron's big hands on her as he soaped her back, and other more sensitive areas of her body. Would they ever make love again, or was her time with him merely a one-night stand, a moment never to be repeated?

Scarlet walked down the hall to Tessa's bedroom and stood in the doorway, unable to go inside. Except for the empty closet, the room was exactly how Tessa had left it a couple of days ago. The stuffed toys and dolls she'd left behind were lined up on her bed, the building blocks and wooden toys Cameron had made for her on the shelves he'd built. The tiny wooden table was set with miniature teacups and pretend food. It was as if Tessa had stepped out of the room and would return at any moment.

Scarlet put her hand over her mouth to stop her sobs. She hadn't allowed herself to cry in front of Cameron, but now, alone in Tessa's empty room, she couldn't stop the sorrow and worry. Was Tessa scared? Did she miss her Dad? Did she miss her?

Would they ever see her again?

After a few minutes, she pulled herself together. She dried her tears and blew her nose. Crying wouldn't help Tessa, or Cameron. She had to be strong for both of them.

With that thought, she went to the office and booted up his laptop. For the next few hours, she immersed herself in website updates and Facebook posts, though the cheery, positive tone she wanted to use was difficult to achieve.

She checked her watch and saw how late it was getting. After powering down the computer, she left Cameron's house. If he came home early, she didn't want him to find her there, uninvited. She wouldn't assume anything about their one night together. If they ever made love again in his house, it would be because he asked her to be there.

When she pulled up to the cottage, dread settled in her stomach. She hated fighting with her sisters. Maybe it was time to cut her leave of absence short and go back to Chicago. The thought of leaving them behind, of leaving Cameron behind, made her queasy. But she might not have any choice. If they were angry with her, she couldn't stay.

*That's right, Scarlet. Run away again.*

With trepidation, she opened her car door and got out. Before she could make it up the stairs of the front porch, Harper and Maggie rushed out of the cottage to greet her. Harper put her arms around her. "I'm so sorry, Scarlet. I was worried about Tessa and I took it out on you."

Maggie grasped her arm. "We should have supported you instead of ganging up on you. This thing with Tessa must be hard on you, too. And if you're starting a relationship with Cam, that's got to be scary for you too."

Scarlet put one arm around Harper and squeezed Maggie's hand. "I'm not starting a relationship with him, not really. Neither of us is in a position for anything permanent. I happened to be there when he needed someone."

To their credit, her sisters didn't argue with her. "Whatever happened between you, we're sorry we made a big deal about it. Can you forgive us?"

Scarlet sighed in relief. "Of course."

"Are you hungry?" Maggie asked.

Trust Maggie to try to feed her. Scarlet gave a shaky laugh and discovered she was indeed hungry. "I could eat."

"Come inside and I'll make something for you."

They walked into the cottage hand in hand. For the first time since she'd returned to Solace Lake Lodge, she and her sisters were truly in sync.

A COUPLE OF DAYS LATER, Lydia texted Cam the name of the lawyer she believed would do the best job for him and Tessa.

"Erin Cochrane is tough and uncompromising when it comes to defending the rights of her clients, especially dads. She has a very impressive track record. But when I talked to her, I was most impressed with her compassion. She's someone who understands," Lydia wrote in her text. "I've made an appointment for you to meet with her in a couple of days."

A series of texts contained details about his upcoming meeting with the lawyer. Cam thanked Lydia and told her he'd be there. She replied that she and Graham would be there, too. There was no way they'd let him go through this alone. A moment later, he got a text from Ethan offering to drive him to Minneapolis. Apparently, his family was circling the wagons to defend him.

Or were they worried the stress would be too much for him. A knot formed in his stomach. Would this lawyer be able to bring Tessa home? If she couldn't...

He couldn't think about that. *One day at a time.*

He stuck his phone in his back pocket and went back to work. For the next couple of hours, Cam helped to move bundles of shingles onto the roof of one of the new cottages. The work required every ounce of his physical strength, but at least it kept him occupied and doing something besides worrying.

"Ah, there's our ladies." Charlie said. Cam followed the direction of his gaze. Scarlet and her sisters were walking toward them pulling the little wagon. "I was beginning to think they forgot about our coffee break this afternoon."

"Not a chance."

The sunshine hit Scarlet's hair, making her bright locks gleam. He loved the color of her hair and the silky feel of it in his hands. He especially liked the way it fell around his face when she was on top of him and leaning over to kiss him...

The memory of making love with Scarlet made him instantly hard. Had it been a one-time thing or the start of something real between them?

He couldn't think of starting something with her while Tessa's future was up in the air. Besides, he had nothing offer her aside from the potential of finding herself in the middle of a bitter custody battle.

The men lined up and Scarlet and Harper distributed coffee and drinks while Maggie passed a container of homemade cookies around. His men made appreciative noises as they stuffed themselves with the sweet treats.

Scarlet approached with a thermos and a smile that didn't quite reach her eyes. "Would you like coffee or a cold drink?"

"Coffee's fine."

For the last two days they'd barely spoken, other than to take his coffee break order or to pass the salt at lunch. He wouldn't blame her if she regretted making love with him. He'd been desperate and needy, and hadn't exactly treated her with kid gloves. He'd pounded into her like a cave man.

It had been the best sex of his life.

He looked into her eyes and for a moment, he swore she was remembering making love with him, too. When she thought of them together, did she remember the soap sliding over their bodies as they made love in the shower? Did she remember the tangled sheets in his bed and the way they'd touched each other?

He wondered if it had been as good for her as it had been for him, and whether she thought about making love with him again.

She blinked a few times and looked away, busying herself by pouring him a cup of coffee. The only thing that gave him hope was the slight tremble of her hand.

"Have you had any news about Tessa?" she asked.

"Laura let her call me last night."

"That's wonderful. How is she?"

Cam sighed. "She sounded confused. She doesn't understand why I can't come out to California and bring her home. She also said Laura wants her to call her boyfriend Daddy."

She sucked in a breath. "I'm sorry, Cameron. That must have been hard for you."

"Yeah." It had killed him to hear his little girl in distress and not be able to do a damn thing to help her. "I tried to talk to Laura, to find out when they might be coming home, but she hung up on me."

"How could she be so cruel? Doesn't she understand how much this hurts both of you?" Scarlet blinked and looked away as if fighting tears.

He touched her arm, surprised at her depth of feeling for his daughter. "Hey, we'll get her back."

Her eyes were shiny with tears when she looked into face, but she blinked them back. "Yeah, we will."

He wanted to take her into his arms and hold her close, to soothe her and make everything better. But he couldn't do that, not with his entire crew, and his brother and her sisters watching. He had to make do with a light squeeze to her arm. "Lydia found me a lawyer. She says she's tough."

Scarlet nodded and composed herself once more. "That's exactly what you need – someone to fight for you."

*What I need is you.* He pushed the thought away. The last thing Scarlet needed was a messed-up fool like him. "Yeah."

"When do you meet with her?"

"Thursday. Ethan's coming with me."

"Good, that's good. Is there anything I can do?"

*Come home with me.* "I don't think so, but thanks."

"Okay."

She gave him a half smile before moving toward Charlie and a couple of the other guys. He tried not to be too obvious about watching her pour them coffee. She laughed at a joke Charlie made and asked about Leo's wife, who was about to give birth.

"She's beautiful, isn't she?"

Cam started at the sound of the feminine voice. He'd been so transfixed on Scarlet he hadn't noticed Maggie standing beside him. She held out a container of cookies and he helped himself to one.

"Scarlet gives off this tough career woman vibe, and she really is a competent, accomplished woman," she said in a quiet voice meant only for him. "But under that sophisticated exterior, there's a very tender, sensitive heart. I hope you remember that."

Maggie walked away and offered her treats to another group of workers. The Lindquist sisters were very protective of each other. And why shouldn't they be? They'd learned at a very young age how easily safety and security could be snatched away.

The last thing he wanted was to bring distress into Scarlet's life. For her sake, he squashed the idea of asking her to come home with him.

An empty ache settled in his chest.

# Chapter Seventeen

AT THE KNOCK, SCARLET opened the door and found Glenn Hanson, Reese's brother and foreman, standing on the veranda with a small wooden box in his hands. "Hi, Glenn. What can I do for you?"

He handed her the box. "We found this under the floorboards in one of the upstairs bedrooms. Reese said to give it to you and your sisters. He thought it might be important."

Scarlet ran her fingers over the initials M.S. carved on the top. A half-forgotten memory suddenly began playing inside her head, as if someone had flipped a switch.

*The strange old house, with all its creaks and noises, frightened Scarlet. She tiptoed to her mom's room and found her sitting on the floor of her bedroom, a box on her lap and handwritten letters and envelopes scattered around her. She had come for comfort, but Mom was the one crying, one hand covering her mouth. Scarlet ran to her, frightened by her sorrow.*

*"Mom, what's wrong? Why are you crying?"*

*Her mom wiped at her eyes, then pulled Scarlet into her lap and held her tight. "I'm fine, honey. Really. I was reading some old letters and sometimes old memories make me sad."*

*"Why do they make you sad?"*

*"Because of all the wasted time."*

*She had no idea what Mom meant, but she didn't want to go back to her room, so she said nothing, content to stay in her mother's arms.*

*"Don't be afraid to love, Scarlet. Not ever."*

*"Okay, Mom."*

The switch flipped off. As Scarlet stood in the doorway staring at the box, her hands began to shake and tears burned her throat. She glanced at Glenn, still standing on the porch and looking uncomfortable. "I—I—it's very kind of you..."

Glenn stepped back. "I'm sorry, I didn't mean to upset you. Reese thought it was important. He would have brought it himself, but he wanted to get home to Abby."

She shook her head. "I'm so sorry. I don't know why I'm crying."

"Scarlet?"

Maggie came to stand next to her. Scarlet handed her the box. "It—it belonged to Mom."

"Oh." Maggie turned to Glenn with a smile. "Thanks for bringing this for us. We appreciate it very much."

With a nod, he turned and hurried down the steps of the front porch, obviously glad to get away from the overwrought female. Maggie closed the door, then guided Scarlet to the sofa and made her sit down. She sat beside her. "Do you know what's in the box?"

"Letters, I think."

"From who?"

Scarlet shook her head. "I don't know. I only know they made Mom sad."

The door opened and Harper walked into the cottage. Her gaze met Scarlet's and she hurried to her, dropping to her knees in front of her and seizing her hand. "What's wrong? What's happened?"

Maggie answered for her. "The workmen found this box under the floorboards in the lodge. Scarlet says it belonged to Mom."

Harper examined the box. "I don't remember ever seeing it before. What makes you think it was Mom's?"

"The initials, of course, and the fact it was found in one of the bedrooms. She must have hidden it there, probably so Grandma couldn't find it." Scarlet inhaled a shaky breath. "And I saw it once before. That summer."

Harper didn't have to ask which summer she was talking about. She ran her hand up and down Scarlet's arm. "Why is it making you so sad, honey?"

Her lower lip trembled. "The letters inside made Mom cry. I'd never seen her cry before, not like that, like her heart was crumbling."

Maggie put her arm around her shoulders. "Maybe we should put it away and forget about it. It's not worth making you cry."

"No!" Scarlet tightened her grip on the box. "We have so little left of our parents. I want to know – I need to know – why the letters in this box upset Mom so badly."

Maggie turned to Harper. "You've got the deciding vote. What do you think? What should we do with this box?"

For several silent moments, Harper caressed the carved initials with her finger. Finally, she looked up at Scarlet, sadness making her normally vibrant blue eyes appear dull and flat. "We've had too many secrets kept from us, too many things we don't understand. I'm tired of not knowing. I say we open the box and if there are letters inside, we read them. We've earned that right."

Maggie gave a brief nod. "Okay. Scarlet, are you ready?"

*I'll never be ready for this.* "Yes."

"You do the honors, Scarlet," Harper said. "Open the box."

Her hands shook as she fumbled with the latch and lifted the lid. As she suspected, the box was filled with yellowing letters. Scarlet lifted the top envelope and read the address. "It's addressed to Abby. Why would Mom have Abby's letters, and why would they make her cry?"

"I don't know." Maggie peered at the postal stamp. "The ink is smeared and I can't make out where it was sent from. All I can make out is the M, so it was likely mailed in Minnesota."

"Or Michigan, Massachusetts or Maryland."

"Who would Mom have known in Maryland?"

"Wherever it came from, we know when it came." Maggie tapped the date stamp with her fingernail. "June 5th, 1975."

"Mom was still in high school. She would have been what? Sixteen?"

"Fifteen," Harper said. "Who's it from?"

Scarlet turned the envelope over but there was no return address. "I guess we'll have to read the letter to find out."

Holding her breath, she pulled the letter from the envelope and began to read aloud.

"My Sweet Randi, I miss you so much. I know the time isn't right for us now, but someday we'll be together. I promise. Nothing and no one will keep us apart. I love you, baby. I know it's hard, but please be patient and give me some time to make things right. I'll see you soon. R." Scarlet's voice shook as she finished, the love and emotion in the words tearing at her heart.

"R? R as in Robert? I didn't realize Mom and Dad knew each other when she was in high school. I thought they met in college," Maggie said.

"So did I, but maybe that was just one more lie we were told." Harper removed the letter from Scarlet's hands. "We know someone else with an R name. Reese."

"Reese? He would have been about five years older than Mom, wouldn't he?"

"Yes. He left Minnewasta as soon as he graduated from high school, and he didn't come back for a lot of years."

"Did they know each other back then?"

"Yeah. He told me he worked at the lodge one summer." Harper shook her head. "But she was fourteen or fifteen and he was about nineteen. What would they have had in common at that age? This sounds like a pretty intense relationship. It's unlikely he's the letter writer."

"Simply because of their age difference?" Maggie's voice rose, her tone incensed. "There are age differences in many relationships. Just because he was five years older doesn't mean they couldn't have cared for each other."

"She was a kid, and he was a young man," Harper insisted. "They were at totally different stages of life."

"Don't discount the possibility they loved each other simply because they weren't the same age," Maggie said stubbornly. Scarlet looked at her, taken aback by her outburst.

Harper shook her head. "I don't buy it. Daddy must have written that letter. They must have known each other back then. Unless..."

"What?" Scarlet asked.

"There is someone else whose name begins with R," Harper said. "Someone the same age as our mother who lived in Minnewasta at the same time. Willy Eklund."

"Willy? What are you talking about?"

"Willy's real name is Richard. He always used his middle name so people wouldn't get him mixed up with his father, who was also named Richard." She bit her lip. "Abby told me that Willy had a huge crush on Mom back in high school. He even wrote poetry for her. But she didn't think he ever told Mom. It's possible Abby didn't know the whole story, though."

Scarlet shook her head. "Why would he sign his name with an R if he didn't normally use that name?"

"Whoever wrote these letters was obviously trying to hide his relationship with Mom. Why else would Abby be the go-between? Maybe not signing the letters was another way of keeping this relationship secret."

"She obviously didn't want Grandma to know about the letters." Maggie gripped the paper in her hands, her lower lip trembling and a tear trailing down her cheek. "She must have been afraid Grandma would disapprove. Why else would she hide them so carefully?"

Scarlet was alarmed by Maggie's emotional reaction. "Are you ok, honey?"

She wiped her face with the back of her hand. "I'll be fine."

Scarlet wished Reese had burned the box. The discovery wasn't worth upsetting Maggie like this.

"I'm sure Grandma would have disapproved of Willy," Harper said. "His mother was an alcoholic."

"Then why would she let Grampa hire Willy if she hated him so much?" Maggie asked.

Harper shrugged. "I don't know. Grandma was a difficult person to understand."

Maggie nodded, her eyes shiny with fresh tears. "She didn't understand us anymore than we understood her."

Scarlet squeezed her hand in silent support. As the youngest, Maggie had been most affected by their grandmother's mercurial ways. And also by her sudden death. However difficult their relationship, Grandma Dorothy was the only mother Maggie had ever known.

"No, these letters must have been written by Daddy. Nothing else makes sense." Harper shook the envelope. "Look at this. He loved her, even back then. He never would have hurt her. This proves he didn't kill her, I know it."

Scarlet's stomach churned, leaving her feeling queasy. "You don't know how he really felt about her. You don't even know for sure he wrote these letters."

"I know it," Harper insisted. "He loved her. All these years, people have believed he killed her out of jealousy and anger and finally, here's the proof that he didn't. He wouldn't hurt her. He loved her. I know it."

Scarlet's hands shook. "I never once heard him call her Randi. Did you?"

"No, but maybe it was a name he used in private. Lovers sometimes have pet names for each other."

She was going to be sick. "I don't want to talk about them anymore!"

"Come on, Scarlet. If we can't talk to each other about them, who can we talk to?"

"I said I don't want to talk about them!"

The walls were closing in on her, the secret she'd guarded so closely for so many years threatening to be exposed.

Harper stared at her. "What's wrong with you?"

Scarlet jumped to her feet, dropping the box to the floor and scattering the contents. "These pieces of paper prove nothing! You weren't there, you don't know!"

She rushed to the door, needing to get away, needing to breathe.

Harper grabbed her arm before she could leave. "What do you mean, I wasn't there?"

Tears blurred her vision. She had to get away before the torrent swamped her and she broke down completely. Then her sisters would know what she knew, and she couldn't let that happen. She pushed Harper's hand from her arm. "I have to go."

She bolted out the door and down the steps, running blindly into the forest. No matter what, she had to protect her sisters from the knowledge that had haunted her all her life.

Harper was wrong; it was no accident. Just as the police had said, their father killed their mother. But what they didn't know was why. Scarlet knew.

Miranda had intended to leave Robert for another man.

CAM CAUGHT A GLIMPSE of Scarlet running through the trees, her red hair visible through the green foliage. She stumbled and fell, then quickly picked herself up and continued to run, soon disappearing into the forest. He slipped off his tool belt and handed his hammer to Charlie. "I have to go. Can you look after things here?"

"Sure, boss. Is something wrong?"

"I hope not."

He ran in the general direction he'd seen he go, unsure of where he was going or why. All he knew was that something had happened, and he had to make sure Scarlet was okay.

The undergrowth slapped against his face and scratched his arms as he pushed his way through. He had no idea if he was headed in the right direction, but he kept moving.

Finally, he found a path of sorts, probably made by deer making their way to the lake. Scarlet may have followed this path. She grew up here and knew every path and hiding place in the forest. But he wasn't sure. There was no sign of her.

Then, he heard it. A keening cry so heartbreakingly sad he knew Scarlet's heart must be shattered. He followed the sound and found her curled on her side in the fetal position, her body shaking with her cries. She ran her fingers through her ponytail, tugging on the strands as if it somehow soothed her. He knelt beside her and touched her arm, fear churning in his gut. She started at his touch and scrambled to a sitting position.

"Scarlet, sweetheart, what's wrong? What happened, baby?"

She swiped at her tears with the back of her hand, a gesture so childlike it broke his heart. "What are you doing here?"

"I saw you running through the trees."

She turned her face away. "You shouldn't have followed me."

"What happened? Why are you crying?"

Her eyes filled with tears again. "Go away, Cameron."

"No." He gently removed a dry leaf from her hair. "I won't leave you like this."

She pulled her knees to her chest and began to rock. "Please, Cameron. Go. I can't...I can't."

He put his arm around her and pulled her close, kissing the top of her head. "I seem to remember telling you the same thing not that long ago. You wouldn't leave me then, and I won't leave you now."

She looked at him, surprise simmering in her blue eyes. The next moment they filled with tears and spilled down her cheeks. Her body shook with her sobs. Cam gathered her into his arms and pulled her onto his lap. His heart ached to see her in such pain. He held her tightly as she clutched the material of his t-shirt and wept.

"It's okay, baby. Everything's going to be okay," he murmured against her sweet-smelling hair. "Let it all go."

She cried as if she'd been holding a torrent of pain inside for a very long time. He knew all too well how grief and anger bottled up inside like that could eat away at a person until there was nothing left but emptiness.

Finally, she cried herself out, her sobs subsiding into soft hiccups. For a long time he simply held her and silently stroked her hair, waiting for her to speak. When she finally did, her voice was quiet and a little raw from her tears.

"I'm sorry," she said against his chest, still clutching his shirt.

"For crying?" He kissed her hair once more. "You don't have to be sorry for that. Not with me."

Her body stiffened. "Please don't tell my sisters. They wouldn't understand."

"What wouldn't they understand?"

"Please, Cameron. Promise me."

"All right. I won't tell them you were crying if you don't want me to." He paused, wondering how far he could push her. "Can you tell me why you were crying?"

She shook her head against his chest. "No. Please, don't ask."

"Scarlet, sweetheart. Look at me."

Reluctantly, she tipped her head back and looked up at him. The bleakness on her face nearly undid him. He gently smoothed her hair from her forehead. "When you stayed with me, when you wouldn't let me push you away..." He stopped, uncomfortable and unaccustomed to speaking about his feelings. But for Scarlet he'd do it. "When you stayed, it meant a lot to me. I didn't realize how much I needed someone to talk to." *Someone to believe in me.*

Her eyes softened. "I'm glad I could help."

"I want to help you the way you helped me. You can tell me anything. I won't judge, I promise."

Her mouth trembled and she once more ducked her head, not letting go of her grip on his t-shirt. "I've never told anyone, not even my sisters. Especially not my sisters."

He kissed the top of her head. "Whatever you're holding inside, it's killing you, baby. It's time to let it go."

"I can't. If they knew..."

"What would happen if they knew?"

"They'd be so hurt, especially Harper. She's believed for so long..." She shook her head against his chest. "I can't take away her hope."

"I know you don't want to hurt anyone, but do you think your sisters would want you to suffer like this? If the tables were turned, would you want them to feel the hurt you feel right now?"

Her reply was muffled against his shirt. "No. Never."

Cam kissed her hair once more, wondering if he had any right to say what he was going to say next. "Do you think your parents would want you to be so unhappy? This is about them, isn't it?"

She flashed him a look of panicked surprise before turning her face away. "Yes," she whispered.

"You found out something, didn't you? About how they died?"

With an unsteady breath, she slid off his lap. He was relieved when she settled next to him on the forest floor. How long she'd stay was anyone's guess. She was like a skittish rabbit, ready to bolt at the first hint of trouble.

She wrapped her arms around her knees. "You promise you won't say anything to my sisters?"

He hesitated. He didn't know if he could promise knowing it would prolong her pain.

She lifted her chin. "Promise me, Cameron, or I'm leaving right now."

"Okay. I won't say anything to Maggie and Harper." He had to hope that unburdening her terrible secret to him would be enough to give her some peace.

She nodded and looked away. "It was here in the woods, not far from here. That's where I heard my parents talking that day."

"That day? You mean the day they died?"

She closed her eyes and nodded again. "Daddy arrived at the lodge unexpectedly. I heard him tell Mom he had some things he needed to say to her, that they needed to work some things out, so I followed them. I thought he was going to tell her he was coming home, that we were going to be a family again. I wanted to find out so I could tell Harper. She'd been so worried."

"So your father had been the one who left the marriage?"

"Yes. He left in the spring. Then when school let out, Mom packed the three of us up and we came out to the lodge."

She fell silent, as if remembering those confusing and unhappy times. Cam touched her hand. "So you followed them through the forest?"

Scarlet roused herself. "Yes. They didn't know I was there. Harper and I had gotten pretty good at being quiet.

We used to follow deer through the forest, and we could get quite close until they caught our scent and ran."

"You heard their conversation?"

Scarlet hugged her knees closer and began to rock. "Daddy was so angry and so sad. Mom said she couldn't go on the way they had anymore. She couldn't live with the lie. She said she loved someone else, that she'd always loved him. Then, Daddy started crying and said he wanted to die, because if he couldn't have her, he'd rather be dead."

*Dear God.* No wonder this secret had been eating away at her. She'd been a child, not much older than Tessa. Cam clasped her hand.

"I'd never seen him like that before, so angry, so anguished, like his heart had been ripped in half. Mom told him how sorry she was. She'd never meant to hurt him." She swiped at tears with the back of her hand. "They must have heard me crying. They found me in my hiding place, told me they loved me, and said I had to go back to the lodge. Mom said we'd be going to a new home soon, but not with Daddy. She said we could still talk to Daddy on the phone whenever we wanted."

"I don't understand. This was traumatic for you, of course, but why couldn't you tell your sisters what you'd heard, if not then, later, as adults?"

She stared at him, her eyes bright with anguish. "Don't you get it? He said he wanted to die. It's not a far stretch to believe he planned to take our mother with him. All these years, Harper has clung to the belief that their deaths were some kind of tragic accident, that Willy had been mistaken when he said he saw Daddy hit Mom with the oar. Maggie's hung onto that belief too, because it's all she's got. But they didn't see him that day. They didn't see how sad he was. He was a man who had nothing left to lose. How could I tell Harper and Maggie what I saw? They'd be devastated."

"Did you actually see him hit her with the oar and knock her into the lake?"

"No, but—"

"Then you don't know for sure. You don't know without a doubt that he killed her and then killed himself."

Her face contorted in pain as tears streamed down her cheeks once more. "It's my fault. It's my fault they died."

Cam reached for her, alarmed at her distress. "Sweetheart, that's not true. None of it was your fault."

"It was my fault!" She pushed his hands away and jumped to her feet. Her sudden movement and her shout spooked a flock of birds out of the trees. With hoarse cries of warning, they took to the air.

Cam leapt to his feet and faced her. "Scarlet, you were a kid. How can their deaths possibly be your fault?"

"If I hadn't followed them, if they hadn't caught me listening, they wouldn't have gone on the lake to get some privacy. They did that because of me." She thumped her chest in agony. "*I* killed them. If they hadn't gone on the lake, maybe Daddy would have calmed down. At least, he couldn't have pushed her into the water. If I hadn't followed them, they'd still be alive."

For a second, he could only stare. Then, he grabbed her shoulders and shook her. "Scarlet! Listen to me! You had nothing to do with their deaths. Nothing you did or didn't do caused them to lose their lives. Nothing." He shook her again, his voice rising in panic. "Did you hear me? You did nothing wrong."

As the seconds ticked by, she stared at him and the bleakness on her face nearly undid him. For years, she'd been carrying around the weight of a guilt she should never have had to bear. He hoped to God he never did something as cruel to Tessa, even unintentionally. He waited, hoping that he'd gotten through to her. That she wouldn't bolt.

Finally, she nodded and walked into his arms.

With a relieved sigh, he lifted her into his arms and gently set her on the forest floor. He sat beside her and pulled her onto his lap again as he leaned against a tree. She rested her head on his shoulder and closed her eyes, exhausted by her confessions. He hoped that speaking her fears and guilt out loud had lessened their hold on her.

She was silent for so long he thought she'd fallen asleep. But at last she spoke, her voice hoarse. "I lied when I said I've never told anyone about overhearing my parents' conversation."

"Oh, yeah? Who did you tell?"

She sighed deeply. "A therapist. I went to see her a few months ago. I wanted—needed to know what was wrong with me."

*What was wrong with me?* "What do you mean?"

She looked away. "I was engaged, twice. The first time was to my high school boyfriend. Right after graduation, we both went to Minneapolis to college. I wanted to get away from the lodge and from Grandma Dorothy. I wanted to live my life, and I wanted to be someplace where everyone didn't know me. For once in my life, I didn't want everyone to know my father killed my mother."

He could understand that. "Small towns are tough that way. They don't let you forget."

"No, they don't." She sighed again before continuing. "Then, Mike asked me to marry him. He totally surprised me. I cared a lot for him, so I said yes."

"You were young. It doesn't sound like you were ready."

"That's what I told myself for a long time, but it was more than that. I went through all the motions of planning the wedding and buying a dress, but the closer it got to the day of the wedding, the more scared I got. I had this dread in my stomach that kept growing. I knew if I went through with the wedding, something terrible was going to happen. Finally, I got so panicked, I couldn't pretend anymore. About two weeks before the day of the wedding, I told Mike I couldn't go through with it. And then I ran."

He brushed a wayward curl from her forehead. "Where did you go?"

"I hid out at a friend's house for a couple of weeks." Her brow furrowed. "Grandma and Grampa were humiliated. I don't think Grandma ever forgave me."

She'd carried a heavy load of guilt for a long time. Cam brushed a kiss over her hair.

"Like you said, for a long time I chalked up my feelings to being young and unprepared for marriage. So when I met Owen in Chicago about three years ago, I thought I was ready. But after we got engaged, I started to have those same feelings again, the same overwhelming fear. I couldn't go through with it. Again."

"Is that when you decided to see a therapist?"

"Yes. I couldn't go on that way."

He stroked her hair. "What did you find out?"

"She made me remember the day my parents died and the terrible conversation I heard. I guess I'd made myself forget it, buried it deep down because it was so painful. But then it all came rushing back. She tried to make me talk about it, but I couldn't. I ran away, again, and never went back." Her small shoulders lifted in a half-hearted shrug. "It seems that's how I handle painful subjects."

"You took the first step. I'm proud of you and you should be proud, too." Cam tightened his hold on her. "When you're ready, you'll go back and do the rest of the work."

"I don't know how proud I feel. Right now all I feel is tired, like I just ran a marathon."

"You should go back to your cottage and lie down for a while."

She shook her head. "I can't, not yet. Harper and Maggie are there. They'll ask a lot of questions, and I'm not ready to answer them. Not yet."

"Then we'll stay here."

She turned to look up into his face. "Don't you have to get back to work? I don't want Ethan to be angry with you."

He smoothed her hair from her face. His heart gave a painful thump at the worry on her beautiful face. "Ethan will be fine. We'll sit here for a few minutes until you're ready to go home."

"Home?" She closed her eyes and rested her head against his chest once more. "I wonder where that is."

He had no reply for that. He simply held her close until her breathing told him she'd fallen asleep.

# Chapter Eighteen

BY THE TIME SCARLET woke, the sun was low in the western sky. She blinked a few times, struggling to return to full consciousness. Her eyes were gritty and swollen from crying, and her left arm, tucked against Cameron's hard chest, had fallen asleep.

*Cameron.* He'd stayed with her. She tentatively laid her hand on his chest and felt the strong, reassuring beat of his heart.

He caught her hand and squeezed it. "You had a nice nap. Feel better?"

"Yeah." She pushed away from him and slid off his lap. Pins and needles shot through her left arm and she winced.

"You okay?"

"My arm fell asleep, that's all." She turned away, and the memory of everything she'd told him came flooding back. She'd never been so exposed, so vulnerable.

But in a strange way, she'd never been so at peace either. She'd told him her most terrible secrets, and he didn't run away. The world hadn't ended. Instead, he'd defended her, told her she wasn't to blame for her parents' deaths. He'd held her and comforted her. She didn't understand why he hadn't run, but she was glad he didn't.

He ran his hand up and down her frozen arm, gently kneading. "Are the pins and needles going away?

"Yes, it's better now. Thank you." She lifted her gaze to look into his face. A five o'clock shadow darkened his strong jaw, making him look even more handsome. Her heart gave an unexpected kick.

"Thank you for staying with me," she whispered. "Those things I told you, like I said, I've never told anyone other than my therapist."

He smoothed her hair, the movement gentle and soothing. "Don't keep all that hurt inside, sweetheart. Talk to your sisters."

She began shaking her head before he even finished speaking. The thought of telling Harper and Maggie about her part in their parents' death caused her stomach to twist painfully. "I can't do that."

After all the years she'd kept the memory locked away, afraid to speak it, she was terrified her sisters would blame her as much as she blamed herself. She couldn't bear the idea of losing them. They were all she had.

"A secret like that will eat you alive. Don't give it the power to hurt you."

She nodded, although she doubted she could ever reveal the truth to them. She got to her feet and Cameron did as well. "I should probably head back to the cottage. I'm sure everyone's wondering where I am."

"Yeah, I should get back to the job site. You sure you're okay?"

She made herself smile for him. "I'm fine." Unable to deny herself, she laid her hand on his cheek, needing to feel one last connection with him. More and more he was becoming a necessity in her life, no matter what she told herself about a relationship between them being too complicated. Cameron's big hand covered hers and his dark eyes held a knowing look, as if he could hear the chaotic thoughts rolling through her brain. She could almost believe in that moment that he could hear the desires and hopes she was too afraid to give a voice to. She could almost believe he desired the same things she did.

Fear gripped her. If she wasn't careful, she'd find herself needing him or, *Dear God*, loving him. Scarlet closed her eyes to break the spell, letting her hand drop from his face. She took a very deliberate step back. "I should go. Thank you. You've been very kind, especially with everything going on with Tessa."

His hand fell away, his gaze now hooded. It was possible she wasn't the only one in hiding. "If you ever want to talk, about anything, let me know."

Scarlet nodded briefly before hurrying back down the trail that led to the cottages. A nagging sense of worry dogged her steps. Perhaps it was already too late. Perhaps she'd already fallen in love with Cameron.

ERIN COCHRANE'S LAW office was in an unpretentious building close to downtown Minneapolis. The offices, though pleasant enough, were crammed with desks and filing cabinets, giving the impression of being undersized for the amount of work being done there. Cam was comforted by the humbleness of the office. It made him believe the lawyer cared more about her clients than a fancy address or the view from a corner office.

Cam and his family huddled around a small table in Erin's office and poured themselves coffee. Everyone had insisted on attending this meeting. Ethan had driven him to the city, and Lydia and Graham had been waiting outside the building when they'd arrived. He was grateful not to have to go through this alone.

Erin sipped her coffee and examined him over her mug. "So, Mr. Hainstock, I've heard from your sister why you're looking to engage my services, but I want to hear the story directly from you."

"What do you want to know?"

"Tell me about your daughter."

Cam shifted on his plastic chair. Was this some kind of test? "Tessa is five years old. She's a very bright and loving little girl. I'm concerned she's not getting the stability she needs from her mother. That's why we're here."

"Why do you think her mother isn't supplying a stable environment for her?"

"Laura dragged her away to California after knowing her current boyfriend for only a short time. I heard from Laura's parents that they spent a few days living out of their car when they first arrived because they hadn't made any effort to find an apartment first. To my knowledge, Tessa hasn't been enrolled in a school yet either."

"And how does that make you feel, Mr. Hainstock?"

He gripped his coffee cup tighter. "Angry. It makes me angry. My daughter deserves better than that."

"What do you want me to do about it?"

*What the hell?* "I want you to help her! I want you to bring Tessa home!"

"How do I know Tessa is any better off with you than she is with her mother?"

Erin's question caught him off guard, but he tried to keep his expression neutral. "You probably already know I've got my own problems."

Erin nodded. "Yes. Your sister told me you're a recovering alcoholic. How long have you been sober?"

"Three years. I knew that if I was going to be any kind of father to Tessa, I had to stop drinking." Cam glanced at his sister. "Our father was an alcoholic, so we grew up without a lot of security. I didn't want that for Tessa."

"Your sister also told me that there's some question about Tessa's paternity."

Hearing the words out loud kicked him in the gut. "Yes. When Tessa was born, Laura claimed she was mine. But now she says otherwise."

"What will you do if DNA testing proves conclusively that you did not father Tessa?"

"Even if she doesn't have my DNA, Tessa is still my daughter. I would still want her to live with me in Minnewasta, to be close to her grandparents and to my family." He paused and fought to keep calm. "You asked me if Tessa would be better off with me than with her mother. All I can tell you is that I love my daughter and I want her to have a happy, stable life. I'm not convinced her mother can provide that. Can you help us, Ms. Cochrane?"

Erin studied him for a moment. "It's not going to be easy, but I think we have a shot. I want you to be prepared for a fight."

Cam nodded, relieved by her answer. "I'm ready."

WHEN CAM PULLED INTO his yard late that afternoon, Scarlet's car was in his driveway. Since the day they'd made love, she'd been very careful about not being at his house when he came home. Maybe she thought he didn't want her. It was also possible she'd decided he wasn't worth the risk. Despite everything going on his life right now, he missed her. She was the one person in the world he really wanted to see, especially today.

He unlocked the back door and hung his keys on the hook. "Scarlet? I'm home."

She came around the corner, her red hair wild and disheveled as if she'd been running her hands through it all day. She'd never looked more beautiful.

"Oh, I'm sorry. I lost track of the time. I'll get my stuff together and go."

"There's no rush. Would you like a cup of tea or something?"

She blinked a couple of times before answering, as if surprised by his question. "Okay. A cup of tea would be nice."

"Great."

He filled the kettle with water and put it on the stovetop to boil before turning back to her. "How are you feeling? Last time I talked to you, you were pretty upset."

She waved her hand in dismissal. "I'm fine. I'm more interested in hearing how your meeting with the lawyer went today."

"It went pretty well, I think. She thinks we have a good chance of forcing Laura to give me visitation rights, especially since Tessa and I have such a strong bond, and I've been supporting her emotionally and financially since she was a baby."

"That's great news, but I thought your aim was to bring Tessa home for good."

"One step at a time. Laura's never going to win any mother of the year awards, but she's not a drug addict or mentally unstable. The court would have no reason to take custody away from her. And as long as she has legal sole custody, she gets to decide where Tessa lives."

"What is your lawyer going to do?"

"She's going to file a petition with the court alleging that I'm the unwed father of the child and that access to me is in Tessa's best interest. We're also going to petition the court to have me named Tessa's father. Laura didn't name anyone as Tessa's father on her birth certificate."

"Do you think she's going to deny to the court that you're Tessa's father?"

"I guess we'll find out. Once the petition to declare me Tessa's father is filed with the court, she'll be served the papers and then she'll have the opportunity to respond. She can either agree that I'm Tessa's father, or deny it."

"What happens if she denies it?"

"I'll have to file a request with the court for DNA testing. We'll find out for sure then." The possibility that the test could prove conclusively he wasn't Tessa's biological father weighed heavily on his heart.

Scarlet touched his hand. "Don't worry, Cameron. A DNA test is only going to prove you're Tessa's father. She looks so much like you. And there's a connection between the two of you that goes marrow deep. Laura can say whatever she wants, but she can't deny the truth."

He squeezed her hand. Somehow, she'd known the exact thing he needed to hear.

The kettle whistled and Cam placed tea bags in two mugs and filled them with hot water. He brought both mugs to the table and set one in front of Scarlet. "I hope we're doing the right thing."

"You absolutely are."

He grinned. "You sound very confident."

"I am. You and Tessa belong together."

He wrapped his hands around his mug and let the warmth seep into his bones. Despite the assurances from his family, he needed a boost of confidence like this from someone firmly in his corner.

He needed Scarlet.

The knowledge took his breath away. It was the first time he'd acknowledged, even to himself, how much he needed her in his life. "Thank you."

She smiled and sipped her tea. Cam removed the teabag from his mug and set it in a saucer.

"I have a confession to make," she said. "I despised Laura back in high school."

"Oh, really?"

"We competed over everything. Sports, class awards and especially boys. For some reason, Laura considered me her main rival."

He could understand why. Scarlet was smart and beautiful and would take the attention that Laura craved away from her.

Scarlet drank some of her tea before continuing. "Laura brought out the worst in me. She always had an uncanny knack of uncovering my most vulnerable spot and then picking at it until I exploded. She figured out my parents' deaths was an issue for me. She made sure everyone remembered their deaths were a murder/suicide."

"That's a cruel thing to do to a kid." But it didn't surprise him. Laura's beauty couldn't disguise the ugliness of her soul. He'd found that out the hard way.

"Yes. But that didn't excuse some of the things I did."

She told him about the schoolyard fights and name calling that eventually culminated in her stealing Laura's boyfriend to get back at her. "That was the end for me. I hurt innocent people, including my own boyfriend, and I embarrassed my grandparents. I'd stooped to Laura's level and I was ashamed. I'm still ashamed."

"You learned from your mistakes. Laura never did. She just kept repeating them."

"Bully for me. My point is, you're a far better parent than Laura ever will be. You're doing the right thing by fighting for Tessa. Don't ever doubt it." She set down her cup. "What's the first thing you're going to do when Tessa comes home?"

"The first thing I'm going to do, right after I give her a big hug and a kiss, is to cook her favorite meal. Spaghetti with red sauce and little meat balls. And you're invited." The exciting prospect of a welcome home dinner with Tessa and Scarlet made him grin.

Scarlet's smile was wistful. "If I'm still at the lodge, I'd love to welcome her home."

Her words wiped the grin from his face, and his excitement fizzled. He'd almost forgotten she was only in Minnewasta temporarily. He couldn't imagine not seeing her every day. "When do you have to go back to Chicago?"

"Late October. My employer was only willing to give me a five month leave of absence, and I can't really blame him. My co-workers can't cover for me forever."

Late October. About eight more weeks. Cam's heart pounded. So little time left...

They sat quietly drinking their tea. Cam struggled with his thoughts. Though they'd only known each other a short time, he couldn't imagine her not being in his life. It felt like he'd known Scarlet forever, like she was a part of him. He couldn't believe he'd have to watch her walk away at the end of October.

But he didn't have a choice. She had a career and a life to get back to. Time was running out. Maybe he should quit wasting it.

Scarlet finished the last of her tea and set her empty cup on the table as she got to her feet. "I should go. Thanks for the tea, Cameron."

She picked up her purse and slung it over her shoulder. Cam rose to his feet and stood in front of her, blocking her escape. "Scarlet..."

*Say it, Cam. Just say it.*

"Yes?"

"Scarlet, I...I don't want you to go."

She stood completely still. After a heartbeat, she whispered, "What are you asking, Cameron?"

He wasn't entirely sure himself. Was he asking for one more night or did he want more than that?

For now, one more night had to be enough. He caught her hand, running his rough thumb over her impossibly soft skin. "I'm asking you to stay with me tonight. I'm asking you to make love with me."

She stared into his eyes, with not so much as a blink to hint at her feelings. "I didn't plan this. I didn't deliberately hang around your house, waiting for you to come home."

"I know."

"I lose track of time when I'm working."

He squeezed her fingers. "I know, Scarlet. I'm not accusing you of trying to manipulate me. That's not your style. I'm asking because I want you."

"Are you sure we're not a bad idea? Especially after everything I've told you."

He couldn't let her believe the things she'd told him changed his feelings for her. "All I know is that when I'm with you, I'm happy."

Scarlet searched his face, as if looking for the truth of his words. Finally, one corner of her mouth turned up in a lopsided smile. "Okay."

"Okay?"

"Okay, I'll stay with you tonight. I'll make love with you." She stepped closer and touched his face. "I'm happy when I'm with you, too."

At her words, Cam's heart expanded, lightened, floated. He pressed a kiss into her palm, his lips lingering over the smooth skin. If this was the only night they had, he wanted to make it special for her.

He led her to his bedroom. When they were standing next to the bed, he cupped her face between his hands and kissed her. Her sigh against his mouth suggested she'd been waiting for his kiss, as if she wanted him as much as he wanted her.

As if she needed him as much as he needed her.

He pushed the thought away and concentrated on unbuttoning her shirt. He didn't want to think right now. He only wanted to feel.

When he finished undressing her, he stepped back and studied her. She was perfect, from her tousled hair to her pink painted toenails. An urge to draw her hit him with unexpected strength. He hadn't experienced such an urge since...he couldn't remember. He wanted to capture that look in her eyes, that combination of desire and vulnerability.

"You're staring." She crossed her arms over her breasts and lifted her chin. "Do I have spinach between my teeth, or something?"

Cam stifled a laugh. "No, your teeth are perfect. Just like the rest of you."

She rolled her eyes. “Hardly. Are you going to get undressed, or are we going to stand here talking all night?”

“Maybe you can help me.”

She stepped toward him, a little grin on her face, as she pulled his t-shirt from his jeans. “Have you suddenly forgotten how to undress yourself?”

“No, but I think I’ll like it better if you do it.”

“Well, then. Let’s find out if your theory is correct.”

He helped her slip his t-shirt over his head. As her clever hands worked to unbuckle his belt, she leaned forward to lick one flat nipple and then the other. Her breasts teased his chest, her taut nipples lightly grazing his skin and driving him wild. Then, she rubbed her palm over the zipper of his jeans. His cock strained against the denim and he had to take a deep breath to keep from losing it right there. His libido hadn’t been so out of control since he was a sixteen-year-old with a raging case of the hots for a cute cheerleader.

“Wench.” He unzipped his jeans and quickly pushed them out of the way. In one quick move, he lifted Scarlet into his arms and deposited her in the middle of the bed before covering her with his body. He braced himself on his forearms to take some of his weight off her. Her eyes were lit with amusement.

“So, have you decided if you like me undressing you?”

“You’re a terrible tease.”

“But you like it.”

He couldn’t help laughing at that. “Yeah, I do.”

She caressed the side of his face. “I’m glad.”

The tenderness in her blue eyes nearly undid him. “I don’t think I can wait very long.”

"Then don't."

It was all the invitation he needed. He pushed at the opening to her body with his cock, then pulled away, teasing her as she'd teased him. She whimpered, her body writhing.

"Impatient?"

She lifted her hips again, panting a little as she did so. "Yes!"

"Let me help you with that."

He inserted a finger inside her and she gasped, her eyes going wide. Her muscles tightened around his finger as her orgasm hit.

"Oh!" Her voice was breathless. "Oh, God!"

His own release was close. When her spasms eased, he left the bed briefly to affix a condom, then returned and covered her with his body once again. Her long legs wrapped around his waist and her arms encircled him, holding him close. He slipped easily inside her and for a moment, he remained still as he savored the exquisite feeling of being surrounded by her slick warmth.

But his impatient body demanded release. He began to move and she moved with him, matching every thrust.

Deeper, harder, faster.

"Cameron."

Her voice was barely a whisper, but he heard the wonder, the need.

The wanting.

He lost all control, all sense of time and space. There was only Scarlet, here in this bed. In this moment, she was his.

*All mine.*

"Cameron!"

Her body stiffened with her climax. He followed her over the edge, his release slamming him with the force of a freight train. Wave after wave of raw pleasure rolled over him, making his body shake uncontrollably. He clung to her, needing an anchor. Needing her.

His heart rate slowed by degrees, as did his breathing. Gradually, he returned to his body. For a short time, he'd been somewhere else with Scarlet, on a journey together to a faraway place. A place only they could go.

Cam chuckled at the notion. Sometimes his mind took weird flights of fancy.

"What are you laughing about?"

"I think I had an out of body experience."

Scarlet kissed his shoulder. "Funny, I was thinking the same thing."

He nestled her close against his side and kissed her hair, glad they'd made the journey together.

# Chapter Nineteen

IF SHE WAS A CAT, SHE'D be purring.

Scarlet snuggled against Cameron's chest, loving the solid feel of him and the spicy, woodsy scent of his aftershave. He gently stroked her hair and she relaxed completely, practically melting into the mattress.

She hoped she made Cameron even one-tenth as happy as he made her.

He pressed a kiss to her forehead. "Stay right here. Don't move."

He slipped out of her arms and off the bed. Without his warmth, Scarlet's skin instantly cooled, and she shivered. She pulled the sheet around her as she sat up. "Where are you going?"

"To my office. I'll be right back."

Bemused, she watched him leave the bedroom. For the first time she noticed that his naked backside was several shades lighter in color than the rest of his tanned skin. And what a backside it was. Silky skin stretched across taut muscles. Her fingers itched to touch him again.

A moment later he returned, a sketchpad and a pencil in hand. He sat on the edge of the bed, his gaze darting between her and the paper. Scarlet clutched the sheet, wrapping it a little more securely around her breasts. "What are you doing?"

"Drawing you." His hand flew across the paper. "I want to capture you in this moment."

Scarlet put a self-conscious hand to her tousled hair. "I'm a mess, Cameron. I probably look like a scarecrow."

"You look beautiful, like a woman who's just been made love to, thoroughly and completely."

His words made her smile. They were said casually, his attention riveted on his sketchpad, his face a study in concentration.

"Well, that makes sense, since I happen to be a woman who *has* just been made love to, most thoroughly and completely. Good job, by the way."

He looked up at her with a quick grin before returning his attention to his drawing. "Glad you enjoyed yourself."

A boldness she didn't know she possessed gripped her. She let the sheet slip down her body to reveal her breasts. "Oh, yes. I enjoyed myself very much."

He frowned at her. "You're distracting me."

"Oh, I'm sorry." She threw back the sheet and sat totally naked on the bed, her legs tucked beneath her. "I wouldn't want to discourage the pursuit of the arts."

Now she had his attention. "Come on, Scarlet. You're not playing fair."

"Oh, really?" She unfolded her legs and then spread them wide. "Am I a bad girl? Maybe I should be punished."

In one swift move, Cameron dropped his sketchpad to the floor and jumped on the bed, trapping her beneath his big body.

"Yes, you're a very bad girl. And I have a suitable punishment in mind for you."

Scarlet was breathless with desire she thought had been fully sated only a short time ago. But it seemed she couldn't get enough of Cameron. "What punishment is that?"

His erection nudged at the opening to her body, but stopped short of sinking inside her. His teasing drove her mad with desire. She lifted her hips, desperate to have him enter her.

"I have my ways."

She had to agree that he did. Did he have any idea what he did to her? One look at the smug grin on his face told her he knew exactly what he was doing.

Cameron slid down her body, kissing every inch of her skin as he went. He stopped to suck hard on her left nipple before doing the same to the right. Scarlet almost flew off the bed. The sensation tittered on the edge of pain but stayed firmly on the side of ecstasy. Wetness pooled between her legs and she squirmed beneath him. She wasn't above begging at this point. "Cameron, please."

He lifted his head from her breast, looking at her with one eyebrow raised and a smirk on his face. "Please, what?"

She groaned. "For God's sake, fuck me!"

His finger found her opening and he plunged inside. Scarlet arched her back and pushed against his hand.

He kissed his way around her breast. "Is this what you wanted?"

"Yes, yes." She was breathless, her heart racing. "But I want more. So much more."

He put another finger inside her. Impossibly stretched, she was at her breaking point.

She'd never had better sex.

"Is this enough?" he whispered.

"No, not enough."

"We can't have you unfulfilled."

To her dismay, he removed his fingers. Before she could utter a protest, he slid down her body to the apex of her thighs, pushed her legs apart, and covered her pussy with his mouth. He licked and stroked and sucked until she was a mass of writhing need.

Then, his tongue found the sensitive nub of nerves that sent her over the edge. Her orgasm exploded out of her in wave after wave of rapture. She heard someone scream and with a start, she realized it was her.

But Cameron wasn't done. He stayed with her, sucking and licking until another orgasm began building once more. This time, when it came, she was more prepared for it. She savored the bliss of her release and the exquisite sensations Cameron had wrung from her body. She had no idea she was capable of feeling such pleasure.

It was all Cameron. She'd never experienced this with any other man.

All too soon, Cameron kissed the inside of her thigh and rolled away from her, leaving the bed as he affixed another condom. Scarlet couldn't do much more than whimper. She was boneless, her limbs as liquid as jelly. She'd never been more completely sated, or happy, in her life. Despite everything going on with Tessa, and despite everything still unsaid between her and Cameron, she'd never known more blissful, joyful happiness.

Because she was in love.

"You're smiling." Cameron returned to the bed and covered her body with his, his breath warm against her ear. His big hand gently caressed her breast.

"Am I?" She could feel her smile stretch across her face. "Maybe that's because I have an amazing lover who knows how to please me."

"Oh, yeah?"

"Oh, yeah." She opened her eyes and laughed at the self-satisfied look on his face. "I shouldn't have told you that. You're probably going to be insufferably smug now."

"I'm simply pleased you're satisfied."

*Oh, yes. Completely satisfied.* "I'm pretty pleased about that, too."

He kissed the end of her nose before straddling her and settling between her thighs. Though she'd thought herself exhausted and completely done, her body began to stir once more at the feel of his erection pushing against the opening to her body. She laughed out loud.

He gave her a bemused grin. "Why are you laughing?"

"Because I can't believe I want you again. I can't seem to get enough of you."

The look of amusement left his face. He tenderly caressed her face. "I can't seem to get enough of you either."

She loved him more in that moment than she'd ever thought possible, more than she ever thought she was capable of. She lifted her hand and ran her fingers through his thick, silky hair. It was on the tip of her tongue to tell him she loved him, but fear held her back. What if he didn't feel the same? What if this thing between them was only about sex for him?

Instead, she made herself smile. "We're pretty amazing together, aren't we?"

"Yeah, we are."

Their lovemaking was less frenzied this time, but no less satisfying. They explored each other's body, discovering where each liked to be touched, caressed, kissed.

When they climaxed together, it was the most beautiful thing Scarlet had ever experienced.

Hollowness slowly replaced her earlier fulfillment. A refrain played over and over in her head.

*I don't want to leave him.*

THE NEXT MORNING, CAM followed Scarlet's car back to the lodge, his body still buzzing from the night before. She was amazing – beautiful, funny, smart and sexy as hell. The things they'd done to each other...

He shifted in his seat, his erection pushing painfully against the zipper of his jeans. After they'd made love that second time, he'd picked up his sketchpad and finished his pencil drawing. He didn't fully understand his compulsion to draw her. He'd never drawn any other woman he'd slept with, but Scarlet was different. He'd needed to record the sexy toss of her disheveled hair and, especially, her smile of satisfaction after making love.

He was probably stupid to become so involved with her when he was in the middle of a battle for his daughter. But he couldn't imagine saying goodbye to her either. He needed her and not simply for sex.

Was he in love with Scarlet?

The thought sent a cold shiver of fear down his backbone. He'd thought he'd been in love with Laura, and she stomped all over his love and his life. He'd nearly drunk himself into oblivion when she'd taken Tessa and left him.

It wasn't fair to compare Scarlet with Laura. But they did have one thing in common; Scarlet was going to leave him, the same as Laura had. But at least this time, he knew it was coming.

He'd be smart about this. He wouldn't let himself get too close. They could have some fun and some great sex while she was in Minnewasta, and part as friends when she left.

A niggling voice in his brain warned that he was fooling himself, but he pushed the voice aside, not wanting to acknowledge it. He had a game plan.

They reached the cottages and parked next to each other on the side of the road. Scarlet got out of her car and walked towards his truck. Cam got out and closed his door.

She looked toward the cottage she shared with her sister. "I'm not sure what to say to them."

"You called Maggie last night. She knows you were with me."

"Yes, but..." She bit her bottom lip, her brow furrowed in worry. "What do I tell them? Maggie asked if this meant we were together, a couple, and I didn't know what to say, so I didn't say anything. What are we, Cameron? Lovers? Fuck buddies? Friends with benefits? What do I tell them?"

She made what they'd shared sound so vulgar. "I'm not sure you have to tell them anything. We're consenting adults, and what we do is no one's business but ours." He cupped her cheek. "But if you want to tell them something, say we enjoy each other's company. And as long as you're in Minnewasta, we'll continue to see each other."

She stared at him, her blue eyes unblinking in that unnerving way she had that completely veiled her thoughts. Then she nodded, wrapping a strand of her hair around one of her fingers and tugging on it. A flash of disappointment raced across her face.

She quickly recovered, released her hair and gave him a smile. "That sounds...reasonable. Let's go have breakfast."

She stepped toward the cottage, but Cam stopped her with a hand on her arm. "Wait a minute, Scarlet. The last thing I want is to hurt you, but this, this thing we have together, is all I can offer. If it's not enough for you, maybe we should end it right now and agree to go our separate ways."

He held his breath as he waited for her reply, unable to read her thoughts as she stared at him once more. He was surprised by how much he feared she would agree and tell him they were finished.

At last, she smiled. "I agree with your proposition, Mr. Hainstock. I needed to know where we stood. I'll tell my sisters we're together, for now. Why shouldn't we enjoy each other while I'm here?"

Cam let out a relieved breath. "Good. Now let's go have breakfast. I'm starved."

When they walked into the cottage, everyone was seated around the table. A sense of déjà vu hit Cam when they all stopped talking and turned to look at them, the way they had the last time they'd slept together and arrived for breakfast the next morning. He didn't much like the family knowing about their sex life, but he could live with it. Scarlet, however, might not be able to, no matter what she'd told him.

"Good morning, everyone," Scarlet said. "Why don't we get a couple of things out in the open right now? Yes, Cameron and I slept together, and we'll continue to do so until I leave here in a few weeks."

Cam stifled a grin. Her directness surprised the hell out of him.

"So I suggest you get used to it and keep your opinions to yourselves. Now, what's for breakfast, Maggie?"

Maggie blinked at her a couple of times before getting to her feet. "I can make omelets for you, if you like."

"Thank you. That sounds great."

Cam caught Scarlet's hand and gave it a squeeze. The little voice in his head screamed that her casual approach to their relationship wasn't what he wanted at all, but he ignored it. He'd been left behind before, but at least this time he knew it was coming.

At least this time, he couldn't be hurt.

# Chapter Twenty

WHEN CAM'S PHONE RANG and he saw his lawyer's name on the screen, he took a few steps away from the worksite. "Hi, Erin."

"Hello, Cam. I'm sorry to take you away from your work, but we've had some news, and I thought you'd like to know right away."

"Yes, I do. What's going on?"

Erin Cochrane's voice came across the telephone as businesslike, but kind. "We've served Laura with our petition. Her lawyer got back to me right away. She's maintaining that Tessa is not your biological daughter and since no father is listed on Tessa's birth certificate, our next move is to file a request with the court for DNA testing."

Cam's stomach dropped into his work boots. He'd hoped to avoid the DNA test because he wasn't sure what it might reveal. "What happens if the test says I'm not her biological father?"

Erin hesitated a moment before speaking. "If that's the case, it gets a little more complicated. We can argue that because of your close emotional bond to Tessa, and the fact that you supported her financially since birth, you should be named her *de facto* parent."

"What does that mean?"

"It literally means you are her acting parent. If the court deems it to be in the best interest of the child, a non-biological person can be named as a *de facto* parent and be given sole or split custody, or visitation rights. I think we can make a solid argument for that, but I can't promise you anything."

Despite Erin's cautious optimism, Cam was afraid Tessa could be lost to him forever. "I see."

"Do you have reason to believe someone else fathered Tessa?"

"No, but then I don't have any proof that I'm her father either. I slept with Laura around the time Tessa was conceived and when Laura found out she was pregnant, she told me I was the father. But I didn't know her well at the time. I found out later she has a hard time with the truth." He sighed. "And I was drinking in those days. A lot. I could have missed some of the cues. But I know, deep in my gut, that Tessa's my daughter. We have a bond, a connection so strong that it has to be based in blood."

"Let's take things one step at a time. First, we'll ask the court to order DNA testing. Once we get the results, either way, we'll come up with a game plan. Deal?"

What else could they do? "Deal."

"Paternity testing usually takes three to five business days from the time all the samples arrive in the laboratory. I'll text you the name and address of the lab in Minneapolis I use. Because we're using the legal test kit that satisfies the chain of evidence requirements of the court, you'll need to go to the lab so the sample you give can be witnessed and documented properly. We will require Tessa's sample to be obtained in the same way."

"Will Tessa have to provide a blood sample?" He hated the idea of causing her any pain, even if it was for a good cause.

"No, that's not necessary. DNA is collected by rubbing a brush gently inside the mouth against the cheek for fifteen seconds. The collection will be safe and painless for both you and Tessa."

Cam sighed in relief. "Good. I'll contact the clinic as soon as I get your information."

"All right. I don't want you to worry, Cam. Whatever happens, we'll figure it out."

"I only want what's best for Tessa."

"I know you do. That's why I'm representing you."

He chuckled at her candid statement. "So, if I'd been some kind of deadbeat dad?"

"I likely would have shown you the door after our first meeting. But you're not. I know you love your daughter."

Cam closed his eyes against the pain. If the DNA test proved he wasn't Tessa's father, he could lose contact with her, especially if Laura decided to stay in California. He'd miss her horribly, but that wasn't the main issue. Laura couldn't be trusted to look after Tessa properly and give her the care and attention she needed. Laura's number one concern had always been Laura.

"Thanks Erin. I appreciate everything you've done for us."

They said goodbye. A few moments later, Cam received Erin's text with the name and contact information for the lab in Minneapolis. He phoned the lab right away and made an appointment for the following Monday. After recording the time of the appointment in his phone, he stuck it in his pocket and headed back to work.

Frustration gnawed at his gut. He hated being so totally powerless. The fate of his daughter was out of his hands, and there was nothing he could do except give a cheek swab and wait. Patience had never been one of his virtues.

*I need a drink.*

He pushed the thought away, frightened by its intensity. His sobriety was hard earned and precious. He couldn't succumb now. Tessa needed him.

His determination calmed him. Tessa needed him to be strong right now. And sober.

So that's what he'd be.

SCARLET SNUGGLED AGAINST Cameron's chest, breathing in his scent and luxuriating in the warmth of his embrace. She loved making love with Cameron. She loved the way he made her feel and the closeness they shared. Cameron took her to heights she'd never reached before. But lying in his arms after making love was fast becoming the best part of her day. There was an intimacy about being together this way that made her feel almost...loved.

She bit her lip. That was dangerous thinking.

"What was that for?" Cameron asked.

Scarlet looked up into his face. "What do you mean?"

"That little sigh and the furrow between your brows. Did you know your forehead wrinkles when you're deep in thought?"

"No, I didn't know. Sorry."

He kissed the spot in question, his warm lips lingering for a moment. "Don't be sorry. What are you thinking about?"

"About how lovely it is to be here with you." It was the truth, or at least part of it.

"And that made you frown?"

"No, not at all. But I was thinking we only have a few more weeks." She was pretty sure that when she returned to Chicago, her heart wouldn't be making the journey with her. She'd miss him terribly, but she didn't want to dwell on it or make him feel bad.

Cameron kissed her hair. "Yeah, I've been thinking about that, too."

"Really?" She didn't dare look into his face.

"Yeah. I don't want to waste a single day of those we have left. Why don't you come to Minneapolis with me tomorrow?"

Tomorrow was Sunday. "I thought your appointment at the lab was on Monday."

"It is. But I thought it might be fun to go into the city a day early. We could go shopping, maybe go to movie or a museum. Whatever you want. Later, we can find a nice restaurant and have dinner, and we can spend the night at Ethan's condo. What do you think?"

She looked up at him with a smile. "I think that sounds nice."

He brushed her hair from her forehead, his eyes serious. "You deserve something nice for a change."

"What do you mean, for a change?"

"Do you realize I've never taken you anywhere, aside from my bedroom?"

"Do you hear me complaining?"

"No, but you deserve more. You deserve a real relationship with someone who takes you places and buys nice things for you."

"I'm not looking for a Sugar Daddy. And for the record, we do have a real relationship." Even if its shelf life was limited.

"I know. I just..." He shook his head.

"Cameron." She clasped his chin and gently forced him to look at her. "You don't owe me anything. I'm happy the way things are. But I would be pleased to go to the city with you tomorrow. You can wine and dine me to your heart's content."

He lowered his mouth to hers, his kiss warm and soft and full of passion. Scarlet loved him so much she could barely breathe.

She didn't know how she was supposed to live without him.

SCARLET THREW SOME panties into her overnight bag. She wished she had something sexier, but all she'd brought with her from Chicago was serviceable cotton. Maybe one of the stops they could make on the shopping excursion Cameron had promised would be to a lingerie shop. Maybe she'd even let him pick out something he wanted her to wear.

"What are you grinning about?" Harper folded the skirt Scarlet had laid out and placed it in the bag.

"I was thinking about shopping. Other than for groceries or hardware, I haven't set foot inside a store since I got here. It'll be fun shopping with Cameron."

Harper picked up a blouse and carefully folded it. "Are you sure you know what you're doing?"

Scarlet's pleasant bubble of happiness burst at her sister's tone. "Please, don't start."

"I hate to keep ragging on you, but I'm worried about you. And I'm worried about Cam, too. So is Ethan. What happens when you go back to Chicago?"

"We've talked about it." She couldn't meet her sister's eyes. "We both know this relationship comes with an expiry date, and we're prepared for that. In the meantime, we want to enjoy each other's company. Is that so terrible?"

"No, of course not. But I don't want you to get hurt."

"Harper, I told you before, I'll be fine." She stopped packing to grab her sister's hand. "I love you for caring, but you have to let me live my life."

From the set of Harper's mouth, Scarlet knew her sister wanted to argue, but instead she nodded. "All right. I'll stop nagging."

"Thank you." Scarlet sighed in relief. She didn't know if her show of bravado could stand up to scrutiny.

"I know you're keeping secrets, whether about your relationship with Cam or something else." Harper's bottom lip trembled. "I want you to know that if you ever want to talk, you can come to me. Whatever it is you think you can't tell me, it doesn't matter. I don't care. I only care about you. I love you, and I only want you to be happy."

Scarlet stared into her sister's blue eyes, eyes so similar to her own. She wanted so much to unburden herself, to tell her what she saw and heard on the last day of their parents' lives. But she couldn't do it. She couldn't ruin her sister's memories. She wouldn't transfer the burden she'd carried all these years to Harper. "I want you to be happy, too."

Disappointment flitted across Harper's face. Whatever else she was feeling was quickly covered with a smile as she squeezed Scarlet's hand. "I mean it. Any time you want to talk, about anything, I'm here."

Scarlet nodded, tears threatening to fall. She quickly withdrew her hand and turned back to her packing. "I should finish. Cameron will be here in any minute."

Harper picked up the blouse she'd abandoned and placed it in the bag. "Yes, of course. You'll be home sometime on Monday?"

"Yeah, probably by noon. Cameron's appointment at the lab is at nine a.m. They told him the cheek swab only takes a few minutes."

"I really hope everything goes well. Cam and Tessa belong together."

"Yes, they do." Again, tears threatened. She had to squeeze her eyes shut once more. When she recovered, she quickly zipped the bag shut and lifted it from her bed. "That should be everything I need."

"Don't forget to take a jacket. I heard it's going to rain tomorrow."

Scarlet had to smile. Old habits died hard. Harper would probably never stop trying to mother her and Maggie, even though they were adults now.

But somehow, it comforted her to know her sister wanted to protect her, even if it was only from a late summer shower.

"I'll make sure to do that." On a sudden impulse, she dropped her bag and threw her arms around Harper, hugging her with every bit of affection she held in her heart. "I love you."

Harper's arms closed around her and held on tight. "I love you, too."

SCARLET'S HAIR GLOWED like burnished copper in the candlelight. Cam couldn't stop staring, mesmerized by her smile and the sparkle in her eyes. He'd always known she was attractive; he'd figured that out the moment he first met her. But tonight, her beauty radiated from somewhere deep inside, as if a candle burned inside her heart. He wanted to bask in the warmth of that candle for the rest of his life.

He had a sudden desire to draw her the way he had the other night. He wanted to capture the glow in her eyes, her happiness.

She cocked her head to one side. "You're very quiet tonight. What are you thinking about?"

"You," he said truthfully. He reached across the table to hold her hand. "I can't take my eyes off you tonight. You're beautiful."

She gave him a self-conscious grin. “It must be the dim light in this place. It’s affecting your eyesight.”

“My eyesight is just fine.” Maybe he was seeing clearly for the first time in his life. “You’re the most beautiful woman in the room.”

She leaned forward and lowered her voice, a smile in her eyes and on her lips. “You don’t have to butter me up, you know. I’m already thinking about what I want to do with you later in bed.”

His cock instantly sprang to attention at her words. His first inclination was to signal the waiter to bring their bill, so he could pay it and get her back to the condo pronto. But when he looked into her eyes, he realized she didn’t quite believe him when he said she was beautiful.

He squeezed her fingers. “I should have told you before how beautiful I think you are. I’ve known it since the moment I met you. But what I didn’t know then was how beautiful you are on the inside. The way you are with Tessa, and with me, that’s true beauty. That’s something that will never fade.”

She blinked several times, and he saw her throat work as if she was swallowing back her tears. “I could say the exact same thing to you, you know. You’re a beautiful man.”

“Physical beauty is nice, but it doesn’t mean anything unless there’s a beautiful heart, too. My dad was a handsome man. I saw the pictures from my parents’ wedding and the way my mother looked at him, like he was some sort of god. But what she didn’t know then was that his heart was black inside. He didn’t care about anyone, not even himself.” He hadn’t meant to bare his soul tonight. And the last person he wanted to think about was his father. He closed his eyes and averted his face.

"You're nothing like him." She held his hand between the two of hers. "You've got a beautiful heart, too. You couldn't be the father you are to Tessa if you didn't. You couldn't say the sweet things to me that you do, couldn't treat me with such tenderness the way you do, if your heart wasn't so completely beautiful."

He stared at her, his heart pounding in his chest. Maybe they could make it work. Maybe they could beat the odds. For her, he wanted to be the best man he could be. He could no longer imagine his life without her in it.

Did that mean he was in love with her? Or had the candlelight gone to his head tonight?

She touched his cheek. "Why don't we get out of here? I've got plans for you, remember?"

"I remember."

The time it took to settle their bill and drive back to the condo gave Cam the opportunity to think. He cared about Scarlet, and he liked her, a lot. But love? He wasn't sure he was capable of the kind of love she deserved.

It was selfish, he knew, but he had to stick to his game plan. He'd take whatever Scarlet was willing to give in the next few weeks. And when the time came, he'd let her go. As long as he was in control, he couldn't get hurt.

He ignored the gut feeling that said he was kidding himself.

THEY ARRIVED AT THE lab the next morning, a full twenty minutes before his scheduled appointment at nine a.m. Cam had woken early, too anxious about the results of the DNA test to sleep. He'd woken Scarlet with a kiss and made love to her before the sun had fully risen. Waking with her beside him, warm and sweet smelling, had eased some of the tension.

But now, as they sat in the waiting room, the tension began to build again. If they discovered Tessa had been fathered by someone else, he'd have a few legal options, but they were far from a sure thing. Fear churned in his gut. He couldn't give up his child. No one could love her, care for her, the way he did.

Scarlet put her hand on his knee, stopping him from bobbing it up and down. "Slow down, Cameron. It's going to be all right."

He hadn't realized what he was doing. Nerves were getting the best of him. "Sorry."

"It's okay. They said the procedure is painless, didn't they?"

"It's not that. What if she's not mine?"

She squeezed his hand. "She is. I can feel it."

"You keep saying that. I wish I could believe it."

"You told me once that no matter what any tests say, she's your baby. She'll always be your baby. Nothing will change that."

Cam rested his elbows on his knees and leaned forward. His boots were scuffed and dusty, and he wondered when he'd last polished them. His memory flashed to Tessa wearing her tutu and trying to walk in his boots, the tops up to her thighs. They'd both laughed when she tripped and landed on the living room floor in a heap of tulle.

"No, nothing will change that."

Nothing would ever change his love for Tessa, but everything could change about their relationship. Laura wanted Tessa to call her new boyfriend Daddy. The idea made his gut twist. Would he know she didn't like apples but loved oranges? Would he read to her before bed each night so she was able to sleep?

A woman in white scrubs appeared at the door of the waiting room. "Mr. Hainstock? We're ready for you now."

Scarlet squeezed his hand one last time and Cam got to his feet. After a thorough check of his identification, they were ready to start. As promised, the procedure lasted only a few seconds and was completely painless. He watched as the technician dropped the swab used to brush the inside of his cheek into a container already marked with his name. She twisted the lid shut.

"We'll seal your sample in a tamper-evident package. When it arrives at the laboratory in California, the staff there will check to see if the package seal is intact. If it is, your DNA samples will be compared to Tessa's. We make every effort to ensure all the evidence arrives at the lab without being tampered with in any way," she said.

Cam nodded and thanked her for her help. When he returned to the waiting area, Scarlet jumped to her feet, appearing anxious. She tried to hide her tension with a smile, but she wasn't fooling him. She was as worried about Tessa's future as he was.

"Ready to go?"

"Yeah. Let's get out of here."

He grasped her hand and they walked out into the September sunshine. The changing color of the leaves reminded him that their time together was growing ever shorter.

"Would you like to stop somewhere and grab some breakfast?" she asked. "You didn't eat anything this morning."

Cam didn't think he could keep anything down. "No, I think I'd like to get home. Unless you'd like to eat?"

"No, I'm fine." She threaded her arm through his. "Let's go home."

Though they said very little on the two-hour drive back to the lodge, Scarlet touched his arm or his thigh every once in a while. She smiled each time he turned to look at her, as if she'd been reading his mind, attuned to his every thought.

He didn't want this time with her to be over. As they approached Minnewasta, he was suddenly seized with a need for her that was so strong he nearly stopped his truck on the side of the road to reach for her. Instead, he gripped the steering wheel and made himself drive on.

"What do you say we play hooky from work today?" Scarlet said.

"I don't know. We both have a lot to do."

She waved her hand as if waving away his concerns. "The world can get by without us for one day. Why don't we spend the day at your place? In bed."

He slid her a sidelong glance. She appeared perfectly calm and composed. Somehow, she'd known how much he needed her.

He wasn't a fool. As long as she was in Minnesota, he'd take anything she cared to offer. At the next intersection, Cam turned toward his place. "That's the best offer I've had all day."

# Chapter Twenty-One

SCARLET ADDED SOME work-in-progress pictures of the lodge to the website and to the Facebook page. The lodge's social media was steadily gaining followers. Many of them were locals who were curious about the progress of the project and whether the lodge really could succeed, but an increasing number of views were coming from out of state. She hoped that interest would translate into bookings once the lodge reopened.

*Once the lodge reopened.* By the time that happened, she'd be back in Chicago. What if Cameron asked her to stay? What would she do?

There was no point pretending, especially to herself. If Cameron asked her to stay, then she'd stay. Even if he said nothing about marriage or made any promises about the rest of their lives together, she wouldn't leave him. Not if he wanted her.

The irony of the situation made her smile. For the first time, she'd found someone she wouldn't, couldn't, run away from, and he might be the one doing the running. Nothing could be settled between them until the situation with Tessa was resolved. Unease made her shiver. If the DNA test proved Cameron wasn't her father, he'd be devastated, especially if it meant he could no longer see her.

She closed her eyes and breathed deeply, one hand over her stomach to stop the ache. Cameron *had* to be Tessa's father.

A week had passed since he'd given his DNA sample. They hadn't talked about it, but she knew they were both on tenterhooks as they waited for the results. She was trying to be patient, but the interminable wait was killing her. Worse, it was killing Cameron. There was a sort of desperation in his lovemaking that had increased as the week wore on. Though they'd talked about all the secrets of their pasts, about things Scarlet thought she'd never be able to talk about outside her therapist's office, somehow neither of them could bring themselves to talk about what would happen if Tessa was no longer in their lives.

The sound of a car driving into Cameron's yard diverted her attention away from her disquieting thoughts. When she went to the window of the office, she saw Harper's truck come to a stop in the side yard. Harper and Maggie got out of the cab, her younger sister carrying a basket. Scarlet went to the front door to greet them.

"What are you guys doing here? Aren't you supposed to be serving coffee at the worksite?"

"Don't worry, we haven't abandoned the guys. We left drinks and cookies at the site. We wanted to see you," Harper said.

"I saw you at lunch."

"It's not the same," Maggie said, setting her basket on the kitchen table and taking out a container of cookies. "The men are there, and we don't have a chance to really talk."

Scarlet nodded. Since she'd been staying with Cameron at his place, and having only the occasional meal with her sisters, there hadn't been much opportunity to share her feelings with them.

"Would you like tea?"

Harper smiled. "We'd love some."

Once the tea was made, Scarlet poured them each a cup. Harper lifted hers to her lips and took a small sip before asking, "How's Cameron coping, really? Every time we ask him, he says he's fine, that he's taking one day at a time. But we're worried about him."

"So am I," Scarlet confessed. "He doesn't talk to me either, but I know he's worried. He doesn't sleep much. I hear him wandering around the house like a ghost in the middle of the night. The other night I woke up at three in the morning to an empty bed. When I went to look for him, he was asleep in Tessa's room." Seeing him sleeping in Tessa's tiny bed had nearly broken her heart.

"He loves that little girl so much," Maggie said. "I can't imagine how scary it is for him to know he could lose her."

"Cameron's devoted to Tessa."

Harper reached across the table to grasp her hand. "And what about you? You spent a lot of time with Tessa over the summer, and I know you two are close. How are you dealing with all this?"

Scarlet's blinked back tears. Trust Harper to see right through her.

"I keep thinking about how she must feel, so far away in California. I worry that she's scared and lonely, and I'm afraid Laura's not looking after her properly. I'm worried about what she's telling Tessa about Cameron. The last time Laura allowed her to talk to him on the phone, she told him her mom wants her to call her boyfriend Daddy. She was confused and scared. She asked Cameron when she can come home." Scarlet's throat burned. "I'm afraid for her."

Harper came around the table to sit beside her. She rubbed her back while Maggie leaned her head against her shoulder, both silently lending comfort and letting her know they were on her side.

"You love Tessa, too, honey. You might as well acknowledge it," Harper said.

Scarlet nodded and dabbed at her eyes. It was true. She loved Tessa as if she were her own child. She'd be devastated if she were no longer in her life.

"Please don't tell Cameron I'm upset. He's got enough to deal with without worrying about my feelings."

Maggie stroked her hair. "You're trying so hard to be brave for him. Who's going to be brave for you?"

"We will," Harper said decisively. "You don't have to be brave because we'll be brave for you."

Tears filled her eyes as she put her arms around Harper. "Thank you."

"You're welcome, honey." Harper hugged her a little tighter. "I know you love Cam, and want the best for him, the same way we want the best for you."

Scarlet leaned back to look into her sister's face. She supposed it was obvious to anyone who knew her as well as Harper and Maggie did that she was in love with Cameron. She couldn't even pretend to hide it.

"For the record," Maggie said, laying her hand on her shoulder. "I think he loves you, too."

She turned to smile at her. She hoped Maggie was right. And she hoped that whatever Cameron felt for her, it was strong enough to weather the storms that were coming their way.

CAM'S PHONE RANG WHILE he was up on a stepladder, nailing strips of pine to the ceiling of the front porch of one of the cottages. When he saw Erin Cochrane's law office calling, a cold bead of sweat broke out on his brow. This was it.

His hand shook as he answered the call. "Hello?"

"Hello, Cam?"

"Yes, it's Cam. Do you have some news for me, Erin?"

The lawyer cleared her throat before continuing. "I do, but it's not good. I'm sorry, Cam, but the DNA test proves conclusively that you are not Tessa's father."

A loud buzzing filled his ears and he swayed, nearly losing his balance on the ladder. He thought he'd prepared himself for this possibility, but he was wrong. Shockwaves screamed through his system.

*I need a drink. Just one drink.*

Erin continued. "I haven't given up. We're immediately filing a motion with the court to name you a *de facto* parent. The courts have granted visitation rights in situations where the adult has had such a close relationship with the child that the child treats them as if they were their parent. That's certainly been the case with you and Tessa. We may not be able to get a shared custody arrangement, but we'll do our best to find a way for you to have some kind of access to Tessa. And I've engaged a private investigator to dig into Laura's activities."

There was no point. He appreciated the effort, but they both knew it was hopeless. Why prolong the agony?

He had to end the call. "Thanks for calling, Erin. I appreciate everything you've done."

"I'll be in touch if I have any more news."

"Thank you." He quickly turned off the phone and rested his forehead against one of rungs as a wave of dizziness overcame him. When it passed, he climbed down the ladder and staggered to the stairs of the cottage, gripping the handrail for support. Charlie was walking toward him carrying a load of pine boards for the ceiling. He hastily dropped the boards and helped Cam down the stairs.

"You don't look so good, boss. Do you want me to call Ethan?"

"No. It's just a bug. I'm going home. I'll see you tomorrow."

Charlie didn't look convinced. "You want me to drive you home?"

"Thanks, no. I'll be fine."

Cam walked to his truck, concentrating on keeping one foot in front of the other and staying upright. When he reached the truck, he climbed inside the cab and turned the ignition.

*I need a drink.*

He tried to fight the feeling, but he simply didn't have the strength anymore. What did it matter now that Tessa was gone?

*Scarlet matters. She needs you to be sober.*

Cam bent over the steering wheel. *Scarlet.* The news about Tessa would kill her. He couldn't tell her right now. He couldn't bear to see the pain in her eyes, couldn't face her tears. If she held back her tears, he couldn't stand her trying to be brave for him.

He just couldn't.

He put the truck into gear and pulled away from the cottages, breathing a sigh of relief when he reached the highway. All he wanted was to drive, to put some distance between him and the devastating news he'd been handed. But he could drive to the ends of the earth and still know he was no longer Tessa's father.

But there were ways to forget.

WHEN SCARLET PULLED up in front of Maggie's cottage late that afternoon, the first thing she noticed was that Cameron's truck was missing. He usually left it next to the cottage during the day and drove it back to his house after dinner. A feeling of foreboding lodged in her stomach. Something was wrong.

Ethan turned to her the minute she walked through the door. "Is Cam with you?"

"No, I haven't seen him since this morning. What's happened?"

He ran his hand through his hair. "Charlie said he went home sick shortly after lunch. He didn't show up?"

"No, I've been at the house all day. I haven't heard from him."

"I didn't think anything of it when Charlie told me Cam went home sick, but I just got a call from Lydia," Ethan continued. "Cam's lawyer called her with the results of the DNA test. Erin said she called Cam right after lunch to tell him the DNA says he's not Tessa's father."

Scarlet leaned against the nearest chair, her legs threatening to buckle. "Dear God."

"And now Cam's missing. I tried to call him, but his phone is off."

"What do we do?"

"We have to look for him. We have to find him before—"

Ethan stopped talking and turned his head. Harper put her arms around his waist and rested her head against his chest.

Scarlet finished for him. "Before he starts drinking again."

Three years of sobriety. He'd quit to be a better father to Tessa. But now that she'd been taken away from him...Scarlet closed her eyes against the pain. She'd deal with Tessa's loss later. Right now, she had to concentrate on Cameron.

The ringing of Ethan's phone made Scarlet jump. He checked the caller ID and quickly answered. "Reese. What's going on?"

Ethan listened silently for a moment before he spoke again. "Scarlet and Harper and Maggie are with me at

Maggie's cottage. I'm going to put you on speakerphone. Say again what you told me."

Reese's voice crackled through the airwaves. "Cam called and asked me to pick him up at a roadhouse outside of Brainerd. He's been drinking. I'm on my way there right now."

Scarlet covered her mouth to stifle a cry. Ethan put his arm around Harper, his face full of misery. He filled Reese in on the situation with Tessa.

"Why did he call you instead of me? I'm his brother. Why wouldn't he trust me?"

"I guess because he knows I'm an alcoholic, too. He knows I've been where he is now."

Ethan sighed, resigned. "What can we do?"

"You can pick up his truck at the roadhouse. I'll leave his keys under the seat. Then, you can stay with him at his place tonight. He shouldn't be alone."

Scarlet brushed away her tears. Cameron needed her to be strong right now. "I'll meet you at his house."

"I'm sorry, Scarlet," Reese said. "He said he doesn't want you to see him like this. Can you stay with your sisters?"

The pain hit hard, fast and unexpected. He was in his greatest hour of need, and he didn't want her. Maggie wrapped her arms around Scarlet's waist and she clung to her.

"If that's what he wants. Tell him I'll see him tomorrow."

"Okay. I'm almost there. I'll call you later, Ethan."

"Thanks, Reese."

He ended the call and for several moments they stood motionless, too shocked to move or speak. Finally, Maggie broke the silence. "I'm going to make tea." She gave Scarlet one last hug before letting go.

Scarlet couldn't move, could barely breathe. Tessa wasn't Cameron's daughter. He was drinking again. It was too much.

Ethan let out a long breath, the sound weary and sad. "Harper, can you drive me to the roadhouse to pick up Cam's truck? I don't want him to be alone for long."

"Of course."

Ethan grasped Scarlet's hand. "He'll be all right." He spoke as much to himself as to her. "This has been a terrible shock for him, for all of us, but Cam will get through this. He'll want to see you tomorrow."

Scarlet managed a nod. She prayed he would get past the loss of his daughter without totally losing his sobriety. She knew how hard he'd worked for it, how much it meant to him.

Cameron might come through it, but she wasn't sure she would. All she could think was that when it mattered most, he didn't want her.

# Chapter Twenty-Two

CAM GLANCED AT REESE as he climbed onto the stool next to him at the bar. The bartender appeared a moment later. "What can I get you?"

"Coffee, black, two sugars," Reese said.

"And you?" The bartender tipped his chin toward the untouched glass of Crown and coke in front of him. "You want another one of those, or do you want coffee, too?"

"No. Nothing."

"Suit yourself." The bartender shrugged and moved away.

"How many of those have you had?" Reese asked.

"A couple."

"How come you haven't touched that one?"

*Good question*. Cam had been staring at the glass for the last thirty minutes. He'd downed the first two drinks within the first ten minutes of arriving at the roadhouse. But after ordering the third, he hesitated. Another drink would lead to another and another and the sweet oblivion he sought. The remembered taste beckoned, enticed, tormented.

So, why was he still sitting here staring at it?

Reese's coffee arrived and he took his time tearing open the paper packets of sugar and pouring them into his cup.

He stirred slowly, his movements unhurried. "Why are you punishing yourself?"

"I'm not doing that."

"Like hell you aren't. First you break your sobriety and then you torture yourself with booze. You might as well hold a loaded gun to your head. Either one is going to kill you, one just faster than the other."

"You don't know what you're talking about."

Reese ignored him. "Ethan told me about the results of the DNA test. You're punishing yourself for not being Tessa's biological father? I hate to break it to you, but that was never within your control."

"I'm not punishing myself, I'm grieving. She's not my daughter! Do you know what that means?" Cam hissed the words at Reese. "I may never see her again. I'll never kiss her goodnight, or teach her how to ride a bike. I won't give her away at her wedding."

His voice caught on a sob. He closed his eyes and held his breath, his hands fisting on the bar. He didn't want to lose it here, with the bartender and the rest of the crowd watching.

"I understand what you're going through, more than you know. You've got two choices right now. You can drink yourself into a stupor, or you can choose to live. As someone who chose the drinking route, I don't recommend it. And since you called me, my guess is that you don't want to take that route either."

"It doesn't matter anymore."

"It matters. What about Scarlet? I've seen the two of you together. She loves you and, unless I'm totally off base, you love her, too. You have a chance for a life with her, maybe more children. Don't throw that away."

"Don't you understand? I was fooling myself into thinking we could have a life together, but I was wrong. Look at me. I'm a drunk. I'll always be a drunk. Scarlet deserves better than that."

"She was hurt when I told her you didn't want to see her. I could hear it in her voice. She wants to be with you, no matter what. She's not afraid of the future, but you are, aren't you?"

"It's for her own good. I'll only make her miserable, like my father made my mother miserable with his drinking."

Reese lowered his voice to a mere whisper that Cam had to strain to hear. "You think you're being so damn noble, don't you? But let me tell you, you're not being noble. You're being a damn coward. You're so afraid of being hurt again, of losing someone else you love, that you're pushing her away before she has a chance to leave you on her own."

Cam curled his fingers around his glass. "You don't know what you're talking about."

"Or maybe you're testing her, to see how far you can push her before she runs away. Then, you can tell yourself she never really loved you."

Despair welled up inside him. "Don't you get it? I'm no good for her. The first thing I thought of after my lawyer told me I'm not Tessa's father was that I needed a drink."

"And yet here we are, staring at that untouched glass." Reese sighed and rubbed a hand across his face. "Are you ready to go home? I don't like to leave Abby alone for long."

Cam silently cursed himself. He'd been so caught up in his own grief and pain that he forgot Reese had his own worries.

He nodded and slid off the barstool, throwing a couple of bills on the bar to cover their drinks. Taking one last, longing look at his untouched drink, he followed Reese out the door.

"Give me the keys to your truck," Reese said once they were outside. "Ethan's going to pick it up and then spend the night at your house."

Cam tossed Reese his keys. "He doesn't need to babysit me."

"Yeah, he does. Trust me, you don't want to be alone tonight."

He immediately thought of Scarlet, the warmth of her body curled next to his, and the sweet scent of her skin. There was no one he wanted to be with more, especially tonight. But no matter what Reese said, she was better off without him.

They drove in silence back to his house. Reese unlocked the house and let him in. "Ethan will be here soon."

"Thanks, Reese. I'm sorry I dragged you out tonight. Say hi to Abby for me and tell her I'm sorry, too."

"I will." He started to leave and then turned back. "You called me tonight because you don't want to repeat your past. You might not realize it right now because you're hurting so much, but you're strong. You stopped at two drinks. A part of you wants to live a good, sober life."

Cam simply nodded, though he couldn't see Reese's logic through the fog of pain and the alcohol he'd consumed.

"What about Scarlet? Is there any message you want me to give her?"

What he needed to say to Scarlet couldn't be said through an intermediary. He had to face her himself. "Tell her...tell her to stay with Maggie tonight. I'll talk to her tomorrow."

Reese shook his head, disappointment evident in the look he gave him. "All right, but I think you're making a big mistake."

The only mistake he'd made was to let his relationship with Scarlet go as far as it had.

THE NEXT MORNING, SCARLET watched Cameron drive past Maggie's cottage on his way to the worksite. Later, when she and Maggie brought coffee and cookies to the men for their morning break, he simply nodded hello to her. The distance she saw in his eyes, as if they'd meant nothing to each other, scared her. The only bright spot was that he didn't appear hung over.

At lunchtime, Cameron was the last to arrive at Maggie's cottage. Harper went to him and gave him a hug, whispering something in his ear that Scarlet couldn't hear. He hugged her back, bending slightly over her small frame, his eyes closed. After a moment, they broke their embrace. Harper seized his hand and led him to the table. Ethan clapped him on the back in silent support and Cameron sat.

Scarlet sat across the table from Cameron, her stomach so tied up in knots she knew she wouldn't be able to eat. Maggie set a bowl of soup in front of her and she managed a few sips, but mostly she stirred the vegetables and bits of chicken around with her spoon.

A somber mood hung over the table. No one said much. Ethan asked Reese a couple of questions about the progress of the renovations on the lodge, and Harper asked how Abby was doing. Reese replied to both questions, but without his usual good humor; the renovations were on target time-wise, and Abby was about the same, whatever that meant.

Scarlet felt Cameron's gaze on her a few times, but whenever she looked up, he looked away. Finally, lunch was over and the men pushed away from the table. She rose to help Maggie clear the table.

Cameron appeared at her side. "Can I speak to you outside, in private?" he asked in a soft voice.

Scarlet looked up into his unsmiling face and she knew. He was going to say goodbye.

She nodded and followed him outside, her gut twisting. If she could avoid this conversation she would, but she didn't have any choice.

Cameron led her into the woods, to the spot where she'd confessed a lifetime of shame and worries. He'd given her comfort there, but this time would be different.

He finally turned to face her. "I'm sorry, Scarlet. I don't want to hurt you, but I think it's best if we don't see each other anymore."

Hearing the words spoken aloud hurt even more than she had imagined they would. She blinked away tears, suddenly angry. "So, do I get any say in this, or have you decided all by yourself?"

"Please don't make this any harder than it needs to be." His throat worked, giving her hope that this wasn't any easier for him than it was for her.

She closed the distance between them and placed her hand on his arm. His skin was warm to the touch. "I know you're devastated about Tessa. But don't throw us away because you're not thinking clearly."

"My thinking is perfectly clear. This has nothing to do with Tessa." He removed her hand. "You're a good person, Scarlet, but we're not right for each other. I've known for a while now that our relationship wasn't going anywhere. The sex was great, but that's all we had."

She stared at him, struck dumb by his words. Every confidence they'd shared, every whispered endearment, meant nothing to him? She felt closer to Cameron than to any man she'd ever known. For God's sake, she'd shared more secrets with him than she had with her sisters.

But for him it was only about the sex!

"I'm sorry. I should get back to work." He walked a short distance away before looking back at her. "Are you going to be all right? Do you want me to send your sisters?"

She snapped to attention. There was no way she'd let him know how much more their relationship meant to her than it did to him. "No, of course not. I'm fine."

He searched her face for a moment, then, after giving her a brief nod, turned and left.

When she could no longer see him through the trees, she sank to her knees, her fall cushioned by a blanket of dry leaves. She stayed like that for a long time, too shocked to even cry.

All this time she'd thought they had something special. How ironic that the first time she was prepared to stay and make a relationship work, the man she loved would be the one to run away.

If her heart hadn't been ripped in two, she would have laughed.

# Chapter Twenty-Three

CAM RECITED THE SERENITY prayer with the small group assembled in the church basement. He needed a meeting tonight, needed the company of fellow alcoholics who could understand at least some of the pain he was going through.

And if he was at a meeting, he wouldn't be at some roadhouse getting drunk. After what he'd had to do today, he wished he could use alcohol to forget the look of hurt on Scarlet's face. But experience told him the relief alcohol provided was only temporary. When he sobered up, Tessa still wouldn't be his daughter and Scarlet would be out of his life.

The pain of acknowledging those two facts nearly brought him to his knees. How the hell could he go on without them?

Reese sat next to him sipping coffee. When it came time to share, he indicated with a lift of his chin that Cam should go up to the podium. Cam resisted, not sure if he was ready to spill his guts, even here. But Reese wouldn't give up.

"Go," he whispered. "You need this."

Cam reluctantly rose to his feet and headed to the podium. He gripped the wooden stand and stared out at the small group, his heart racing. "Hello, my name is Cam and I'm an alcoholic."

"Hello Cam," came the reply.

"It's been one day since my last drink. I broke my sobriety of three years when I discovered that the child I'd called my daughter for the last five years wasn't mine and that I'm going to lose her forever."

He paused and lowered his head. The black despair that had been with him since Erin Cochrane first broke the news about Tessa's parentage hovered on the edge of his consciousness. He had nothing to fight for anymore.

Cam closed his eyes and concentrated on his breathing. *In and out, in and out.* The only thing he had left was a fervent desire not to turn into a bitter, angry, drunk like his father.

He lifted his head and looked at the crowd. "My first inclination when I heard the news was to drink, to forget. There's a woman in my life, a woman I care about very much. She deserves better than me. How can I be with her when at the first sign of trouble I turn to alcohol? I can't promise her, or even myself, that it won't happen again. I can't, I won't, break her the way my father broke my mother. He promised her a hundred times he'd stop drinking, and he broke every one of those promises. He made her believe she was the reason he drank, that it was all her fault. By the time she died, my mother had nothing left, financially, emotionally, spiritually.

"I can't do that to the woman I care about. So, I broke it off. She doesn't realize it yet, but she's much better off without me. Maybe...maybe someday she'll forgive me."

Cam resumed his seat and a couple more people got up to share. One was a woman who had killed a teenager while driving drunk. Her grief and guilt, even after ten years, filled the church basement.

He listened and said a prayer of thanks that it wasn't him. He was sure everyone else in the room did the same thing.

After the meeting, he helped himself to coffee and cookies at the back of the room, reluctant to leave and go home to his empty house. He made small talk with a few people while he sipped his coffee, but eventually he couldn't put it off any longer. People were filing out and it was time for him to go.

As he left the church, Cam spotted Reese and fell into step with him. "You want to grab a coffee?"

"No, I need to get home to Abby. I've been away from her long enough today."

When they reached the sidewalk, Reese stopped and turned to him, his voice low. "So you've broken off with Scarlet?"

Cam looked away. "Yeah. Like I said, she's better off."

"Is she? I was there at that roadhouse with you. You could have drunk yourself into oblivion, but instead you stopped after two drinks."

"I can't promise that the next time I'll do the same thing. I can't promise her anything."

"I think you're wrong, Cam. You're a lot stronger than you give yourself credit for. You've been dealt a lousy hand, and you've bent, but you haven't broken. Don't send Scarlet away."

"It's too late. We're done. She was always leaving anyway."

"Don't put this on her. If you're done, it's because you ended it."

Reese was right. None of this was Scarlet's fault.

"I've got to go. I'll see you at work tomorrow."

"Yeah."

"I know what you said about it being over with you and Scarlet, but I want to say the love of a good woman can make all the difference in your life. It has for me. If there's any chance of getting back with her, take it."

He'd deliberately hurt Scarlet, letting her think their relationship meant nothing to him aside from the sex. He'd probably never forget the look of stunned disbelief and pain on her face. After what he'd said to her, there was no hope for reconciliation. He'd burned that bridge to cinders.

"ARE YOU SURE THIS IS what you want to do? You still have four more weeks left of your leave of absence," Maggie said as she pulled Scarlet's clothes out of the closet, removed the hangers and tossed them on the bed.

Scarlet folded a sweater and placed it in her suitcase. "Yes, I'm sure. It's time for me to go. My co-workers are getting snowed-under trying to do my share of the work, and my manager is getting impatient. I can update the website and manage the lodge's social media accounts from Chicago. I'll need you guys to send me pictures of the progress on the renovations."

"Yes, of course. We can do that." Harper carefully folded a T-shirt. "I know everything you say is true but please, between the three of us, let's be honest. You're leaving early because of Cam."

Scarlet sighed and sat on the edge of the bed. She'd given her sisters an edited version of the conversation she and Cameron had had two days ago, in which they had mutually decided to go their separate ways.

*Liar*. She'd been unceremoniously dumped.

"We all knew our relationship had an expiry date. I was always going to go back to Chicago. I decided to leave a little earlier, that's all."

She didn't add that if he'd asked, she would have given up her life in Chicago to be with him.

The truth was she couldn't see Cameron every day and pretend she didn't love him. Retrieving her things from his house had nearly killed her, especially when she looked into Tessa's room. Time to go back where she belonged and get on with her life without him.

Maggie sat on the bed beside her, and Harper reached out to tug a lock of Scarlet's hair. "Don't be too angry with Cam. Losing Tessa has broken his heart and his spirit. Maybe he's saying things he doesn't really mean right now."

Scarlet shook her head. He'd been pretty clear that he didn't want her. "I know how devastating losing Tessa was for Cameron. She was his baby..." She closed her eyes. She couldn't talk about Tessa or she'd cry. Again. "I'm going to miss you guys a lot. You have to promise to keep in touch."

Maggie hugged her. "Of course. I'll text you so often you'll tell me to shut up."

Scarlet held her close. "Never."

"When are you going to drive back to Chicago?" Harper asked.

"Tomorrow morning, bright and early. I'll load my things in my car tonight and be ready to go first thing."

Harper tugged on her hair again, her smile pensive. "I'm going to miss you very much. It's been so wonderful having both of my sisters home the last few months."

The three of them had grown closer in ways Scarlet had never thought possible. It was wrenching to leave them, but she had no choice. "It's been wonderful for me, too."

"Group hug!" Maggie put her arms around both of them.

Scarlet hugged them both, laughing through her tears. She already missed them and she hadn't left the driveway. How was she going to survive the rest of her life?

SCARLET PUT THE LAST suitcase in the trunk of her car and slammed the lid. The only thing she had left in the cottage was a small overnight bag with a few toiletries and a change of clothes for tomorrow. Everything else was ready to go.

Except maybe for her.

Cameron chose that moment to drive by, presumably on his way home after work. Since their breakup, if she could call it that, he hadn't come for lunch at the cottage. He'd been avoiding her as efficiently as she'd been avoiding him.

He slowed down as he passed, and their gazes collided. Without thinking, she stepped toward his truck. But before she could reach him, he jerked his gaze away and accelerated.

His truck sped past the cottage and disappeared around a corner.

She had her answer. She really did need to leave. Staying any longer would only make it more difficult for both of them to move on, and she had no wish to make Cameron suffer. He'd been through enough.

Her cell phone rang and she pulled it from her pocket, grateful for the diversion. A name she didn't recognize displayed on the screen. "Scarlet Lindquist speaking."

"Scarlet, hello. I'm so glad I caught you. You're my last hope."

"I'm sorry. Do I know you?"

"I'm sorry. I should introduce myself. My name is Meredith Anderson and I was at the wedding show in Minneapolis this past summer. I picked up one of your brochures."

"Oh, I see." It would be nice if she could line up another wedding for the lodge for next summer. Her heart stuttered a little when she realized she wouldn't be around to organize the event. "When is your wedding?"

"That's the thing. It's in four weeks. Can you help us?"

"Four weeks? Meredith, I hope I didn't give the wrong impression at the wedding show. I did say the lodge was under construction. We're only taking bookings for weddings and events scheduled for next year."

"It's a small wedding," Meredith pleaded. "Under fifty people. Our venue had a huge flood. A water pipe burst in the basement and some of the walls collapsed. There's no way they're going to have the building ready for our wedding in four weeks. I've been searching all over the city for a new venue, even as far away as St. Cloud. Everything is booked. We don't know what to do!"

Scarlet heard her sniffle, obviously holding back tears, and she sympathized with her predicament, but didn't know what she could do to help. "We're still under construction here. Workers and construction materials and equipment are everywhere. A couple of things are done, but—"

"I don't want much," Meredith interrupted. "As long as we have somewhere to hold a small ceremony and a simple dinner, that's all we need. I saw the pictures of the wedding you hosted earlier this year. It was lovely and simple. That's all we want."

"That was my sister's wedding in June. It was warm enough to hold the ceremony outside and have the reception in a tent on the grounds. We can't count on the weather cooperating like that in late October."

"But you said a couple of things are done. It doesn't have to be fancy."

"No, but you'll need a functioning kitchen, and plumbing and electrical that works. What about hotel rooms? If your guests are coming from the city, they'll likely need somewhere to stay. Our guest rooms aren't ready yet."

"Maybe there's a hotel close to the lodge where they can stay," Meredith suggested, clearly not ready to give up.

Scarlet supposed they could stay at Miller's Resort down the road, if rooms were available. The dining room of the lodge was ready; the only change had been to replace the windows overlooking the lake with energy efficient French doors that allowed guests to go out on the new deck. But the kitchen still had a long way to go before it could be considered usable.

The whole idea was unfeasible. And besides, she was on her way back to Chicago.

"I'm sorry, Meredith. I'd really like to help you, but we're in no position to host a wedding so soon. If you're willing to wait until next spring—"

"We can't wait." She was crying in earnest now. "My fiancé is in the military, and he has to deploy a week after we're supposed to get married. And...and I just found out I'm pregnant. Mike wants to make sure we're married before he leaves, so that if something happens to him... if something happens, the baby and I will be looked after."

*Good God.* Scarlet bowed her head and tugged on her ponytail with her free hand. "You must be thrilled about the baby," she offered.

"Yes, totally. The timing could have been better, but we've always wanted children. There was a time we didn't think it would happen."

"Have you thought about having a civil ceremony at city hall?"

Meredith inhaled deeply as if trying to get herself under control. "Yes, we have. If we don't have any alternative, that's what we'll do. But both of us wanted a celebration, nothing fancy, just something to mark the occasion with family and a few close friends. And my mother is kind of old fashioned about these things. She's been looking forward to my wedding for a long time." She took another unsteady breath. "I'll let you go. I'm sorry to have bothered you."

"Wait." She was probably going to regret this. "What's the exact date of your wedding?"

"October twentieth. Why? What are you thinking?"

"I don't want you to get your hopes up because this is a long shot. I'll speak to our construction managers and see if there's anything we can do to be at least partially ready in time for your wedding."

"Oh, thank you, Scarlet! That's wonderful!"

"I'm not making any promises, Meredith," she warned. "If they say there's no way the lodge can be ready in time, then we can't help you."

"I understand, and I appreciate your willingness to at least try. Thank you so much."

"Don't thank me yet. I'll call you as soon as we decide. Like I said, I can't promise anything."

"I understand. I look forward to hearing from you soon."

Scarlet said goodbye and hung up the phone. This was insane. She was all set to leave for Chicago first thing in the morning. Committing to this wedding would mean she'd have to stay for another four weeks.

Meredith's story had truly touched her, but maybe that wasn't the only reason she was thinking about staying. In her heart of hearts, she knew she was having a hard time saying goodbye to Cameron. Dragging out her departure, however, wouldn't be good for either of them.

For better or worse, she'd made a promise, and now she had to keep it. Reese might say there was no way they could be ready in time and the whole exercise would be moot. But if he said it was possible...

Scarlet wasn't sure which scenario she was hoping for.

## Chapter Twenty-Four

"WHAT'S THE DATE OF this wedding again?" Reese asked.

"October twentieth. Exactly four weeks from tomorrow," Scarlet said.

"I don't know," he said, shaking his head. "There's still a lot to do. I'd say the biggest stumbling block would be getting the kitchen in shape. How could you feed guests without a functioning kitchen?"

"Where would people stay?" Cam asked. The idea of hosting a wedding had come out of left field, but he found himself rooting for the bride.

Scarlet's gaze briefly met his before skittering away. "I know they can't stay at Miller's that weekend. I checked, and they're completely booked. Maybe they could stay at one of the other resorts or hotels in the area."

"If the guests are staying at another resort, they might as well hold the wedding there as well," Ethan said. "If we're going to do this, it's all or nothing."

Harper nodded. "I agree. If we go ahead with this, we can't cut any corners just to get done. The project can't suffer. So how can we make this happen?"

Cam had to admire his sister-in-law's can-do attitude. The whole renovation project was a testament to her tenacity and spirit. But even Harper might have to concede that this tight timeline would be a challenge.

"All the equipment and appliances for the kitchen have been ordered. I can check with our supplier to see if they can deliver in the next four weeks," Maggie said.

"That's a good place to start," Ethan said. "If we can't get the commercial appliances in time, I don't think there's any point pursuing this further. Let's call the supplier right now."

Maggie retrieved the paperwork for the items that had been ordered along with the business card of the salesman. She punched his number into her phone and put the call on speakerphone.

"Pete Barker speaking."

"Hi, Pete. This is Maggie Lindquist from the Solace Lake Lodge. We placed an order with you for our commercial kitchen equipment almost three months ago. At that time, we told you we wouldn't be ready to take possession of the equipment until early in the new year, but something has come up and we're wondering if it's possible to take possession immediately."

"Immediately?"

"Yes, as in right away."

"I can find out for you," the salesman said. "What's your purchase order number?"

Maggie read off the number. The salesman repeated it back to her and then asked her to wait while he checked.

Cam found himself holding his breath while they waited. If they went ahead with this wedding, Scarlet would stay another four weeks. Despite knowing the best thing for Scarlet would be for her to go, he couldn't help hoping she'd stay. When he'd seen her packing her car to leave, a piece of his heart froze inside his chest. Though it was agony to see her every day and not be able to touch her, he couldn't imagine her gone either.

"Hello, Maggie. It's Pete here again. We have the commercial refrigerator, the dishwasher and the freezer you ordered in stock, but the range is on back order with the manufacturer and we don't expect to receive it for several weeks. I talked to my manager, and what we can do is offer you a floor model from our store. But it's a higher end range." He gave her the name and model number of the range, and Maggie wrote it down. "It has all the features of the one you ordered and a few more, but it costs nearly a thousand dollars more, even with a floor model discount. If you're interested, we can deliver it to you in the next few days."

"Can you give us a couple of minutes to discuss this, Pete? I'll call you right back."

"Sure thing."

Maggie hit the off button, then used her phone to look up the commercial range Pete was proposing to sell to them. "I remember this one. I'd even considered it."

"Why didn't you buy it in the first place?" Ethan asked.

She shrugged. "The money, I guess. This range is a real Cadillac and since the reviews on the range I ordered were very good, I didn't think it was necessary to get the most expensive range they had in the store."

"So you're okay with it?"

"More than okay."

"Okay, we know we can get the equipment for the kitchen," Ethan continued. "The dining room should able be to accommodate a ceremony and a dinner for the small wedding Meredith wants. Can the kitchen itself be ready in time? What about guest rooms? What do you think, Reese?"

"I know for sure we can't get everything done in time. But maybe if we put all our resources into a couple of key areas, we might be able to pull it off."

"What do you propose?" Harper asked.

"I've had the crew working on the event center for the last couple of weeks. If we concentrate on the kitchen and on the new wing of guest rooms instead, we might be able to get them finished."

Ethan nodded. "Cam, what about you? Do you think you could get one or two of the new cottages ready in time?"

Cam hesitated. To this point, his priority had been to finish the exteriors of all eight cottages so that his crew could finish the interiors over the winter. But if he had to, he could change gears to completely finish two of them in the next few weeks.

But should he do it? He could tell Ethan it wasn't possible to complete two cottages. Then Scarlet would go back to Chicago.

"Yeah, we can get a couple of the cottages ready," he said. He hoped he was doing the right thing.

"Good." Ethan turned to Scarlet. "Will you be able to help? We'll need you to work with the bride. And Harper will need help getting fixtures and furniture for the guestrooms and cottages. What do you say? Will you stay?"

Scarlet stared at Ethan, her face pale and her blue eyes wide with what looked like anxiety, or possibly indecision.

She'd only said a few words through the whole discussion. Her gaze slid to his, before quickly shifting back to Ethan. "Yes, I can help."

Cam let out his breath. Conflicting emotions swirled through his head – elation, trepidation, fear. She was staying four more weeks. He'd see her, but there'd be no closeness between them, no sharing of confidences, no touches. He'd made sure to stomp out any tender feelings she might have once had for him.

A powerful craving for a drink nearly brought him to his knees. He recited the Serenity Prayer to himself and concentrated on breathing. He only had to get through the next four weeks.

*One minute at a time. One hour at a time. One day at a time.*

Harper and Ethan looked at each other.

"I think we're doing this," Harper said. "Are we crazy?"

"Probably." Ethan pulled her into his arms and laughed.

Maggie picked up her phone. "I'll call Pete back and tell him we'll take his deal. When should I tell him to deliver?"

"As soon as they can," Reese said. "The appliances can be stored in the dining room until we're ready to install. That way, at least we know we have them."

Maggie nodded and headed to the other room to make the call. Reese left the cottage to go back to work. Harper turned to Scarlet. "I guess you can call the bride and tell her the wedding is on."

"Yeah, I guess I can." She didn't look happy about the prospect. "I should call my manager, too and let him know I won't be coming back to work next week after all."

"I'm sorry, honey," Harper said. "Do you think he's going to be difficult?"

"I'm not sure."

Cam clenched his fists. If the man dared to say one unkind word to her...

"If he gives you a hard time," Ethan said, "I'll tell him where he can stick his job."

That made Scarlet smile. "Thanks Big Brother, but I can take care of it."

"You're sure you're okay with staying?" Harper asked.

Her smile disappeared. "Yes, of course. After all, I'm kind of responsible for getting us into this predicament. The least I can do is help out."

Her gaze once more briefly landed on him. It was obvious his presence made her uncomfortable. He headed for the door. "I'd better let the crew know there's been a change in plans."

"Why don't you join us for dinner tonight? About six?" Harper said.

He glanced at Scarlet. If his coming to dinner upset her, he'd stay away.

"You should come." Scarlet's smile appeared forced. "Maggie said she was making something special tonight."

They were going to have to get used to seeing each other. And besides, the evenings were long and empty in his house. The silence weighed heavily on him. "Okay, thank you. I'll be here at six."

He left the cottage and closed the door softly behind him. Once on the other side, he exhaled. The next four weeks would test his strength. He hoped he passed the test.

# Chapter Twenty-Five

HARPER HELD ONE END of the tape measure while Scarlet measured the space in the living room where the sofa bed was supposed to go. While they measured, painters rolled the walls of the cottage in a soft gray paint and carpenters hung cabinets in the kitchen.

"Eighty-five inches. We've got to be able to fit in a queen sofa bed and at least one side table in this area." Scarlet wrote the measurements on her clipboard.

"We'll need to look for a sofa bed with sleek arms that don't take up too much space," Harper said.

"For sure. Did you add the lamps to the list of stuff we need to get?"

"I did." Harper sighed. "I hope we don't forget anything important."

"We won't. And if we do, we'll wing it."

They'd all been working feverishly for the last two weeks. The new guest wing of the lodge was nearing completion and if all the furniture, appliances and fixtures they'd ordered arrived in time, they'd be ready. The cottages were taking a little longer because there was so much more to do. Cameron had hired extra tradespeople to handle some of the tiling, painting and finishing carpentry. The trades were practically tripping over each other, but somehow it was working.

As long as they didn't have any major setbacks, they might pull this off.

Ethan and Cameron walked into the cottage. Ethan gave Harper a kiss. Cameron's eyes met hers. It was a sweet kind of torture being so close to him every day and yet so far.

Ethan put his arm around Harper's shoulders. "What are you guys doing here? I thought you were going to Minneapolis with Maggie today."

"We are, but we just found out from our supplier that their sofa beds are out of stock, and they can't guarantee when they're getting their next shipment. We're going to shop for them while we're in the city. Guess we'll have to buy retail."

Scarlet added, "We're meeting our bride Meredith tonight at the condo. She's going to go over her food choices with Maggie, and we'll nail down a few details, like the flowers. We should be back by about noon tomorrow."

Ethan hugged Harper to his side and kissed her once more. "I'll miss you."

Harper kissed him back. "I'll miss you too."

Scarlet looked away, pretending to check her clipboard. She loved her sister, and Ethan was like a brother to her, but it was hard to witness their love for each other and not feel hollow inside.

Her phone beeped with an incoming text. Scarlet pulled it from her pocket, glad for the distraction. "It's from Meredith."

She silently read the text. "Uh-oh."

"What's wrong?"

"She's asking if we can accommodate more overnight guests. Apparently, her mother-in-law has invited two more families, eight people in total."

"There's no way we can finish another two cottages at this late date," Cameron said.

"Even if you could, I don't know if our supplier could furnish it in time," Harper said. "What about the other two cottages, the ones we're staying in?"

"That's a great idea, except where are we going to live?" Ethan asked.

"You can stay with me for a few nights," Cameron said. "You two can sleep in my bed, and I'll stay in Tessa's old room."

Harper shook her head. "No, Cam. You can't."

"It's time I cleaned it out anyway. I'll box up her toys and send them to her."

Scarlet looked at her clipboard once more, the lump in her throat making it hard to swallow. Boxing up Tessa's things made her absence feel so final. She really was never coming home.

The thought made her so sad she wanted to weep. But she held it together for Cameron's sake. The last thing he needed was her tears.

"What about Maggie and Scarlet? Where are they going to stay?" Harper asked.

"We could rent a room at a hotel in the area," Scarlet offered.

"That's a possibility, but I have another idea," Ethan said. "What if we rented a motorhome?"

"Can you look into that while we're in the city?" Harper asked. "Then we can give Meredith some news when we see her tonight."

"I'm on it. I'll call you as soon as I find out something."

Harper reached for Ethan's hand. "Come on, you can walk me back to our cottage so I can pick up my overnight bag."

Scarlet watched them leave hand in hand. If only she and Cameron could have that...

*Stop it!* She had to halt that line of thinking or she'd go crazy.

"I should go, too. Maggie will be waiting for me."

"Have a safe trip, Scarlet," Cameron said.

"Thank you."

When she looked into his eyes, his loneliness reached into her heart and squeezed.

"I can help you clear out Tessa's room. You shouldn't have to do it alone." The words came out of her mouth before she had a chance to think over the wisdom of her offer.

If his face had been expressionless before, it was stony now. "I appreciate the offer. But this is something I need to do myself."

She nodded and did her best to smile, even though her heart had been smashed against a wall. She'd offered to help out of friendship and even that had been rejected.

"I'd better get going." Clutching her clipboard against her chest, she turned to leave.

Before she could make her escape, he touched her arm. "Scarlet, wait." Cameron let his hand drop to his side, his voice no more than a whisper. "It's better for me to pack up Tessa's things by myself because I don't think I can do it without crying. I'm not comfortable letting anyone see me that way."

White hot anger bubbled to the surface. "Don't forget who you're talking to, Cameron. I *have* seen you that way, and you've seen me. Maybe we both need a good cry and a chance to mourn. But you're too damn stubborn to even grieve, or let me grieve. You've got your emotions so tightly packed inside that one day they're going to explode. And this time, I won't be there to pick up the pieces."

Without another word, she ran to the door.

CAM TIGHTENED THE LAST screw on the front porch light of one of the new cottages, the final touch before guests arrived. He and his crew had put in many long hours in the past four weeks, and he was proud of what they'd been able to accomplish.

If he was completely honest with himself, he was grateful for the work that filled his days and left him too tired to do anything but fall into an exhausted sleep every night. At least he didn't have time to dwell on everything he'd lost.

The craving for a drink still haunted him, but he was coping. Being busy and focused helped. But he worried about the future and the long, cold Minnesota nights to come.

He pushed the worries from his mind. *One day at a time.*

The wedding they'd been madly preparing for was today. It was a bright, crisp fall morning, and the leaves of the poplars and birch were putting on a show of their finest colors. Cam stood on the front porch and gazed over the sea of yellow and red and orange to the sapphire blue of the lake below. Guests were scheduled to arrive soon, and he was sure they'd enjoy this view.

Cam sighed. When the wedding was over, the guests would leave and so would Scarlet. Maybe he'd see her again, catch an occasional glimpse when she came to visit her family. But her life was far away from Solace Lake. Away from him.

He'd never felt more alone.

Cam shook off the melancholy and straightened his spine. He had work to do. He'd promised Maggie he'd be her sous-chef and assist her with the preparation of the food.

He drove his truck down to the lodge and parked around the side of the building. The landscaping wasn't complete, but it had been cleaned up enough to look tidy. In the spring, bushes and flowers would be planted and the parking lot paved. He'd been skeptical about the lodge's future at the start, but now he was feeling optimistic that Ethan and Harper would make a success of the place.

Entering the front doors, he was greeted by a display of chrysanthemums in a myriad of fall colors. But the star of the show was the view of the lake visible from the front entry. With some engineering magic, Reese had taken out a wall to make that happen. The result was spectacular.

To the left of the front door, a reception area had been set up. Eventually there would be a proper desk and office, but for now a tablecloth covered a plastic folding table. Harper was behind the table organizing the keys to the rooms. A key card system would be installed over the winter, but for now they'd go old school.

"How's it going?" he asked her.

"Okay, I think. I keep worrying that I'm forgetting something."

"You're going to be fine."

Harper's smile held a touch of sadness. He knew she didn't want Scarlet to leave any more than he did. "So are you, Cam."

"Yeah." He swallowed around the sudden lump in his throat. "I'd better go see what Maggie needs me to do."

"Have a great day."

"Thanks."

Maggie's kitchen was a celebration of efficiency and stainless steel. The gleaming work surfaces and appliances were the centerpieces, but the kitchen also had a couple of homey touches, like Maggie's grandmother's apron that she'd framed and hung on one wall, a touching reminder that this kitchen and the lodge belonged to a family.

"Hey, Maggie. What do you need me to do?"

Maggie smiled at him in relief. "It's not glamorous, but I really need you to peel potatoes. Meredith wants a homestyle meal, so we're having roast chicken and mashed potatoes, all sourced locally."

"I can handle that. Point me in the direction of the spuds."

She pointed to one of the sinks. "Over there. The potatoes are next to the fridge. Have I told you how grateful I am for your help?"

"Stop. I'm glad to be of some use, even though this wedding stuff is out of my wheelhouse."

"I have a feeling we're going to get real experienced at putting on weddings."

He was a quarter way through a twenty-pound bag of potatoes when he heard his cell phone ring. He let it go to voice mail.

"Aren't you going to get that?" Maggie asked.

"I'm a little tied up right now," he said, indicating his wet hands. "If it's important, they'll call back."

A few minutes later, a ping indicated he'd received a text message. Maggie looked up from the chicken she was basting. "Sounds like someone really wants to talk to you."

Cam put down his paring knife and dried his hands on a towel. "Maybe Ethan needs something."

He pulled his phone from his back pocket and read the message: *Urgent. Call Erin Cochrane immediately.*

"That's odd. Erin Cochrane has an urgent message for me." Cam dialed the number given.

Maggie set her baster on the counter. "Your lawyer?"

"Yeah." His heart raced. He hadn't heard from Erin in weeks.

Erin picked up on the first ring and spoke before he had a chance to say hello. "Cam! I've got some amazing news. The DNA tests were wrong."

Cam's hand shook so hard he nearly dropped the phone. "What? How can they be wrong?"

"I've had a private investigator follow Laura for the past few weeks, to make sure everything was on the up and up with her. He snapped some pictures of her and Tessa and another little girl about the same age as Tessa. This child has long brown hair and is about the same height and weight and age as Tessa."

"Okay." He gripped the countertop, no clue as to where she was going with this.

"When the investigator showed the pictures to the people at the DNA lab, the technician swore the other child was the one she obtained the DNA sample from."

Cam's heart threatened to beat its way out of his chest. "Is she sure? I mean, how do we know for sure it wasn't Tessa?"

Maggie stopped working to stare at him. Erin continued, her voice excited. "The technician signed an affidavit, swearing to it. What color are Tessa's eyes?"

"Dark brown."

"This kid's eyes were blue, according to the technician. Cam, this is enough for the court to order retesting. I've applied to family court and the judge agrees. The court takes a dim view of someone deliberately trying to deceive it."

His head was spinning. "When will she be retested? How soon can we find out the truth?"

"That's the really good news." He could hear the excitement in her voice. "I've applied to the court to have the testing done in Minneapolis, since Laura can't be relied on to be truthful. The judge agrees. Tessa will be home tomorrow. You've been given temporary custody pending the results of the DNA testing."

Cam couldn't stand up. He dropped to his knees on the kitchen floor.

Maggie was at his side in a moment, her face full of worry. "What's wrong? What happened?"

"She's coming home, Maggie," he said through his tears. "Tessa's coming home."

Maggie slid to the floor beside him, her hand over her mouth and her eyes wide. "Oh, my God!"

"Cam! Are you still there?" Erin said through the phone.

"Yes, yes, I'm still here."

"Apparently, the child Laura tried to pass off as Tessa is the daughter of a friend of the boyfriend's. On the pretext of taking the two girls on an outing, Laura brought the other little girl for the swab test at the lab. She was trying to convince the boyfriend that Tessa is his. They were in a relationship in Minneapolis when he lived here, shortly before she met you."

"Where was Tessa while Laura was in the lab with this other child?" He put his arm around Maggie as she cried.

"Outside, in the car, crouched on the floor of the back seat. Tessa told our investigator that Laura had ordered her to stay put and not tell anyone what happened or she'd be punished."

Rage poured through Cam at the thought of his little girl alone and afraid, bullied and threatened by her mother, the one person who should have been protecting her. He wished he could wrap Tessa in his arms right now and let her know everything was going to be all right.

"Why was Laura so bent on passing Tessa off as this other guy's child?"

Erin sighed, the sound of it exhibiting her disgust. "She said he was the love of her life. He wanted children and she wanted to present Tessa to him on a silver platter."

His thoughts flew to Scarlet as they so often did. She would never pull a stunt like this. She'd made mistakes in her past, but she would never knowingly hurt or deceive anyone. She was the most honorable woman he knew. "Laura has no idea what love means."

"I have to agree with that observation," Erin said dryly. "I'll text you the details of Tessa's flight right away. She's been removed from Laura's custody by the Department of Children and Family Services and will be flying unaccompanied tomorrow. Can you meet her at the airport?"

"Are you kidding? Of course I can!" The earth would have to open up and swallow him whole before he wouldn't make it to the airport tomorrow. He sobered a minute. This had to be confusing for Tessa. "How's Tessa doing? Where is she? Is she scared?"

"I spoke this morning with the foster mother she's been temporarily placed with, and yes, she's confused about everything that's happened. But when she was told she was coming home to you, she seemed relieved. I'll text you the foster mother's phone number so you can call Tessa yourself."

"Thank you, Erin. Thank you for everything. I can't believe..." Emotions threatened to overwhelm him. He couldn't go on.

"I'll let you go for now, Cam. I'll be in touch soon about all the formal legal stuff. Congratulations."

"Thank you. And please thank the private investigator for me."

"I will. Goodbye."

Cam hung up the phone and turned to Maggie. "Tessa's coming home tomorrow."

She threw her arms around his neck in a giant bear hug. "Yes!"

Harper ran into the kitchen. "What's going on? I heard a lot of yelling. Why are you on the floor? Are you hurt?"

"Tessa's coming home," Maggie cried.

Harper's face went blank. "What? How?"

Cam relayed everything Erin had told him. "I can't believe she's coming home."

"Oh! Oh! I have to tell Ethan! And Scarlet!"

Harper raced from the kitchen, and he and Maggie laughed when they heard her excitedly calling Ethan's name. Cam pulled himself to his feet and dragged Maggie with him.

Maggie grasped his hand. "This is a miracle. I'm so happy for you and Tessa."

"It's not over yet. She has to be retested. We could still find out I didn't father her."

"I have a good feeling. Laura wouldn't have gone to such lengths if she didn't believe Tessa was yours."

A moment later, Ethan and Harper ran into the kitchen, followed closely by Scarlet. His gaze connected with hers immediately and in it he read her surprise and joy. He wanted to pull her into his arms and hold her, to tell her he was sorry for the way he'd treated her.

To tell her he'd needed her all along.

Fear stopped him cold. For the last couple of weeks, he'd played her words over and over in his head. *This time, I won't be there to pick up the pieces.*

She was done with him.

"Is it true?" she asked breathlessly.

"Yes, it's true. Tessa is coming home tomorrow."

Ethan embraced him in a tight hug. Cam hugged him back, all the while watching Scarlet's face. Though she smiled and laughed, tears streamed down her cheeks. He remembered what she'd said about not allowing her to grieve. Had she grieved for his little girl, too? Had he underestimated her feelings for Tessa? For him?

Despite his joy, his heart ached. Whatever her feelings had been, he'd thrown them away. It was too late to get them back.

# Chapter Twenty-Six

AFTER STAYING LATE at the lodge the night of the wedding to make sure no one needed anything from the front desk, Scarlet arrived back at work by seven the next morning. Once she'd learned that Tessa was coming home, the rest of the day had gone by in a blur. Aside from a couple of minor hiccups, Meredith and Mike's wedding went off without a hitch. The ceremony was intimate and beautiful, the couple obviously very much in love. Scarlet had to hold herself together when Mike promised to always love Meredith, to trust her, and always be her friend.

What she wouldn't give to have Cameron say those words to her.

It was never going to happen. But at least Tessa was coming home to be with Cameron. She was confident that this time the DNA tests would prove he was her father. She was so happy for him.

She only wished she could be part of their lives.

She'd barely slept, her emotions too jumbled to allow any rest. She was thrilled to be seeing Tessa again, but sad that their time together would be short. With the wedding guests leaving later in the day, most of them after breakfast, there was no reason for her to stay any longer.

Except that everyone she loved was here.

The weather cooperated for the second day in a row with bright cloudless skies. Light streamed into the dining room as guests helped themselves to the breakfast buffet that Maggie and the others had set up. Maggie manned the omelet station while Cameron, Harper and Ethan made sure the trays of food on the buffet table were kept filled. Scarlet started another urn of coffee and walked around the dining room refilling cups and making sure everyone had everything they needed. She was refilling her coffeepot at the urn when a tingle skittered down her spine. She sensed Cameron's presence even before he spoke.

"Hey. How are you doing this morning?" he asked.

"I'm fine." She turned to him with her best smile. "The question should be, how are you doing the morning? Are you excited to see Tessa?"

"More than excited. I can't believe she's coming home. I thought I'd never see her again."

"I'm really happy for you, Cameron, and especially for Tessa. Nobody loves her like you do. You'll give her a stable, loving home."

His gaze was warm with gratitude. "Thank you. I appreciate you saying that."

She looked away, afraid she'd fall into the dark depths of his eyes and never surface again. "When do you leave for Minneapolis?"

He looked at his watch. "In about an hour. I spoke to Tessa last night, and I promised her I'd bring her favorite stuffed bear to the airport with me. It's in the truck. I spent last night unpacking all the things I'd packed up a couple of weeks ago. I never did get the courage to send them to her in California."

"I hope this experience hasn't been too traumatic for her."

"Me, too. As soon as the tests prove I'm her father, I'm going to do everything in my power to make sure I get sole custody so Laura can never pull a stunt like this again."

"The courts are crazy if they don't give you custody."

"Thanks. I think so, too." His expression sobered. "Scarlet, about what you said to me a couple of weeks ago. I'm sorry I didn't let you help me clean out Tessa's room, and I'm sorry I didn't let you grieve. I realize now you needed to mourn Tessa's loss as much as I did. I was so tied up in my own grief I couldn't recognize yours or anyone else's. I'm sorry."

She fiddled with the lid of her coffeepot, unable to meet his eyes. "I understand, really I do. Losing Tessa was such a blow." She forced herself to stand straighter. "But it's over now. You can concentrate on being her dad."

"Yeah."

She picked up the coffeepot and offered him another bright smile. "I'd better get back out there. Please tell Tessa I'm glad she's home."

"You can tell her yourself. I'm going to bring her back here to the lodge."

"Oh." As much as she wanted to see her, she wasn't sure she'd be able to hold it together when she did. "That's wonderful."

"Scarlet." He touched her free hand, his voice barely a whisper. "I've missed you."

She pulled her hand away. "Please don't say that."

"Why not? It's how I feel."

A sudden epiphany struck her. She needed someone who was in it for the long haul. Someone who would stand beside her in good times and in bad. She'd finally figured out that she didn't want to run anymore, and she needed someone who felt the same way. She needed someone who needed her.

She turned to face him. "When we thought Tessa was gone, I wanted to stand beside you, but you wouldn't let me. When things go bad in the future, will you cut me loose again? I can't play that game, Cameron."

She walked away, making sure her smile was firmly in place. None of their guests would ever guess her heart had splintered to pieces. Again.

CAM ARRIVED AT THE Minneapolis airport about fifteen minutes before Tessa's flight was scheduled to arrive. When the arrivals board flashed a notice saying her plane would be delayed by thirty minutes, he nearly put his fist through a wall. Instead, he concentrated on breathing deeply to calm himself. Then he went to one of the airport shops to buy Tessa another stuffie, a gopher with a bandanna around his neck proclaiming "I love Minnesota." It wasn't much, but at least the shopping had killed some time.

He passed an airport bar and for one wild moment, considered going inside. For a glass of coke, he told himself. To pass the time.

Then, he thought about Tessa and how much she needed him, especially today. He'd spend the rest of his life battling the beast, one day at a time. With help from friends and family, he'd do it. He had to.

He turned around and walked away from the bar.

Finally, Tessa's plane landed. Cam paced at the bottom of a set of stairs, anxious for the doors to open and the passengers to disembark. A few people began trickling out, their suits indicating they were in Minneapolis on business. Then the doors slid open and he saw her, holding the hand of a female flight attendant. They walked down the stairs and he could see Tessa scanning the crowd. When she caught sight of him, she shouted, her free arm waving madly.

"Daddy, Daddy! I'm here!"

She practically dragged the flight attendant the rest of the way down the stairs. When she reached the bottom, she let go of the attendant's hand and pushed past the barrier that prevented him from coming to her. He got down on one knee and she ran into his arms.

"Daddy, I missed you so much." Tessa's small arms clasped him tightly around his neck, as if she was afraid to let go. "I didn't like California."

"I missed you, too, baby." He held her close and breathed her in. *Thank God.* "I missed you like crazy."

The flight attendant came to stand next to them and gave Cam a polite smile. "It's pretty obvious you're Tessa's father, but I'm required to see some ID."

"Of course." Cam rose to his feet, Tessa clinging to his leg, and pulled his wallet from his back pocket. He slid his driver's license out of the plastic pocket and showed it to her.

She examined it, and then him, and smiled again. "Thank you, Mr. Hainstock. I'm happy you two have been reunited. Tessa talked about you the whole flight."

Cam extended his hand. "Thank you for looking after her. Her safe arrival means the world to me."

"It was no trouble. She was an angel. Best of luck to you both. Goodbye, Tessa."

"Bye, Patty!"

Cam picked Tessa up and nestled her into the crook of his arm. "Are you ready to go home?"

"Yes!"

"I was thinking we'd go to the lodge first so you can say hi to Uncle Ethan and Auntie Harper. They really want to see you. Would that be okay?"

She nodded solemnly. "Uh-huh. Will Scarlet be there, too?"

"Yeah, she's there. Did you want to see her?"

Tessa nodded again. "I missed her a lot."

He didn't have the heart to tell his daughter that Scarlet's stay at the lodge would be short. Or that he'd blown any chance of a future with her. "Let's go home, pumpkin."

She placed her small hand against his cheek. "I love you, Daddy."

Cam said a silent prayer of thanks as smiled into his daughter's eyes. "I love you, too, baby. To the moon and back."

"To the moon and back," she repeated.

They collected Tessa's luggage and then headed to his truck. All the way home, she talked about Scarlet and the things they'd done over the summer. Despite Tessa's happy chatter and the songs they sang together, Cam's heart grew heavier with every mile. It was so unfair that Scarlet was leaving at the same time Tessa was coming home.

He couldn't blame her. She needed someone steady in her life, and he'd cut and run. But he'd done it for her. If he succumbed to alcoholism again, he didn't want to drag her down with him. He'd had no choice but to end their relationship. Aside from giving up booze, it was the toughest thing he'd ever had to do.

When they arrived at the lodge, Cam parked outside the front doors. The parking lot was empty, and he presumed all the wedding guests had gone home. By the time he unbuckled Tessa from her booster chair and set her on her feet, everyone was out on the front step. Tessa spied Scarlet and, with a small cry, ran to her. Scarlet opened her arms and gathered her close.

"I love you, Scarlet," Tessa said. "I missed you so much."

Scarlet kissed her hair. "I love you, too." Tears streamed down her cheeks. "I thought about you the whole time you were gone."

"Did you go for walks on the beach when I was away?"

"No, not once. It wouldn't have been any fun without you."

Tessa pushed Scarlet's hair from her forehead to look into her face. "Can we do that tomorrow?"

Scarlet's gaze collided with his over Tessa's shoulder. He knew she couldn't promise her anything. She let go of Tessa and straightened to her full height, her smile wobbly. "It's a little too cold now for walks on the beach. Why don't you say hi to Ethan and Harper and Maggie? They've been dying to see you."

Tessa happily complied. While the others made a huge fuss over her, Scarlet stood to one side and watched. Though she put on a brave face, Cam knew her well enough to realize she was holding back tears. Tears of joy, or tears of regret? Whichever they were, he hated to see her cry.

Maggie smoothed Tessa's hair as Ethan held her. "I made your favorite for supper, spaghetti and meatballs. And chocolate pudding for dessert. Are you hungry?"

"Yes!"

Maggie laughed. "Good! Let's all go inside and sit down together."

He and Scarlet followed the others into the lodge's dining room.

"Are you okay?" he whispered.

She blinked at him, hastily wiping an errant tear with her hand. "Yes, of course. Just emotional over Tessa's return."

He nodded. Her attachment to Tessa, and Tessa's to her, had been far stronger than he'd realized. He was afraid of Tessa's reaction when she found out Scarlet would soon be leaving. And, he realized, he was afraid for Scarlet, too.

One of the dining room tables was already set for dinner. Maggie and Harper brought the food from the kitchen and they all dug in. The conversation centered on all the fun everyone was going to have at the lodge over the winter. No one wanted to remind Tessa of her time in California or her mother, though she didn't seem to be missing Laura at all from what Cam could see.

"This winter we'll go skating, Tessa," Harper said. "When we were kids, Grampa used to shovel off the snow on a piece of the lake so we could skate. It was such fun, especially when he cleared off a really big piece and I could feel like I was flying down the ice. Do you remember, Scarlet?"

"Yes, of course. It was fun." She smiled, but she looked anything but happy.

"Will you teach me how to skate, Scarlet?" Tessa asked, a meatball stabbed on the end of her fork.

"Tessa, I'm sorry but I won't be here over the winter. Remember I told you that I live in Chicago, and that I was only here at the lodge to help out for a few months?"

Tessa's face fell and she set her fork on the plate, her meatball abandoned. "Yes, I remember."

"It's time for me to go. But I'm very glad I had a chance to see you before I left."

"Can't you stay?"

"I'm sorry, honey, but I can't. I have a job I need to get back to. They miss me." Scarlet paused as if searching for reasons why she had to leave. "And I miss my friends."

"But I'll miss you! I missed you the whole time I was away. You have to stay."

Scarlet's careful façade began to crumble. "I'm sorry, Tessa. I have to go."

"No!" She jumped out of her chair. "Don't go!"

When she ran to Scarlet and threw her arms around her, Cam's heart ached for his two girls. Scarlet wore a stricken expression and her lip trembled. She pulled Tessa onto her lap and gathered her close.

"Honey, sometimes things don't work out the way we want them to, and we have to be brave and do the best we can. Even though we won't be together, you'll always live in my heart, and I'll live in yours. You can think about the fun things we did over the summer whenever you want to."

"It's not the same!" Tessa cried.

She smoothed her hair. "No, baby, it's not. But I want you to know I'm going to think about you a lot. I'll never forget you."

Her last words were barely a whisper. When his gaze met hers, her stark pain broke his heart.

And then anger filled him. She didn't have to go. They could be together...

*No.* She was right. She needed someone who was in it for the long haul and that wasn't him. He couldn't promise her anything, least of all his continued sobriety. His anger dissipated.

But selfishly, he wanted her to stay.

Tessa's sobs gradually subsided into soft hiccups. Harper brought both her and Scarlet tissues and helped Tessa blow her nose and wipe her eyes. When she was done, Harper held out her arms to her. "Tessa honey, come with me into the kitchen. We can help Maggie bring in the dessert."

Tessa reluctantly gave up her hold on Scarlet and allowed Harper to lift her into her arms. She laid her cheek against Harper shoulder's and clung to her.

"Ethan, why don't you come into the kitchen and help us?" Harper said.

He nodded and followed them out of the dining room, leaving Cam alone with Scarlet.

"I'm sorry," she whispered. "I didn't mean to upset Tessa like that on her first night home."

"It's not your fault. She's grown very attached to you."

"Yes." She swallowed. "I think it's best if I leave right away, first thing in the morning. There's no point delaying my departure if it upsets Tessa every time I see her."

*No, not so soon!* "I suppose that's for the best."

"Yes, I suppose." She didn't sound convinced. "Will you tell her, or do you want me to talk to her this evening?"

"I'll tell her tomorrow. I think she already understands that you have to leave. There's no point upsetting her even more tonight."

She got to her feet and stared in the direction of the kitchen, wringing the tissue between her hands. "Maybe I should leave now, before she comes back. I couldn't bear to make her cry again."

Cam stood and faced her. "You don't have to do that. I'll take her home as soon as dessert's over. She's had a big day, and she needs some sleep."

"Yes, poor little angel." Scarlet's lip trembled again. "I hope she feels better in the morning."

"Scarlet."

He reached for her and pulled her into his arms. Her body molded perfectly against his in the way he remembered. He tightened his hold as he inhaled her sweet scent and let the silky texture of her hair caress his cheek. Her arms came around his waist, holding him as if she didn't want to let him go. Cam closed his eyes and swallowed hard, afraid this might be the last time he touched her.

When she pushed gently against his chest, Cam dropped his arms and let her go. He wished he could take away her pain, he wished things were different between them. He wished...

Wishing did no good. He had to deal with reality in the here and now. And his reality was that Scarlet was moving far away.

He blinked back tears. "I'm going to miss you, Scarlet."

"I'll miss you, too," she whispered.

Tessa ran into the dining room, her previous upset seemingly forgotten. "Daddy, Maggie let me make the whipped cream! We're going to put it on the chocolate pudding she made!"

"Sounds delicious, pumpkin." Cam marveled at her resilience. After everything she'd been through, she was still a happy child. But he didn't want to push his luck with more bad news for her.

None of them could handle any more bad news tonight. Especially Scarlet. She'd turned away to compose herself when Tessa ran into the room. Though she was smiling now, Cam knew it was a thin veneer.

"Maggie showed me how to make it. Can we make chocolate pudding at home sometime, Daddy?"

Cam smiled at Maggie, grateful that she and the others had been able to distract her. "Maggie will have to show me how and then we can try it."

"Anytime," Maggie said.

She set a tray with six tall parfait glasses on the table and handed them around. The glasses were filled with creamy pudding and topped with a generous dollop of whipped cream covered with bits of shaved chocolate. He was sure Maggie's pudding was delicious, but he had no appetite for it.

But for Tessa, he'd fake it.

He stuck his spoon in the pudding. He was right; the pudding was chocolatey and creamy and complete delectable, but he couldn't eat more than a few spoonfuls. Tessa couldn't eat much either. After her first few enthusiastic spoonfuls, she'd slowed down and was now only eating a bit of the whipped cream. She looked suddenly very tired and worn out.

"I'm full, Daddy."

"Tessa, how about I put your pudding in a container and you can take it home with you?"

"Okay, Maggie."

Maggie kissed her head and taking her parfait glass, retreated to the kitchen. Cam took that as his cue to leave.

"Come on, Tessa. Let's get you home."

She said nothing as he helped her into her jacket and fastened the string of the hood under her chin. Then, she looked at Scarlet. "Goodbye Scarlet. I love you."

"I love you, too." Her voice wobbled.

Maggie handed him a plastic container filled with Tessa's pudding. He kissed her and Harper goodnight and shook hands with a solemn-faced Ethan. Cam imagined the look on his brother's face mirrored his own.

Cam picked up Tessa and headed for the door, needing to get away. But he couldn't go without one last glimpse at Scarlet. When he turned to her, she gave him a sad smile.

"Goodbye," she whispered.

"Goodbye."

Tessa fell asleep as soon as he started driving. Cam smiled at her in the rearview mirror, so grateful she'd been returned to him. He'd do his damnedest to be a good father to her and give her everything she needed.

Everything but Scarlet.

# Chapter Twenty-Seven

TESSA SNUGGLED AGAINST Graham's shoulder while Lydia smoothed Tessa's hair.

"It's so nice to have you home, sweetheart," Lydia said. She turned to Cam. "It feels like a miracle, doesn't it?"

"It does."

He and Tessa had gone through DNA testing again and three days later the results were back, confirming he was her biological father. The relief and joy had been overwhelming. As soon as the results were in, Erin Cochrane began working to secure sole custody. He'd never have to say goodbye to Tessa again.

It still didn't feel quite real. In the two weeks since Tessa had been home, he'd woken several times in the middle of the night, convinced he'd dreamt the whole thing. Only when he went to her room and saw her sleeping in her bed amongst the stuffed toys he'd retrieved from a box in the basement, did he believe it was true. His little girl was home.

Graham and Lydia and Drew and Carrie had arrived at the lodge a couple of hours ago. They'd wanted to see Tessa since the day she got home, but Lydia wanted to give her time to settle in first. She was afraid that so many changes in her life would be confusing, but Tessa had resumed her old life with him as if she hadn't been away a day.

Harper had invited everyone for an early Thanksgiving celebration now that they had plenty of space with the new wing of rooms completed. With the kitchen up and running, Maggie was eager to try out some new dishes to see what they thought. It was a joyous family reunion.

Except, Scarlet wasn't there.

Cam longed for her. He knew he'd miss her, but he hadn't expected to feel her absence like a physical pain. It wasn't only the sex, though he longed to make love with her again. He missed talking with her, hearing her voice, her laugh, being around her. He missed the way she used to touch him, a squeeze to his hand, a pat to his shoulder, a simple gesture to show she cared and was right beside him.

He had to get over her before he lost his mind.

"Ethan told me you hosted a wedding last month," Lydia said. "How did that go?"

"It went surprisingly well." Harper set a tray of mugs filled with hot chocolate on a side table while Maggie passed a plate of cookies. "We scrambled like crazy to get things ready, but we did it. I'm really proud of what we accomplished in such a short time."

"We've got a lot of renovations to finish over the winter, like the rooms upstairs in the lodge and the other six cottages. And there's lots of other things to do, like hiring a hotel and restaurant manager. We need someone with experience to keep us on the right track." Ethan stacked logs in the massive stone fireplace. "Scarlet booked another wedding for late May, so everything needs to be in place by then."

"How is Scarlet? I was hoping to see her here this weekend," Lydia said.

Harper's gaze briefly connected with Cam's before she shifted her attention to Lydia. "She's fine. She went back to work in Chicago a couple of weeks ago."

"We were hoping she could come home this weekend, but she wasn't able to make it," Maggie added. She accepted a mug of hot chocolate from Harper and sat in the loveseat next to Carrie. "It doesn't feel right to be celebrating Thanksgiving without her. Especially since..." She stopped and looked down at her mug.

"Especially since what?" Cam sat straighter, his senses on high alert.

Maggie and Harper exchanged a glance before Maggie spoke again. "Harper and I have been reading our mother's letters, the ones Reese found upstairs beneath the floor boards. We came across some new information."

"What information?" If they knew something, they had to tell Scarlet.

"Cam, this isn't the time." Maggie glanced at Tessa.

He got to his feet, too agitated to sit. "What information? If you know something new about your mother, Scarlet has to be told. Did you know she blames herself for her death, for both your parents' deaths?"

Harper stared at him. "Blames herself? What are you talking about? She was eight years old when they died."

Lydia stood and put her hand on Cam's shoulder. She turned to speak to her husband. "Graham, why don't you and Drew and Carrie take Tessa for a walk outside? It's such a beautiful, sunny afternoon."

Graham nodded, immediately taking the hint. “That sounds like a great idea. I’d like to see if the lake has frozen over yet.”

Tessa scrambled out of Graham’s arms and ran to Cam, her brow wrinkled in worry. “Are you mad at Scarlet, Daddy?”

Cam picked her up and held her close, inhaling her sweet little girl scent. “No, pumpkin. I’m not mad at Scarlet. I could never be mad at her.”

She put both her small hands against his cheeks and looked into his face. “Me neither. I love Scarlet.”

*So do I.*

The thought surged its way to the forefront of his mind as if it couldn’t be contained any longer. *I love her.* He’d loved her from the beginning, from the night of Ethan and Harper’s wedding when he saw her holding a sleeping Tessa. But he’d been too stubborn and too scared to admit it. Instead, he’d let her walk away.

How could he have been so stupid?

He kissed Tessa’s cheek and set her on her feet. “Go with Uncle Graham. Your jacket is in the closet at the front door.”

Graham nodded and took Tessa’s hand. “Come on, sweetie.”

Cam waited until they left the room and Tessa was out of earshot. “What have you learned?”

Harper sat beside Maggie in the seat Carrie vacated. “We thought they were all old letters from a boyfriend our mother had as a teenager, but there were newer ones, some dated only a few weeks before she died.” She grasped her sister’s hand. “It appears she was having an affair.”

Cam dropped into a chair. "So, Scarlet was right. She heard your mother tell your father she was in love with another man."

Harper sucked in a breath. "Oh, my God. Why did she never say anything?"

"She didn't want to hurt you or ruin your memories of your parents. Were you able to figure out who Miranda was having the affair with?"

"No," Maggie said, shaking her head. "All the letters, even the ones going back to when they were kids, are simply signed 'R'. At first, we thought the letters might be from our father, Robert, but now we know that's not the case. After reading all the letters in chronological order, it seems our mother and R were in love as teenagers but our grandparents disapproved of him and forbid her from seeing him. We're not sure why they objected to their relationship."

"For about fifteen years, there's no letters. Then nearly three years before she died, R starts to write to her again," Harper continued. "It's obvious from the letters they're having a sexual affair, but I think he loved her. He's begging her to leave our father and marry him. He says they should have been together all along."

Lydia held out a box of tissues, and Maggie grabbed one and dabbed at her eyes. "It's so sad. When two people love each other, they shouldn't be kept apart."

Harper shook her head. "What about our father? He was a good man, Maggie. Maybe he worked too hard and spent too much time away from us, but he didn't deserve to be cheated on."

Maggie wiped her eyes as fresh tears rolled down her cheeks. "No, he didn't."

He hated to see Maggie so distressed. He found it odd that she and Harper disagreed so vehemently about their mother's affair. But maybe it wasn't surprising since Harper had known her parents, and Maggie was too young to have any memories of them. She wouldn't have known whether her mother was worthy of her sympathy.

Ethan turned to Cam. "What did you mean when you said Scarlet feels guilty about their deaths?"

Even though he had promised he wouldn't, he told them Scarlet's story about following her parents that day. "All these years, she's believed that if she hadn't followed them, they wouldn't have gone out in the canoe to get some privacy."

"Poor Scarlet," Harper said. "Why did she keep this to herself? Why didn't she tell us?"

Cam shifted uncomfortably in his seat. Scarlet would not be happy that he was sharing all her confidences. But there had been too many secrets, too much darkness, in the Lindquist sisters' lives. It was time to throw open the doors and let in some light.

"I know it doesn't make sense, but somewhere down deep in her eight-year-old heart, she's afraid you and Maggie would blame her for your parents' deaths the way she blames herself. She's afraid of losing you."

Harper's hand flew to her mouth. "Poor Scarlet."

Ethan sat beside Harper and put his arm around her.

"She didn't want to hurt you, Harper. I'm sorry to be the one to cause you pain, but she can't go on blaming herself like this."

"You're right, she can't." Harper took another tissue from Lydia and blew her nose. "I'm glad you told us."

"There's something else." He hesitated, weighing his words. "I know you believe your parents' deaths were an accident, and that Willy was wrong when he said your father hit your mother with an oar, but Scarlet thinks it's true. The last words your father said to her was that no matter what happened, she had to remember he loved her. Scarlet heard him tell your mother that without her he had nothing to live for."

Maggie sucked in a breath. "Did she actually see what happened? Did she see our father strike our mother?"

Cam shook his head. "No, Maggie. No, she didn't."

Maggie sighed in relief. "Thank God. But you're saying Scarlet believes our father planned to kill our mother when he went out on the lake with her? Because she was leaving him?"

"That's what she believes. Your mother told Scarlet you were all going to live someplace else, without your father."

Harper blew her nose once more. "All these years I've fought against the idea that Daddy killed her. Even though the inquest said he did, it didn't jive with the man I knew. He was kind and funny, and I know he loved us kids. I couldn't believe he would do this to us. But maybe he snapped. Maybe I have to accept that he did kill her."

Ethan rubbed her back, trying to give comfort. Cam closed his eyes. He hated upsetting Harper like this, but he was glad to spare Scarlet the pain of telling her secret to her sisters. He would gladly bear any pain for her.

"Harper, you need to tell Scarlet about the letters, and you need to tell her you don't blame her for what happened. She needs to know."

"Yes, she does." Harper looked at Maggie and squeezed her hand before turning back to him. "And I think you should be the one to tell her."

"No." He shook his head, shocked she would suggest it. "She doesn't want to hear from me."

"You're wrong, Cam. She loves you, and I think you love her, too. You need to go to her."

He jumped to his feet and began to pace. "I'm no good for her. She needs someone stable, someone who's not going to turn to alcohol at the first sign of trouble."

"You had a slip, but you didn't go over the deep end. You didn't fall back into alcoholism, did you?" Ethan said. "Give yourself some credit."

"Scarlet believes in you," Maggie said, her dark eyes shiny with tears.

Cam bowed his head. More than anything in the world he wanted a life with Scarlet. But he was scared. What if he messed up, maybe not with alcohol, but in some other way? He couldn't risk Scarlet's happiness.

Lydia laid her hand on his arm. "When are you going to forgive our father, Cam? You've been hanging on to such anger for so long, it's eating you alive. And now you're about to throw away your chance for happiness because of it."

He looked at her in surprise. "That's not true."

"Isn't it? You're angry because of the way he treated our mother. You're angry because he wasn't the father we needed him to be. But I think most of all, you're angry with him because you think you're so much like him."

Cam flinched, her words hitting hard. "I *am* like him. I look like him. I'm a drunk like him."

She cupped his face with her hand as a tear slid down her cheek. "No, you're nothing like him. He never stopped drinking because he didn't want to. He was content to blame everyone but himself for his drinking. You found the strength to quit so you could be a good father to Tessa, and a good brother to us. He wanted to be an artist, but things didn't work out the way he'd planned and he took out his frustration for his failure on our mother and on us. You found a way to channel your creativity into your furniture and home designs. You're a better man, and a better father, than he ever was, so don't use him as an excuse not to be happy."

He stared at her. "I didn't know he wanted to be an artist."

"Yes. Mother told me he even went to art school at the Illinois Institute of Art in Chicago, but he had to drop out when she got pregnant with me. They had to get married and move to Wisconsin to take over the inn so they could make a living. She told me he never forgave her."

"Was that why he trashed my drawings when I was a kid?"

"I'm sure it was. Maybe he wanted to save you from dreaming for something he thought could never be. Or maybe he saw your talent and was jealous of it." Lydia grasped his hand. "Hanging on to your anger only hurts you.

Let it go and forgive him. It's what I've had to do. And forgive yourself. You deserve happiness."

Cam pulled Lydia into his arms and held her tightly. He could never forget the past. He didn't know if he was capable of the forgiveness she was asking of him, or if their father was worthy of such forgiveness.

And forgiving himself? He couldn't begin to imagine how to do that.

CAM AND TESSA WENT home shortly after dinner with a promise to come back to the lodge the next morning to spend the day with his family. After bathing Tessa and reading her a story, he tucked her into bed and kissed her goodnight. She was asleep by the time he turned off the light and closed her bedroom door.

He was alone for the rest of the evening with only his thoughts for company. They rumbled through his brain like thunder threatening to explode into a summer storm.

Lydia's revelations today stunned him. He'd never once considered that his lack of forgiveness for his father, and for himself, was preventing him from finding peace in his life. Or love.

He ran his hand through his hair, trying to make sense of his feelings. He tried to imagine what Scarlet's reaction would be if he did as Harper asked and delivered the news about her mother's letters in person. She'd be angry he hadn't kept her confidences. But secrets like that needed to be brought out into the light where they lost their power. He wanted to give Scarlet relief, to let her know Harper and Maggie didn't blame her for anything.

He paced his kitchen, unable to settle in one spot. If he showed up at Scarlet's door unannounced, she might tell him to get lost. But somehow, he didn't think so. He ran his hand over his kitchen table, remembering her enthusiasm for his work. She'd believed in him, as much as he believed in her. He realized that now.

She'd told him she needed a man who didn't cut and run at the first sign of trouble. God, how he wanted to be that man.

But he was scared. He was afraid of disappointing her the way he always thought he'd disappointed his father. He was afraid of being rejected by her the way his father had rejected him.

The realization hit him hard. It all came back to his father. He dropped onto one of the kitchen chairs, rested his elbows on his knees and stared at the floor. Lydia said he needed to let go of the anger he'd harbored for his father before he could allow himself to be happy. That he needed to forgive himself for his drinking. How did he even do that?

He thought about what his sister had said about their father studying art. He must have been very talented to get into such a prestigious school. To have the career he wanted snatched away must have been a terrible blow.

He didn't remember his father ever sketching or painting, even as a hobby. It was as if he'd totally rejected his former ambitions. Maybe it had been too painful to pick up his sketchpad. Or perhaps he'd been punishing himself for having such dreams. He certainly punished himself and his family with his drinking.

Cam could understand his father's disappointment at having to drop out of art school, could even sympathize with it. But he couldn't sympathize with the way he'd handled his disappointment. He'd heaped blame on his mother for getting pregnant and ending his dreams. Maybe that was why she'd enabled his drinking. She was trying to assuage her guilt for making him drop out of school.

Instead of keeping his love of art alive by painting in his spare time, or finding a way to turn his art into a part-time job, he chose to be a martyr. If he couldn't have his art on his own terms, he didn't want anything. Not even his family.

And now Cam was doing the same thing. If he couldn't be one hundred percent sure that he and Scarlet would always be together, that they would always love each other, he was prepared to throw her love away entirely.

Cam got to his feet, too agitated to sit. He walked quietly to Tessa's closed bedroom door and rested his palm against the wood. He didn't want to make her pay for his mistakes, and especially not for her grandfather's. But by denying her Scarlet's love, that's exactly what he was doing.

He didn't want to repeat his father's mistakes.

For reasons known only to him, his father had been incapable of accepting the disappointments life had thrown at him. His resentment had had profound effects on his own life and the lives of his children and wife. But it was over now. Cam could choose to live his life on his own terms.

*I forgive you, Dad. I'm sorry you were so unhappy.*

A huge weight of anger and resentment lifted from his shoulders. Cam sucked in a breath at the sensation of lightness.

He deserved to be happy with the woman he loved. Maybe he'd stumble and fall and turn to drinking again. But maybe he wouldn't. There were no guarantees in life. Or in love.

He turned away from Tessa's door and hurried to the kitchen, knowing what he had to do.

Cam pulled out his cell phone and hit his brother's number. Ethan answered immediately. "Hey. What's going on?"

"Can you and Harper look after Tessa tomorrow? I'm driving to Chicago."

Ethan laughed. "We would be happy to, buddy. Good luck."

"Thanks."

To convince Scarlet he wanted a forever with her, he'd need all the luck he could get.

## Chapter Twenty-Eight

SCARLET FOUGHT AGAINST the cold November wind howling down her street. If she'd been smart, she would have taken her car to the grocery store instead of walking the ten blocks. If she'd been even smarter, she would have ordered in pizza.

But she'd been too restless to stay cooped up in her apartment any longer. During the work week, she managed her restlessness by taking on extra projects and staying so busy she had no time to brood. The weekends were different. She had too much time to think and to wonder how Cameron and Tessa were doing. Their happiness was always on her mind, and she wondered if they missed her, even half as much as she missed them.

She'd needed this walk, even though the wind was biting cold and her two bags of groceries were getting heavier by the minute.

A block from her building, she noticed a truck parked in front that looked like Cameron's. Her heart lifted in joy before she told herself there were probably hundreds of trucks like his in the city. She had to stop seeing his face in the crowds, seeing reminders of him everywhere she looked. She had to stop thinking about him, dreaming of being in his arms again. If she didn't stop loving him, she'd lose her mind.

But when the truck door opened and Cameron stepped out onto the sidewalk, she stopped walking, incapable of putting one foot in front of the other. Her lungs threatened to explode as she stood on the sidewalk staring at him. She reminded herself to breathe.

He walked toward her. "Can I carry your groceries for you?"

She hadn't spoken to him in two weeks and his first words to her were about groceries?

"Why are you in Chicago? Is Tessa sick? Is she all right?"

"Tessa is fine." He took the bags from her cramped fingers. "She's barely mentioned her mother since she got home. She seems very happy to be back in Minnesota."

Scarlet let out a relieved breath. "Good. I'm glad she's happy." If Tessa was okay, why was Cameron here?

He cleared his throat. "I have a message from Harper and Maggie. They thought it should be delivered in person."

Sudden panic swirled in her gut. "Is Harper all right? Maggie? What's happened?"

"Everyone's fine, Scarlet, honestly."

Her heart fell. So, he was here on an errand from her sisters, not because he wanted to see her. Why did they think this message needed to be delivered in person? And why by Cameron? They knew how hard seeing him was for her.

He nodded toward her building. "Do you think we can go inside? It's cold out here."

"Yes, of course."

She fished her keys from her purse. If he was coming all the way from Solace Lake with a message from her sisters, she could at least let him deliver it in the warmth of her apartment.

Scarlet opened her door and turned on the lights. Cameron followed her inside with the grocery bags, and she pointed to her kitchen. "You can put them on the counter. Would you like some tea?"

"Sure."

She filled her kettle with water and set it on the stove to boil. As she was pulling cups from the cupboard, her hands shook. He unnerved her, making her tiny apartment seem even smaller with his large presence. And she didn't yet know what he came all the way to Chicago to say to her. It must be important.

He emptied the bags and put the milk and other perishables in the fridge.

"Where does this go?" he asked, holding up a can of chicken noodle soup.

"You can leave it on the counter. I was going to have that for supper. What about you? Are you hungry?"

"Starved," he said. "I didn't stop to eat."

It was almost an eight-hour drive from Solace Lake to Chicago. Maybe he'd been in such a hurry to see her he hadn't stopped to eat.

She pushed the wishful thinking from her mind. "We can go out and get something. There's a great little Italian place a few blocks from here."

He shook his head and smiled. "I'd rather stay here. If it's okay with you."

"Of course." His smile appeared nervous and she wondered at the reason. She hid her anxiousness with a smile of her own. "Luckily for you, I recently laid in a few supplies."

While the soup heated, Scarlet filled her teapot with hot water and loose tea and set it aside to steep. She found a can of tuna in the back of her cupboard and made them each a sandwich. For dessert, she set the cookies she'd purchased on a plate. It didn't seem like much.

"I always said Maggie got the cooking gene in the family. Are you sure you don't want to go out?"

He set his hand on her arm. "It's fine, Scarlet. Really."

It was the first time he'd touched her since he arrived. His warm fingers burned a hole through her thick sweater. A trail of fire ran straight to the apex of her thighs, as if he'd touched her in her most sensitive spot, the way he'd done so many times before.

She stepped back, afraid if she let herself bask in his warmth she'd do something to embarrass herself, like jump into his arms. Turning away, she busied herself filling two bowls with the soup and bringing them to the table.

"Everything's ready. Why don't you sit down?"

They ate in silence. Scarlet nibbled at her sandwich, her stomach too tied up in knots. Cameron obviously didn't have the same problem. He wolfed down his food and then reached for a couple of cookies. Scarlet poured tea for them both, using a strainer to catch the loose leaves.

Cameron swallowed a bit of cookie and sipped his hot tea. "You're not eating."

"I'm fine." Time to end this charade so he could leave. "What message did Harper and Maggie send you to deliver?"

He set down his cup. “It’s about your mother’s letters. They said they weren’t only letters from her teenage boyfriend. It looks like their relationship resumed about three years before her death. They were having an affair.”

Scarlet sat back in her chair, shocked, though not sure why. She’d known all along her mother was having an affair. “They’re sure?”

His eyes were steady and calm. “Yes.”

He told her what Harper and Maggie had told him about the letters. “I’m sorry, Scarlet. There’s more,” Cameron said.

“More?” She sucked in a breath and turned her face away, tears burning behind her eyes. She couldn’t take much more.

“I told them,” he said. “I told them about what you saw and heard on the day your parents died. They don’t blame you, sweetheart. They want you to know you had nothing to do with their deaths. Nothing.”

She clapped her hand over her mouth to stop her sob but tears spilled over onto her cheeks. She shook her head. “You shouldn’t have. You shouldn’t have. You promised.”

Cameron came around the table to kneel beside her. He caught her hand and placed a kiss in the palm. “I had to, sweetheart. I couldn’t let you suffer anymore. All these secrets that the two of us have been carrying around inside for so long, they’re killing us. We both have to let them go. We can’t let the past have power over us anymore.”

Scarlet wiped her cheek with the back of her hand. “What do you mean?”

"You need to forgive yourself for the role you believe you played in your parents' death, and I..." He stopped and took a deep breath before lifting his gaze once more to look into her eyes. "I had to forgive myself for being a drunk. I was so afraid of hurting you that I walked away, but I realize now there are no guarantees in life. We have to love each other and hope our relationship weathers all the storms."

He got to his feet and pulled her up with him. "I love you, Scarlet. I want to spend my life weathering those storms with you. I promise you right here, right now, I'll never leave you again. I'll never push you away. I'll always stand beside you."

She was thrilled to hear him say he loved her. But they needed so much more than love.

They needed trust.

"Cameron," she whispered. "I love you, and I've dreamed of having you say those words back to me. I know you think you mean what you say right now, but how can I be sure? Before, when things got rough, you turned away from me. I can't do that anymore. It's too hard."

He cupped her face with his big hands. "I won't go anywhere, Scarlet. I'm not scared to love you anymore. I believe in you, in us. Yes, I was afraid of hurting you, but I was more afraid of being hurt again, rejected. All this time I told myself I was doing the right thing, the noble thing by leaving you. I was saving you from living with a drunk. But what I was really doing was saving myself. I was leaving you before you had a chance to leave me. But I'm not scared anymore. I need you, and I want to be the man you need me to be."

She looked into his dark eyes and knew he'd stand by her no matter what life threw at them. In that moment, she knew she could always trust him. She gave him a tremulous smile. "Can you say it again?"

"I love you."

She wound her arms around his neck. "Maybe once more."

He grinned and the beauty of his smile made her heart sing. She vowed to make him smile every day for the rest of their lives.

"I love you, Scarlet."

She'd never get tired of hearing him say those words. And she'd never get tired of saying them back to him.

"I love you, too, Cameron."

# Epilogue

SCARLET FINISHED TYING Tessa's new skates and then steadied her as Cameron fastened the strap of the hockey helmet under her chin.

"Let's go, Daddy!" she said impatiently.

"Hang on a second. Let's wait for Scarlet." He flashed a smile at her. "Even if she is a slowpoke."

"Slowpoke? I can skate rings around you, Hainstock." She gave them both an indulgent smile. "You two go on ahead. I'll catch up as soon as I get my skates on."

"Okay, sweetheart."

Cameron led Tessa to the chair he'd brought out to the large patch of ice on the lake that he and Ethan had cleared of snow. Tessa pushed the chair around the ice, encouraged by her father's praise.

"Scarlet, look! I'm skating!" Tessa called.

"You're doing great!"

Scarlet smiled fondly at Cameron and Tessa. *Her family.*

Sometimes it was hard to believe how much her life had changed in such a short time. In a week, she and Cameron would be married in a simple ceremony at the lodge. Tessa would become her stepdaughter. Happiness made her heart swell with joy.

Still, despite her joy, questions about the past nagged at her. Who was the man her mother had loved as a teenager and continued to love as a married woman? Had she really been planning to run away with him?

She tightened the laces on one skate and pulled on the other. Somehow, she had to find the answers to those questions or they'd never leave her and her sisters in peace.

But how could she uncover the truth after so many years when almost everyone involved was dead? She closed her eyes and sent a silent prayer heavenward.

*Mom, Daddy, please help us find the truth so we can have peace.*

Harper and Maggie joined her on the bench and set their skates beside them. Harper unlaced her boots. "I haven't skated since we were kids. I hope I remember how."

"If you have trouble staying on your feet, maybe Tessa will let you borrow her chair," Maggie teased.

"Smart ass." Harper paused and looked out at the frozen lake. "It's going to sound a little crazy, but I feel like Mom and Daddy are nearby when we're out on the lake."

Scarlet smiled at her sister. "I think that's a nice sentiment." If Harper was comforted by the belief, she was happy for her.

Maggie finished lacing her skates and got to her feet, doing a little spin on the ice in front of them. She stuck the pick of her skate into the ice to bring herself to a stop.

"Still got it," she said with a grin. "Thank you, Grandma, for all the figure skating lessons."

She skated off, did a couple of little jumps, then skated backwards towards them, her skates criss-crossing in perfect precision.

"Show off!" Scarlet shouted. Maggie made a little bow and laughed.

"Are you guys ready?"

"Give me a minute," Harper said.

"Scarlet!" Tessa took a few tentative steps without leaning on the chair. "Look at me! I'm skating!"

"You are! You're skating all by yourself, Tessa," Scarlet called. A minute later, Tessa lost her balance and fell on her bottom. With a helping hand from Cameron, she pushed herself to her feet once more and took a few more steps. Scarlet's heart filled with love.

"Isn't she adorable?"

"She is. And you're going to be a wonderful mother," Harper said. "Now, help me up. I may need to lean on you a bit."

Scarlet and Maggie got her to her feet and Harper took a few tentative steps. "I think it's coming back to me, but don't let go."

Scarlet gripped her waist. "We've got you, sweetie."

They each took one of her hands and slowly made their way around the perimeter of the ice surface. As the sun lowered in the western sky, Scarlet gazed out over the frozen surface of the lake and in the distance, she saw a flash of yellow. When she looked more closely, she saw a yellow canoe drift across the ice. Two people were inside the canoe, their paddles moving in perfect synchronization. The fading sunlight glinted off a woman's red hair. Scarlet blinked, and when she looked again, they were gone.

She gasped. It happened so quickly, she couldn't be sure it had been real.

*Of course it wasn't real.*

"Scarlet? Something wrong?" Harper asked.

"No, no. Everything's fine." She couldn't stop herself from looking one last time, but there was nothing in the distance except the frozen lake topped with frothy drifts of snow.

"You're sure?" Harper had always had a knack for reading her. As much as she trusted her and Maggie, she wasn't ready to share what she'd seen, whatever it was. She made herself smile.

"I'm sure."

Ethan approached and came to a quick stop in front of them, his skates sending up a small shower of ice. "Can I take my wife off your hands, ladies?"

"You are welcome to her. Good luck!" Maggie said with a laugh.

"Hey!" Harper laughed, too, then happily skated off with Ethan, who held her securely.

"I'm going to do some spins," Maggie said. "You okay, Scarlet?"

"I'm fine. I'll catch up with Cameron and Tessa."

With a wave, Maggie skated off. Scarlet hurried in the opposite direction, reaching for Cameron's outstretched hand. He brought her gloved hand to his mouth for a kiss. "I love you," he said.

"I love you, too. To the moon and back."

Cameron grinned at her. "To the moon and back. Come on. Let's take Tessa for a spin."

"Let's go all the way around the rink one more time before it gets too dark. Think you can keep up, Tessa?"

"Yes!"

They skated on and Scarlet listened to Tessa's excited chatter with half an ear. Maybe what she'd seen had simply been a trick of the light. It was possible she'd so wanted a glimpse of her parents that her mind conjured them up for her. Or maybe it was something more.

Scarlet glanced over her shoulder, hoping to catch a glimpse of the canoe and its passengers once more. There was no one there, but she could feel their presence. A feeling of warm happiness swirled in her chest and radiated through her body.

*Mom, Daddy, I love you.*

"Are you two ready to go inside now?" Cameron asked.

"I'm ready," Tessa said. "Can we have hot chocolate?"

Scarlet smiled. "Absolutely. With whipped cream, too. Let's go home."

Cameron leaned over for a brief kiss. "There's nowhere else I'd rather be than at home with my two favorite girls."

Scarlet smiled back at him, her heart overflowing with love. "Nowhere else at all."

The End

Thank you for reading "Secrets and Solace." Are you ready for the next Love at Solace Lake story? Check out the blurb for "Truth and Solace", Maggie's story and book three in the series:

*THE TRUTH COULD DESTROY them. Or set them free.*

Maggie Lindquist left Solace Lake determined never to return. Circumstances have pulled her back and she's helping to restore her family's dilapidated fishing lodge. When she agreed to the plan she didn't expect to have to work side by side with the man who abandoned her ten years earlier. She didn't expect to like him, or want him ever again. But can she trust him as she once did?

Luke Carlsson rushes home to tend to his ailing mother. Her lengthy illness means he needs to stay, at least temporarily. And to stay, he needs to work. Solace Lake Lodge offers him a job and an opportunity to work with the woman he's never stopped loving. But the restoration is unleashing secrets hidden for decades and no one is left unscathed. Especially not Maggie and Luke, whose love needs to be resilient enough to forgive, and strong enough to build a future together.

Scan the QR code for your copy of TRUTH AND SOLACE!

# A NOTE FROM JANA

Reviews are the life blood for authors. I hope you enjoyed SECRETS AND SOLACE, and if you did, I would appreciate you letting other readers know. Please leave a review at the retailer where you purchased the book, on Goodreads, or on your own blog. If you leave a review, I would love to read it! Please email me the link at Jana@JanaRichards.com.

You can stay up to date with me and my upcoming new releases, sales, giveaways and contests by joining my newsletter. You'll receive a FREE ecopy of **HOME TO SOLACE LAKE** as a thank you for signing up. This romantic novella is available only to newsletter subscribers. I'd love to have you on board! Here's the blurb for **HOME TO SOLACE LAKE**:

> After Jerry Fields buried his mother twenty-two years ago, he cut all ties to the small town in Minnesota where he grew up. He swore he'd never return. But when his biological father, a man who never acknowledged him, leaves Jerry his entire estate, curiosity has him returning to Minnewasta. Why did Earl Rogers will him everything he owned when during his lifetime he didn't give Jerry a minute of his time?
>
> Denise Rogers wants to save the business that her deceased husband loved so much. But when her father-in-law Earl leaves all his property to his illegitimate son, saving the business gets much

more complicated. Denise is determined to buy the property from Jerry Fields to keep it from being demolished and turned into condos. She wants to continue to run the business as a marine repair shop, knowing it's what her husband would have wanted. But events throw her plans into disarray and she has to give up on her dream. Until Jerry offers to work with her over the summer to help her buy the property.

Jerry can't stomach the idea of putting his half-brother's widow out of a job and a home, so he decides to stay in Minnewasta to help her. At the end of the summer, Denise will purchase the property from him and they'll go their separate ways. But as they work together, their feelings for each other deepen into love, and they uncover long-held secrets that force Jerry to question everything he thought he knew about his parents. Can Jerry overcome past hurts and fears for a chance at love?

Sign up using the QR code below for Jana's newsletter and receive your FREE copy of **HOME TO SOLACE LAKE!**

# Don't miss out!

Visit the website below and you can sign up to receive emails whenever Jana Richards publishes a new book. There's no charge and no obligation.

https://books2read.com/r/B-A-YISD-FRLZC

# Also by Jana Richards

**A Left at the Altar Romance**

Her Best Man

There Goes the Groom

Always a Bridesmaid

**Love at Solace Lake**

Lies and Solace

Secrets and Solace

Truth and Solace

Christmas at Solace Lake

**The Victorian Mansion Series**

Rescue Me

Take a Chance on Me

**Twice in a Lifetime Series**

I'll Be Seeing You
Never Can Say Goodbye
When I Was Your Man

**Standalone**
A Long Way From Eden
Seeing Things

Watch for more at https://www.janarichards.com/.

# About the Author

When Jana Richards read her first romance novel, she immediately knew two things: she had to commit the stories running through her head to paper, and they had to end with a happily ever after. She also knew she'd found what she was meant to do. Since then she's never met a romance genre she didn't like. She writes contemporary romance, romantic suspense, and historical romance set in World War Two, in lengths ranging from short story to full length novel. Just for fun, she throws in generous helpings of humor, and the occasional dash of the paranormal.

In her life away from writing, Jana is a mother to two grown daughters, grandmother to an amazing granddaughter, and a wife to her husband Warren. She enjoys golf, yoga, movies, concerts, travel and reading, not necessarily in that order. She and her husband live in western Canada with a senior calico cat named Layla and an acquarium full of unnamed fish. She loves to hear from readers and can be reached through her website.

Read more at https://www.janarichards.com/.

www.ingramcontent.com/pod-product-compliance
Lightning Source LLC
LaVergne TN
LVHW020655110826
845149LV00012B/2006

* 9 7 8 0 9 9 5 2 7 9 1 4 8 *